,ook at me," he said. "You're going be okay. I'm here," Sam said.

reached out, catching her hands gently in his. His
1 was cool and wonderful, the gesture infinitely
1forting.

oe met his eyes. A subtle shift came over his
.ures, a tightening of the lips, his pupils eating
the steel-gray irises. There was concern there,
something else now, too. Desire. Possession. He
:d her hand to his lips, brushing the lightest of
ses across the back of her fingers.

: gesture was courtly, barely qualifying as a true
;, but a flood of tingling arousal swamped her
1 from head to foot. No one had ever touched her
ntimately with so little flesh.

POSSESSED BY A WARRIOR

SHARON ASHWOOD

Published in Great Britain 2014
by Mills & Boon, an imprint of Harlequin (UK) Limited,
Eton House, 18-24 Paradise Road, Richmond, Surrey, TW9 1SR

© 2014 Naomi Lester

ISBN: 978 0 263 91394 1

89-0514

Harlequin (UK) Limited's policy is to use papers that are natural, renewable and recyclable products and made from wood grown in sustainable forests. The logging and manufacturing processes conform to the legal environmental regulations of the country of origin.

Printed and bound in Spain
by Blackprint CPI, Barcelona

Sharon Ashwood is a novelist, desk jockey and enthusiast for the weird and spooky. She has an English literature degree but works as a finance geek. Interests include growing her to-be-read pile and playing with the toy graveyard on her desk.

Sharon is the winner of the 2011 RITA® Award for Paranormal Romance. She lives in the Pacific Northwest and is owned by the Demon Lord of Kitty Badness.

For Mom, who taught me never to give up.

To love someone deeply gives you strength.
To be deeply loved gives you courage.

–Lao Tzu

Chapter 1

Sam Ralston shed his robe, tossing it to the floor. He'd done so a thousand times, in many contexts. Most involved women.

This time, however, he was staring at a wall of knives. They were eight inches in length, set about four inches apart, each point aimed straight out like the quills of an angry porcupine. In the half light, the blades gleamed softly, stainless steel polished to the understated efficiency of a showcase kitchen. The wall of blades blocked the room from end to end, leaving only a narrow gap near the ceiling.

Getting over the wall was his first challenge. Sam gave a derisive sound that wasn't quite a laugh. It echoed oddly in the otherwise bare room, adding nothing to the gray-on-gray atmosphere.

Trust *La Compagnie des Morts* to come up with an obstacle course designed to shred the runner right at the start. Everything that came after would be painful in the extreme, even for vampires.

But Sam was one of the Four Horsemen, *La Compagnie*'s crack unit named after the riders of the Apocalypse: Death, Plague, Famine and War. Units like theirs were called in after the CIA, the FBI, MI5 and all the rest of the international alphabet soup had failed to get results. Then they swept in and saved whatever needed saving.

As jobs went, the hours were bad but it was never boring.

Sam was War, and he was better than any trial the Company of the Dead could dream up. He'd proven it, mission after mission. Nevertheless, the Company put all their operatives to the test every so often, which was why he was standing in their Los Angeles facility, wearing nothing but running shorts, sneakers and fangs.

He flexed his knees and leaped. The gap was too narrow to land on top of the wall—that would have been far too easy. Instead, Sam caught the edge with his right hand, forcing himself to pause in a kind of one-armed pushup before he swung his feet onto the ledge. He felt the muscles in his shoulder and stomach bunch to hold his weight. The maneuver was almost perfect, but one blade kissed his left calf, leaving a trail of blood to snake down his leg and into his shoe. He cursed, mentally docking himself a point.

Without pausing at the top, he flung himself onto the mat on the other side. Wooden arrows hummed through the air, whispering against the back of his neck, skimming his chest right above the heart. He rolled, grabbing a SIG Sauer from the rack on the wall and taking out the two mechanical bowmen within seconds. He dropped the gun, knowing there were only two bullets inside. Miss once, and he'd be staked.

Dispassionately, Sam scanned the room for the next course on the menu. The room was lined in more stainless steel, and he could track his movements in a blurry reflection. Dark hair, gray eyes, a body coiled more like a beast than a man. No more emotion than a machine.

He heard a door open, and an enormous wolf bounded forward. A werewolf, actually. Famine, one of the other Horsemen—but the fact they worked together didn't mean

Kenyon would give him an inch. For the first time, Sam felt his stomach tighten. Everything so far had been a test of strength or coordination. Kenyon, on the other hand, had a very crafty mind.

The wolf stopped a few paces away, crouching with a warning growl. Pale gold eyes raked over Sam, sending an electric prickle across his shoulders. He growled right back, feeling the low rumble in his chest. His fangs were down, adrenaline bringing out his own beast. His calf stung from the knife wound, and he could smell the blood, the coppery scent almost, but not quite, like a human's. From the gray wolf's twitching nose, he'd noticed it, too.

Kenyon sprang. Sam leaped to grab the wolf in midair, twisting so that they both fell hard to the floor. Kenyon writhed, jaws snapping, hind legs slashing. Sam straddled the beast, the coarse hair rough against his skin. At the same time, he had the wolf's head between his hands, trying to immobilize him. They were matched for strength. Sam's only hope was to keep him off balance.

It might have worked, except Kenyon chose that moment to shift. The burst of energy sent Sam sailing backward. His back had barely hit the floor when Kenyon was on top of him, huge hands around Sam's throat, shutting off all air.

"Sucker," Kenyon gloated. A manic grin lit his Nordic features.

Sam replied with a hard right jab.

"Ungh!" Kenyon fell sideways, releasing Sam's neck.

Sam got to his feet and glared down at the werewolf, putting one foot across his throat. "Vampires don't have to breathe, remember?"

Kenyon rubbed his face and swore.

"Time." The voice came from somewhere in the ceiling. "Two minutes, fifteen seconds."

Sam grunted. Not bad. Not his best speed, but close. He

held out a hand to Kenyon, who took it and pulled himself up.

"You're not even sweating," the wolf complained.

"Cardio only applies if you have a pulse."

Kenyon gave him a scathing look. He'd heal quickly from Sam's punch, but he'd have a black eye first. "I should have had you."

"Dream on, dog breath."

The door opened again, and this time one of the human technicians came running in holding Sam's cell phone. Sam exchanged a look with the wolf, seeing his own question in Kenyon's eyes.

The tech waved Sam's iPhone, a harried look on his face. "For you. It's Death."

"Sam, I need you and the others at Oakwood pronto. Code…whatever. Code the whole damned spectrum. Just get your butts over here."

Jack Anderson, also known as Death, threw the phone onto the seat beside him, needing both hands on the wheel. He should have been using the hands-free option, but driving with undue care and attention wasn't Jack's issue.

It was the jackass trying to make a hood ornament out of his Porsche that was the problem. Not that anything could outrun his silver Porsche 911 GT2 RS—or at least not here, on the back roads of Wingman County, where soccer-mom SUVs and handyman trucks ruled the two-lane highways. Except the car behind him was a black Mercedes SLS complete with a sniper in the passenger seat.

Jack navigated a sharp turn, hugging the cliff and ignoring the sheer drop to his right. A bullet punched through the back windshield and tore through the leather seat. *Bloody barbarians!*

He could have sworn the bullet had glinted like silver.

They know I'm a vampire. Jack stepped on the accelerator, taking advantage of a straight stretch of road to leap ahead. Then the downshift, left turn, and he was on the wooded road leading home.

The next bullet made a spiderweb of the windshield. *Who are these guys?* They were bad shots, or maybe just not up to Jack's standards. Sam would have taken out a tire and sent the car over the cliff. *That* was how you ended a car chase: one bullet, no fuss.

He'd picked up the yahoos on his tail about halfway home, just after he'd left the populated part of the coast. They'd started shooting as soon as he was on the treacherous cliff road and couldn't get away. Jack drove as fast as he could, but the twists and turns held him back. The fact that it was two in the morning and pitch-black didn't help, either. Vampire night vision only did so much.

Just like his so-called immortality had its limitations. He was hard to kill, but a silver bullet or a fiery crash could take him out. Whoever was behind this attack had done his or her homework.

What do they want? There were plenty of people who wanted him dead. Okay, extra-dead. Re-dead. Whatever. Which ones were these?

Another turn, this time to the right. Now it would be safe to jump out of the car, vampire-quick, but he was almost home. He could do it. He could beat them.

He could see the massive iron gate of Oakwood, his mansion with its handpicked security staff. Oaks flanked the entrance, huge, gnarled sentries. *Thank God.* Jack's heart leaped with relief. *Safe.*

Then, finally, a bullet took out the rear tire. The Porsche bucked and slid. Jack swore, one curse running into the next. He'd been going too fast, and…

Chapter 2

"Is there a problem, Ms. Anderson?" said the attorney, who was visibly sweating in his penguin suit of funereal black.

Is there a problem? Chloe mused, tears threatening to seep through her defenses. *Let's see. My billionaire playboy uncle Jack wrapped his Porsche around the oak tree out front because he supposedly drank too much at the yacht club, and now our dysfunctional relations are circling like hungry raptors. And, oh, yeah, he named me executor. Fun times.*

The sarcasm couldn't shut down the pain squeezing her heart. She already missed her uncle like crazy—but right now it was her job to be cool, collected and businesslike.

"No, there's no problem," she said in a tight voice, memories choking her until her words were little more than a whisper.

Thankfully, she hadn't been the one to identify Jack—his butler had done that honor before she'd even arrived at Oakwood. The faithful old servant had quit after that. She didn't blame him one bit.

Chloe swallowed hard, feeling faint as she unfolded the scrap of notepaper with the combination to her uncle's private wall safe. It was slow going because her hands were clumsy and sweaty. The cause wasn't nerves, exactly. It was more like her body's attempt to melt away so she wouldn't have to deal with whatever was behind that steel door. Opening the safe was like admitting Jack was gone. She didn't want to believe it.

What happened, Jack? Did you really drive home drunk? For a moment, tears blurred the numbers on the notepaper. *It just doesn't make sense. None of it does.*

For one thing, Jack was never a drinker. Chloe had told that to the police. They'd given her a pitying look, as if she were a rosy-cheeked innocent. In the end, they hadn't listened to a word she'd said.

Her tears dried as she felt a pair of steel-gray eyes boring a hole between her shoulders. Irritation flooded her, momentarily washing out grief and the daunting sense of responsibility thrust on her as executor. *Is there a problem? Oh, yeah, there's a problem. The room is a thousand degrees, my feet hurt in these stupid shoes and that guy over there is giving me the screaming willies.*

The guy in question was named Sam Ralston. He'd shown up for the funeral along with two of Uncle Jack's other friends. They were big, handsome men, pleasant, mixed with the other richy-rich guests well enough, but there was something off about the lot of them. Something *other.*

Who was Ralston to Uncle Jack? It was hard to say. Although she referred to Jack as her uncle, he was actually a distant cousin, and she'd never quite worked out his place in the family tree. Even though Jack had been her guardian after her parents' death, he'd not been around a lot of the time. At fourteen, it wasn't as if she'd needed supervision 24/7—at least not once the initial shock had passed. So, there were chunks of Jack's life she knew nothing about, Sam Ralston among them.

Jack had named him as the other executor, which was why he was here with her and Mr. Littleton, the family lawyer. Whatever was in the safe Jack had installed in his palatial bedroom would have to be documented as part of the estate, even if it was meant for Chloe.

Too bad. When she'd found out Ralston would be her partner in settling the estate, Chloe had actually shivered, as if someone had opened a refrigerator door right behind her.

"Do you need help?" Ralston asked, his baritone voice threaded with impatience.

"No," Chloe returned.

"You know you need a key, too. The safe has a double lock."

"Got it." She turned and gave Ralston a look over her shoulder.

The view, at least, was no hardship. More than once, she'd found herself staring at him, her body clenching with an unexpected and unwelcome fever of desire. He was somewhere in his thirties, tall and hard-bodied, with thick dark hair combed back from a broad forehead. He had the kind of face advertisers of leather jackets and fast cars would have liked—strong bones, a few character lines, and a dark shadow of beard no razor could quite obliterate. His nose was blade straight, his lips full and sculpted above a slightly cleft chin. The set of his head and shoulders said he owned whatever room he was in, and the rest of the planet besides.

Yummy and forbidding at the same time.

At the moment, he was returning her glare with a face carefully scraped clean of expression—and yet every line of his body screamed "Hurry up!"

So what's the rush? she wondered. He'd been like this—barely repressed urgency—ever since he arrived.

A career as a wedding planner had honed Chloe's skills at reading people. Too many couples ordered an event based on what they thought was correct rather than what was in their hearts. Chloe was good at ferreting out the truth from a shared look, an inflection in the voice, a finger drawn down the picture of a fluffy white dress in a magazine.

Just like her gut said Ralston and his buddies might have fat wallets and Italian-cut suits, but they'd break heads just as easily as they tossed back their single-malt whiskey. Now he was standing a little to the side, just out of the splash of late afternoon sunlight pouring through the French doors—a shady guy staying in the shade.

Ralston shifted, making a noise like a stifled sigh.

"Cool your jets," Chloe said evenly. "Whatever's in here is what Uncle Jack left me."

"He already left you a nice bequest," Ralston pointed out.

"So?"

Chloe cursed the lawyer for staying tactfully silent. She turned back to the safe and away from Ralston.

"Whatever is in the safe is going to be the interesting part." He sounded amused, the first sign of warmth she'd seen in him. "He liked his secrets."

"How do you know?"

"I know—knew—Jack." Now he sounded sad. She liked him better for it.

"How did you come to know him?"

He gave the same nonanswer he'd given her once before. "We hung out in a few of the same places."

Chloe began spinning the dial on the safe, her mouth gluey with unease. What was in there? Gold bars? The deed to a private island in the Caribbean? A stack of bearer-bonds with tons of zeroes? Jack had possessed a Midas touch, turning every business venture into a wild success.

Poor Jack. People would remember his *GQ* style and his tragic death, but Chloe would remember him starting a game of hide-and-seek with her when she was six. He'd sent the care package of flowers and chocolate when her engagement had fallen apart. He'd always been there, a steady friend and the best of listeners in a world where people were too busy to slow down and truly care. Sure, he'd had money, but he'd always offered his heart, too. People—especially their family—had never stopped grabbing long enough to notice.

Chloe swallowed hard, her fingers fumbling with the dial. The safe lock clicked. She swallowed again, feeling as though she was gulping down the entire situation and it was stuck painfully in her throat. Blinking to keep her vision clear, she took the key to the second lock out of the pocket of her sleeveless, indigo sheath dress.

The key slid into the lock. Chloe turned it and then pushed down on the long handle. The safe opened on a silent glide of hinges. It was wide enough that she had to step back to accommodate the swing of the door.

The men were suddenly behind her, Ralston so close that she could feel his lapel brush her shoulder. The lawyer was a bit better about personal space, but she could sense him hovering. If curiosity had a frequency, theirs was vibrating high enough to shatter glass.

All three of them made a noise when they saw what was in the safe. There was nothing but a white box about eight inches tall and maybe four feet by three feet, with a note taped to the lid. Chloe reached in, pulling the note off. The clear tape made a ripping sound as it pulled a tiny patch of the box's white lid away with it. She unfolded the note and felt the men lean in as she read.

Chloe,
If you're reading this, I'm gone. Keep this secret and
safe. When the story comes out, you'll know what to
do with it, and I know you'll do the right thing. Trust
Sam. Be careful.
Love you, kid,
Jack

Chloe reread the note. *Trust Sam.* Why? With what?

"What could it possibly be?" asked Littleton, a little breathlessly.

"Let's find out," said Ralston, lifting the large white box out of the otherwise empty safe.

Chloe took it out of his hands before he had taken one step away from the safe. "Uncle Jack left this for me, remember?"

His eyes flared with surprise, as if people rarely snatched loot out of his grasp. "I was just going to put it on the bed."

Chloe looked up into his steel-gray glare and smiled sweetly. "Thanks. I can manage."

Her heart kicked a little at Ralston's frown—part fear, part perverse enjoyment. He was a bit too pushy for his own good. *Trust Sam.*

She walked the few steps to Jack's orgy-sized bed. The whole room was in a black-and-white color scheme, making the scene look like a homage to liquorice allsorts. When she set the large white box on the ebony silk counterpane, the mystery of the package seemed even more emphatic.

The room was utterly silent, the rasp of Littleton's rapid breathing the loudest sound in it. Chloe felt for the box's opening. There was no tape. The lid lifted off, revealing a nest of blue-white tissue paper, the type meant to keep cloth from turning dingy with age. Ralston was at her elbow, close enough that her skin tingled with the breeze of his movements. Even now, her body felt magnetized to his nearness.

He pulled back one piece of tissue at the same moment that Chloe picked up the other. Despite the fact that they were strangers, they shared a look. It was utter astonishment.

"A wedding dress?" Chloe asked aloud. She touched the beaded bodice with one finger. The glittering stones were cold. Definitely not plastic. She's seen a lot of dresses in her career, and she could tell the work was exquisite.

"What the hell?" Ralston looked utterly stunned. "Jack would never have married."

"When the story comes out," Chloe said, repeating the note Jack had left. "What story? What was Uncle Jack doing with a dress?"

Ralston's eyebrows shot up with sudden dark amusement. "Well, it's tiny. At least we know it wasn't for him."

Chloe smiled, but her mind was already racing ahead. There were only so many reasons Jack would lock something away for safekeeping, whether it was treasure or weapons or even a gorgeous dress: because it was valuable, because it was meant for someone important to Jack or because dangerous people wanted it for the wrong reasons.

She was willing to bet the confection of lace and satin was all three.

Chapter 3

Death. That had been Jack's code name.

So who killed Death? It was almost a joke.

Irony sucks. Sam finally left the bedroom, taking a last look at Chloe Anderson bent over the white froth of the wedding dress. The image of her, sad and beautiful, stroking the symbol of so many feminine hopes and wishes—it brought a rush of something that was neither lust nor hunger, but held a hint of both. Strangely unnerved, he had elected to retreat. He could tell she wanted to be alone with her memories of Jack, and Sam appreciated that. The soft-spoken beauty was the only one in the family who seemed to care the man was dead.

And someone had to do the weepy thing. Sam was better at revenge.

The thought made his fangs descend, prepared to rip and tear in savage retribution.

His mind went back to Jack's last phone call, wringing each word dry of meaning. Jack had been running from his killer. Ambushed. Not much made Death run.

Sam banged out of the side door of the house, grateful to be in the clear air. The sun had just dipped behind the trees, making the outdoors safe for the undead. He took a huge breath, smelling green trees and the sweet pungency of the sun-warmed dirt. This was what he liked: solitude and no walls to hem him in. The past few days at Oakwood had been pure torture.

The people were the worst, and not just because they were a banquet of veins he couldn't touch. They were nasty. He didn't mind good, honest greed, but he couldn't stand all the whispered speculation about who would score big-time in Jack's will. And Sam called himself a mercenary. He was a rank amateur compared to Jack's aunt Mavis and that litter of useless, grasping cousins.

No wonder Jack was so good at covert operations. He'd needed them to survive his relatives.

Jack *had been* good. There went that verb tense thing again. It was hard to think of Jack in the past.

Sam swore under his breath. What were the Horsemen going to do now? There were only three of them left: Sam, the werewolf Kenyon, and Dr. Mark Winspear, the vampire they called Plague. Jack was—had been—their team leader.

He started toward the gate, his shoes crunching on the white gravel drive. It was so clean, Sam could imagine the hired help dusting each tiny pebble every morning, working inch by inch across the broad sweep that led back to the road.

Sam walked through the gates, approaching the oak tree where the Porsche had crashed. The tree had survived better than the car, but not by much. It would have to be felled before there were any serious windstorms. One heavy branch dangled from the trunk, hanging on by a thin layer of bark.

Plague was frowning at the ground around the roots of the oak. He was tall, olive-skinned, and dressed in chinos and a short-sleeved shirt. The doctor looked enviably casual.

In contrast, Sam felt hot and irritable in the black suit

he'd put on for the paperwork-signing and safe-opening portion of the entertainment. "Find anything?"

Winspear looked up, his dark eyes serious. "About half a mile down the road. Shell casings. The local cops missed them. Kenyon is going over the woods again, sniffing for more. Maybe he'll find a bullet in a tree."

His voice still held a faint trace of an indefinable accent. Despite the English-sounding name, he'd once mentioned growing up in Italy. The last of the Horsemen to join, he was by far the most private. No one could actually say they knew Mark Winspear. Still, he was the best at what he did. He was not only an accomplished doctor, but was what the vampires called an "eraser"—someone who possessed a rare ability to manipulate human memory.

"Kenyon looked at the casings and believes the bullets were silver," the doctor added. "We'll know more once we've gone over the car."

"So it was assassination," Sam said, stating what was rapidly becoming the obvious.

The doctor was peering awkwardly under the dangling branch, examining the marks in the soil, and made a sound that held a world of resignation. "The car had to be going eighty, by the amount of damage. That raises questions. Jack loved his Porsche too much to risk it at that speed on these roads. And you know how slim the odds are of a vampire actually getting drunk, despite the headlines."

Playboy Dies Living Fast and Hard. Sam swore. "He might have been drugged. Can you do a tox screen?"

Winspear's mouth was a grim line. "The body was badly burned, but if it's possible, I'll get the information we need."

He looked stricken, and for a moment Sam felt sorry for him. It didn't seem right that he had to do an autopsy on a friend, but who else had the expertise to examine dead vampires? Not the city morgue.

Sam shifted impatiently. "You have any theories about all this yet?"

Winspear stood, folding his arms. "I don't like to speculate before I have all the facts."

"Jack had a lot of enemies. We all do. We need some way to narrow down the list."

Winspear shrugged. "What stands out? What was Jack up to during the last month?"

"I don't know." The Horsemen had been taking a short break from the job and from each other—a necessary thing when so much of their work was all about death and carnage.

"I can't answer that, either—I was out at my cabin. It was just by chance that I'd arrived back in town when you called."

Sam grunted in irritation. Patient deduction wasn't his forte. He liked the part where he got to hit things. "Jack seems to have been close to his niece. He might have mentioned something. Small details can provide clues."

"Maybe." Winspear looked away.

Sam understood his doubts. The Horsemen were the only ones who knew who and what Jack really was. The rest was all playacting, learning to fit in with the latest slang and electronic gadgets. Remembering to hide every second of every day.

An unexpected jolt of melancholy hit Sam. He swatted it away with an answering annoyance. "I'll ask some questions. A few odd things have come up in the estate."

Winspear raised a dark brow. "Such as?"

"He left his niece a wedding dress." The image of Chloe and the dress came back, along with that strange, restless feeling.

"A dress hardly seems alarming. Unless it was, as I have heard human girls exclaim, a dress to die for?"

Sam closed his eyes, fighting down a sarcastic retort. "Never mind. It's a puzzle piece I can't make fit."

"Then I would talk to the niece. Maybe there's a dressmaker or a delivery company that can provide a clue."

Sam gave a small, ironic salute. "Shall do."

Winspear looked dubious. "Can you talk to—what's her name? Chloe? Or do you want me to do that?"

"I think I can handle her." In fact, handling her sounded like a solid plan—he could spend hours executing that particular mission, if he left his scruples at the door.

A faint trace of a smile lurked in Winspear's face. "I'd be careful if I were you. She looks like the smart, quiet type. They're dangerous."

"I'm a vampire. She's just a wedding planner."

Winspear gave a rare, low laugh. "So was Cinderella's fairy godmother. Don't underestimate her."

Sam stuffed his hands in his pockets. "I'll steer clear of mice and pumpkins."

It took little time for Sam to track Chloe down. She had taken the dress from Jack's suite to the room where she was staying. The door was ajar, allowing Sam to pause a moment before he had to knock. He used the time to study the location, as he always did before mounting an assault. It was a large chamber, one window, sparse furniture. Definitely a feminine space, with flowery prints on the walls and bedspread.

Chloe was standing in the middle of the room with her back to the door, looking sleek and polished from her high-heeled shoes to the twist in her dark blond hair. She was staring at the dress. It was hooked to the front of a huge, mahogany wardrobe, the dark wood showing off the white foam of lace.

Sam knew nothing about gowns, but he was pretty sure

this one was exceptional. There was something in the proportions and detailing that said this wasn't some off-the-rack number.

The same could be said for Chloe. The curve of her spine drew his eyes, his gaze lingering on her exposed neck. Ever since he'd arrived at Oakwood, she'd drawn him. Sam desired women and had them, well and often, but few provided more than a moment's interest. War was not prone to the softer emotions—they were anathema to everything he was.

This woman, though, brushed his senses like the scent of a delicate perfume. She was pretty, but it was a sense of poised energy that made her remarkable—like an arrow about to fly. He couldn't help watching, expectant for the moment, wondering what would happen if she finally sprang loose.

Sam imagined that release of energy, feeling it with his whole body. It would be exquisite. The thought made his fangs descend, and he quickly began thinking of dull paperwork instead. *She's not for you. Women like her die around creatures like you.*

She turned, her brows drawing together when she saw him there. "Something I can help you with?" Her words were quiet and low, but her voice resonated right through him.

You have no idea. A sudden stab of hunger pushed to the fore, reminding him again of what he was: a weapon meant for blood sports. She looked soft and delicious, as if she would taste of summer. Once again, his body tightened in anticipation.

Sam swallowed hard, wrestling himself as he had Kenyon's wolf, holding back the snapping jaws of the beast. *Small talk. Make small talk.*

"I can't help wondering what Jack was doing with that." He nodded toward the dress.

She relaxed a bit. "Me, too."

"It's good quality, isn't it?"

"Yes." She folded her arms and walked toward it. Sam trailed after her, using the moment as an excuse to get closer. The room was redolent with her perfume—something that reminded him of sunshine and lemonade.

He realized he was stalking her, and forced himself to stand still. "Should it be out of the safe?" he asked.

"Maybe not, but I can't learn anything about it when it's locked away."

Sam nodded. She had a point. "That's right. You're the wedding expert. Any insights?"

With a professional air, Chloe eyed the dress. "There's no label, but I'm sure it's made to order. The beading is hand-done. It's probably unique."

"Expensive?"

"It's worth a fortune. That's Italian silk or I'm a duck."

Sam slanted a glance at her. She was definitely not a duck. "None of your relatives tried to make off with it yet?"

She gave a rueful smile. "They don't know about it. Fortunately, the last of the happy horde is leaving in the morning."

"How long will you be here?" He wouldn't be leaving a moment sooner.

She looked up. Her eyes were dark blue. "Until the end of the week or so. After that the house will be going on the market."

"You don't waste time."

She gave a soft sigh that made his skin tingle. "It's not me. Everyone wants their piece of the estate."

Sam watched her eyes sparkle with tears. Forgetting himself, he brushed her wrist with his fingertips, the lightest gesture of sympathy. One he would never normally make. She blinked, folding her arms across her stomach. Sam dropped his hand, the feel of her skin clinging to the pads of his fingers. *Silky.*

He forced his mind to the task of asking questions, doing his best to shut off his senses. The woman was like a drug, scrambling his thoughts. "Was Jack close to any family but you?"

"Not really. My father, but he died when I was fourteen. Along with my mother." She looked away. "Long story."

Something told Sam now was not the moment to ask for details. "No one was close, but the rest still think they should get a piece of all this?" He made a gesture indicating the house.

"Of course." Chloe made a slight movement, almost a shudder, as if she was trying to shake off a distasteful memory. "Jack had a talent for making money."

He also had centuries of financial experience, but Chloe didn't know that.

"Who were Jack's friends?" he asked abruptly.

"I thought that was you."

Winspear was right. He sucked at interrogation. Frustration made him resort to his usual bluntness. "You're in the wedding business. You said the dress was unique. Is there any way to figure out who owned it?"

"What did you say you did for a living?" She narrowed her eyes.

Too blunt. *Oops.* "Trust fund baby," Sam said lightly. "I don't do anything." *But I want to know Jack's exact schedule for the last six weeks.*

The set of her mouth said she didn't believe him. "But obviously you like solving mysteries."

"Why not?"

"Well, here's one for you to chew on. I don't think Jack died the way the police say he did."

Sam nearly started. He kept his voice very neutral. "Oh?"

Chloe sat on the edge of the bed, looking suddenly tired and much younger than she had a moment ago. "Jack had a hidden side. I don't think most people even noticed, but if there was a loud noise, he'd reach for a gun even if he wasn't wearing one. I never knew what that was all about, but I'd bet good money you and your friends do."

A very, very smart girl.

"Did Jack have enemies?" she asked, her voice even.

"They're mostly dead." *Or undead.*

Her hand, so fine-boned and soft, made a fist. "I think you guys missed one."

"What are you talking about?"

She shot him a look. "You've got that whole brothers-in-arms vibe going on. I think you watch each other's backs pretty closely, and I don't mean around the boardroom table. Well, try this one on. I don't think Uncle Jack smashed up his car by accident."

Sam stayed mute.

Chloe pushed on, her jaw set in a stubborn line. "He never drank as much as he pretended to. The whole playboy thing was a game, like a mask he wore when it suited him."

Her fierce tone was doing something to Sam's insides, a painful, hot, sweet feeling radiating from deep in his gut. He was getting turned on in a big way. *Oh, good timing, Ralston.*

"I don't know," he said casually. "Once in a very rare while, Jack could tie one on."

Chloe grimaced. "He wasn't stupid. Not where the Porsche was involved."

God, she did know her uncle. Jack loved that car. This whole conversation offended his sense of fair play. *She de-*

serves to know she's not the only one who thinks Jack was killed. But if he broke cover, it wasn't just his existence on the line. *Women like her die around creatures like you.* The thought repeated in his mind like a tolling bell. He knew that from bitter experience. Everything about who he was, what he did, invited danger.

"Leave it to the police," he said reasonably. "They know what they're looking for."

Her eyebrows shot up. "Which is why your two friends are all over the scene of the accident? They've been there since day one like a pair of designer-casual bloodhounds."

Sam stomped on a snort of laughter before it could get away. "You're imagining things."

"Lame." The heat in her eyes said she didn't like being dismissed.

"You're just upset because he died suddenly. It's understandable."

"Lame." A flush of pink was climbing her cheeks. "I'm not a clueless child, Mr. Ralston. Don't try to hide information from me."

Irritation flashed through him. "What do you think happened? One of your relatives hired a gunman to get Jack's estate?"

Her blue eyes didn't waver. "I bet you'd know how to find out if they did."

He gave up. "I can't help you."

"Then get out of my bedroom."

Her expression was hard. Unexpectedly, Sam felt it dent his ego. He wanted to reach across the gulf his job and his nature put between them. It was a rare impulse, and one he couldn't do a damned thing about.

Probably just as well.

His gaze wandered to the wedding dress, taking it in for a brief moment. Marriage was just one more human entanglement he'd left behind, but for a split second he wondered what it would be like to be that unguarded with somebody. It had been too long to remember.

Sam turned and walked out of the room, leaving Chloe alone on the bed.

For now.

Chapter 4

Chloe curled up under the covers, her eyes sandy from lack of sleep. The room should have felt restful, for this was where she'd slept most of her teenage years—but too much had dramatically, tragically changed.

Someone had murdered Jack, she was sure of it, but she had no proof. She'd tried talking to the police, but they couldn't—or wouldn't—help. They'd treated her like a kid too young for grown-up worries. It pushed every one of her buttons. Still, how could she blame the cops? All she had to go on was Jack's character and the suspicious behavior of his buddies.

In the dark quiet of the bedroom, she surrendered to pain and loss, letting the pillow muffle her sobs. She just couldn't grasp the fact that she wouldn't see Jack again. Ever. For as long as she drew breath. But it wasn't just grief she felt. Hot, frustrated anger sliced along her raw nerves. She wanted to act, to avenge, but she didn't know how.

Chloe sniffed and rolled over, the sheets sticking to her hot skin. Outside the window, wind hissed through the trees, making a lullaby of the restless breeze. Chloe's mind ticked on.

Suspicion just wouldn't stop clawing at her. She knew

she was right to speak up, but other people reacted like she was a hysterical freak—even Sam Ralston. Once she'd asked him about Jack's accident, it had been like talking to a wall, his handsome face wiped of expression.

Oh, well. At least stone-faced was a change from broody or bossy, which seemed to be his other settings. Too bad he had a magnetism that turned her insides to pudding. *Yeah, right. A broody, bossy blank wall with gobs of animal magnetism. Every girl's dream.*

She had worked long enough in the marriage business to know what she wanted in a man: dependable, home-oriented, quiet and sensible. None of her family's nasty competitive streak. An independent business owner or middle-ranking executive would be perfect. Solid, but not flashy.

Chloe pulled the blanket under her chin. *Someone who likes gardening and country fairs.*

Not Sam Ralston.

She rolled over again and froze.

What was that? It wasn't a sound so much as the sense of the air being displaced. As if something had passed in absolute silence. Chloe held her breath, listening.

The wind soughed outside. Almost beyond her range of hearing, she could hear the clock on the grand sweep of stairs chime half past midnight, and then the house was still once more. Logic said she'd been imagining things. There was no one there.

And yet every nerve ending strained with apprehension. A bead of sweat trickled down the small of her back, making her shiver.

She heard a faint exhalation of breath.

Not her own.

Someone's in the room with me!

Without moving a muscle, she scanned the darkness.

The bedroom curtains were partially open, admitting just enough moonlight to separate one blob of furniture from the next. Opposite the foot of the bed, the wedding dress hung on the wardrobe door like a filmy ghost. She wasn't about to leave the dress unattended, but having it near made her feel closer to Jack so she'd left it there for the night. She suddenly wondered if that had been a wise thing to do.

Beside the tall wardrobe lurked a darker shape, and it was slowly moving. Like a stain, it crept across the white cloud of the dress, making the garment shift. The moonlight caught the crystal beads, making the bodice glitter with shards of cold light. Chloe heard the soft rustle of silk, and then the dress seemed to bob in the air.

Someone was stealing it. Outrage sparked through her, followed by flat-out disbelief. She was right there, mere feet away! Why would anyone risk her catching them? *And who knows I've got it?*

Aunt Mavis? Her hand snaked out from beneath the comforter, finding the switch of her bedside lamp.

"Don't." The male voice was hard and cold and not one she recognized.

The sneering tone made her more defiant than smart. Chloe swore under her breath and flicked the switch anyway.

She felt the rush of air as the figure lunged across the room. The china lamp exploded as it hit the floor. Chloe yelped in surprise, instinctively rolling away to avoid the spray of shards. Rough hands grabbed her by the back of her nightgown, forcing her facedown on the mattress.

"Don't," the voice repeated, the sneer turning to something more sinister.

Chloe panted in fright, her face turned away from her attacker and pressed hard into the bed. He had her arms pinned behind her back at a painful angle.

Let go of me! she screamed in her head, but somehow the words couldn't find her tongue. She was paralyzed, the man's hot breath stroking her skin as he chuckled, long and low.

"Can I trust you not to move?" he said.

It was then she felt the cold kiss of a gun muzzle against her spine. She sucked in a stuttering gasp. She felt his lips brush her ear. "I'd rather not shoot. I'd rather leave without attracting attention. Get it?"

"Y-yes," she whispered, feeling a hot sting as tears filled her eyes. She squeezed her eyelids tight, stifling a sob. She wanted to scream so badly, but her voice had abandoned her. She'd taken self-defense classes, but the gun trumped any tricks she knew. She'd never been so terrified in her life.

She felt a sudden weight on her back as the thief straddled her, pinning her arms with his body and squeezing the air from her lungs. Her head was turned to the side, but it was still hard to breathe. Chloe struggled, gulping air that stank with her attacker's sweat.

She sensed him grabbing a pillow off the bed. A moment later, the cool cotton muffled her face, filling her nose and mouth. A gun might make too much noise, but suffocation was silent.

Desperate, Chloe tried to squirm away.

"Damn you!" he muttered, and she felt his grip tighten.

Fighting would only get her killed a different way, but Chloe couldn't stop. The will to survive was too strong. She bucked hard enough that the pillow slipped and she gasped in precious oxygen.

Wham!

Her eyes went wide as the bedroom door slammed against the wall. The pillow fell away and a flare of sudden light filled the room as someone turned on the overhead. The thief swore, pushing Chloe's face against the bed with his bare hand. Her mouth flooded with the metallic taste of fresh panic.

"Get away from her!" someone barked. Someone used to shouting orders. It sounded like Faran Kenyon.

"Now!" That one was Ralston!

Chloe felt her attacker's weight shift.

The deafening noise from his gun came from right above her, making her skull ring.

Oh, God!

A hot spray of blood spattered the pillow in front of Chloe. She recoiled, covering her head, and realized a beat later that she could move her arms. Her attacker had leaped off the bed.

Or been blown off. She scanned the sheets in front of her, crimson spreading across the white like bright drops of paint. Nausea lurched in her throat.

Ralston vaulted over the bed with an unholy snarl, leaping for her attacker. Chloe twisted around to catch a glimpse of a dark-clad man lunging toward the window. She covered her face as the window smashed, her own scream sounding muffled because she was still deaf from the gunshot.

Her attacker disappeared in a hail of glass. Ralston skidded to a stop as he reached the gaping mess where the window had been. Kenyon joined him a second later. Both had their weapons up, standing to the side of the window frame and scanning the grass below.

Chloe could guess what they were thinking. Her room was on the second story, but a porch roof jutted out below. Someone could use that as a halfway point while jumping to the ground.

"Do you see him?" Ralston demanded. He was wearing nothing but worn jeans and sneakers, his torso bare. His big body was still ready to spring, coiled muscles drawn tight.

"Not from here," Kenyon replied.

"Go."

Kenyon turned, running for the door and thumbing on his cell phone as he went. By the time he reached the door, someone on the other end of the connection had answered. "Close the gates!"

Chloe could make out the words, but beyond that was nothing but the muffled ringing from the gunshot. For a moment, her emotions felt the same: numb, stunned, distant.

I nearly died.

"You okay?" Ralston stared out the window, still scanning the darkness.

She cleared her throat. "I think so." The words quavered.

"Good."

As her pulse slowed, Chloe studied his back, her gaze tracing the muscles and bones of his broad shoulders. Half naked, he looked far more at home than he had in a suit.

It was as if, stripped of clothes, the real man was visible. Sam Ralston moved with an animal grace that stirred something primitive in her. Her fear responded to his blatantly male presence, wanting all that size and strength on her side.

"Is he gone?" she asked, her voice shaking.

"Not for long," he replied, his head moving slowly as he scanned the grounds. "He's going to pay for this."

Finally, Ralston turned away from the window, a furrow between his dark brows. His gaze flicked over her face. "You're not okay. You're pale."

"So are you."

His gaze flicked around the room. "It's the smell of blood."

"I hate it, too." Chloe hiccupped, feeling a wave of nervous energy shudder through her. The numbness was fading. She wanted to scream. Or cry. *He held me at gunpoint. He tried to smother me.*

The very idea was surreal. For a moment, she doubted that it had happened at all.

"You're safe now." Ralston took a quick step toward her. The speed of it, the size of him made her flinch. He stopped, looking at her for a long moment. Chloe felt her pulse speeding again, pounding in her head.

Slowly now, he set his gun on the nightstand and put his hands on his hips, a gesture that showed his broad chest. His gray eyes were dark and angry. "Do you know what he wanted?"

Chloe felt slightly dizzy. Adrenaline aftermath and unexpected desire hit her like strong brandy. *Sam rescued me!* A wave of new emotions—ones she couldn't even name— lapped dangerously at the edges of her thoughts. "He was after the dress."

They both looked over at the gown, which pooled like a deflated cloud on the carpet. Sam crossed over to it, picking it up by the hanger and replacing it on the wardrobe door. The gesture was surprisingly careful.

Something about it—the crumpled dress or the way he handled it—made her start to cry in soft, gulping sobs. Chloe covered her face, horrified at the pathetic sounds coming from her throat, but the feel of the pillow against her face, the attacker's hands on her skin played over and over again in her mind.

The bed dipped as Sam's weight settled next to her. He pulled a blanket around her, his gestures efficient but gentle, as if he were holding himself firmly in check. "It's over. He's gone."

"Then why am I crying?" she snapped. She was weirdly angry, as if it were all Sam's fault.

"You're in shock," he said quietly.

"I don't cry."

"I know." He sounded apologetic.

She wanted to demand how he could possibly know what she did or didn't do, but it was clear he was just being kind. Biting her lip, she struggled to stop weeping. She craved Sam's protection but was furious that she needed it. *I've got to pull myself together.*

Frustrated, her mind lunged for specifics. Something besides the horrible feeling of being pushed and crushed and threatened that played over and over in her head, like a bad song that just wouldn't shut up. "How did he get in?"

"Probably the window. I don't know yet."

Yet? That meant the mysterious Mr. Ralston was going to investigate. She swallowed down a fresh batch of sobs. "How did you know I was in trouble?"

"I heard something break."

"Uh-huh." That sounded too pat. Chloe's mind grappled for some way to probe his answer, but she was still too overwhelmed. "Thank you for saving me."

He gave her a guarded look. "No problem. I was hoping to hit the guy in the leg so we could catch and question him. Didn't quite work out that way. I overcompensated my aim. I didn't want to risk shooting you by mistake."

"I appreciate that."

"Yeah." Sam touched her arm gently. She would have expected him to crush her to his chest, do the manly-man protective thing, but he didn't. He was being careful about how he handled her. He knew enough to give her distance, as though he'd dealt with situations like this before.

Chloe realized she was thinking of him as Sam now, and not Ralston. Sam, her savior. Super Sam. Oh, what the heck, he'd earned some girlish gratitude. She was just glad her mind was starting to function again.

A babble of voices came from the hallway. Was her hearing just coming back or had they been out there all along? She slid off the bed, feeling a little unsteady.

"Where are you going?" Sam demanded.

She gestured helplessly at the door. "My aunt. My cousin. People. They're wondering what's going on."

Sam held up a hand. "Let me."

He pulled open the door, looking like the sexy trades-man from a bored housewife's daydream. From where she stood, all she could see was the curve of Sam's shoulder and his denim-hugged backside. That would set the fam-ily's collective imagination spinning. *Go me.*

While he stood in the hallway, Chloe changed into a pair of yoga pants and a T-shirt. She saw with disgust the nightgown she'd been wearing had splatters of blood on it. She balled up the garment and threw it in the garbage can. There was blood on the sheets, too, and glass on the floor, but suddenly she was too exhausted to deal with any of it. She perched on a corner of the bed far from the blood, wishing she could just lie down.

No, no lying down. Not here. She could still feel the echo of a hand crushing her face into the bed.

"How are you doing?" Sam asked as he came back into the room.

The question wasn't the vague politeness of a stranger. To her utter surprise, Sam crouched in front of her, study-ing her face. His expression was concerned, almost tender. He reached out, catching her hands gently in his. His skin was cool and wonderful, the gesture infinitely comforting. "Look at me," he said. "You're going to be okay. I'm here."

Chloe met his eyes. A subtle shift came over his features, a tightening of the lips, his pupils eating up the steel-gray irises. There was concern there, but something else now, too. Desire. Possession. He lifted her hand to his lips, brush-ing the lightest of kisses across the back of her fingers.

The gesture was courtly, barely qualifying as a true kiss, but a flood of tingling arousal swamped her skin from head to foot. No one had ever touched her so intimately with so little flesh.

She gasped lightly, and the skin around his eyes flinched, a predator narrowing his focus. Now it was her neck that prickled with the faintest frisson of fear.

It was too much. Chloe looked down, unable to hold his hypnotic gaze a moment longer. Heat flooded her face. "Chloe?"

His voice was soft, intimate. It sucked her down further, so she fought it, clawing her way back to the present. She'd just been attacked. Sam had chased the bad guy away.

Memory slammed back, ripping the cobwebs away.

"I wanted to fight," she said. "I wanted to cry out."

He made a noise as close to a sigh as someone like Sam Ralston would make. "You did what you needed to. It's called surviving. That's how we're programmed."

She took a steadying breath. "You didn't freeze. Neither did your friend. How did you just happen to be there with guns?"

"I always carry." In a blink, his face was back to his blank-wall setting. Sam rose and put an appropriate distance between them.

Chloe folded her arms, feeling suddenly as if a fire had been doused, leaving her in the cold. What had just happened? Had she asked one question too many? Too bad, because every answer he gave prompted a dozen questions more.

There was a sharp rap on the door. Sam opened it, looking relieved. Kenyon pushed his way in, a grumpy look on his face. His blond hair looked mussed, as if he'd been pushing his hands through it. He stopped, giving Chloe a once-over. "You all right?"

"Sure," she replied.

"Anything?" Sam asked his friend.

"Nope. The security here means well, but what can you expect?"

Sam swore lustily. "How can that happen? I shot him in the shoulder. He was bleeding."

"They don't have our training. Trampled the trail. Messed it up."

Chloe caught the shut-up look Sam shot his friend. *What training?*

Kenyon either didn't notice the look or pretended not to care. "So what was that guy after?"

"The wedding dress," Sam replied, gesturing toward the place where it hung.

Kenyon gave it a curious look. "Seriously?"

Then something seemed to catch his eye. Suddenly alert, he crossed to the wardrobe. He pulled a small Maglite flashlight from the pocket of his cargo pants and shone it at the beading around the gown's low neckline.

Chloe got to her feet, still feeling shaky. "What do you see?"

"Interesting decoration. It's not all crystals."

Chloe had noticed that, too. There was elaborate embroidery all around the neckline, much of it gold wire couched with silk thread and dotted with seed pearls. Dozens and dozens of set stones had been added to the design, giving a shimmering fire to every movement of the dress. "The headpiece has similar decoration. I think the pearls might be real."

Kenyon looked up, an odd expression on his face. "So are the stones."

Chloe gulped. "What do you mean?"

He gave a wry smile to Sam. "You remember last March?"

"That can't be right," Sam said dully. "Tell me you're kidding."

"You know your guns, I know my luxury goods."

Sam cursed. "We should have known the moment this turned up in Jack's safe. Though how he ended up with them…"

"Were you looking for a wedding dress?"

"No." Sam suddenly looked offended. "What in the nine hells was Jack up to?"

"What are you talking about?" Chloe demanded, her voice going shrill.

Kenyon pulled out his light again and played it across the bodice of the dress, making the stones dance with white fire. "These are diamonds. Whatever bride belongs to this dress could have bought a small country with this dowry. In fact, if I'm right, one almost did. I think these are the lost diamonds of the Kingdom of Marcari."

Chapter 5

Chloe's gasp hit Sam hard. He whipped around, alert to whatever had startled her and ready to smash it. But nothing was there. Her shock had simply been at Kenyon's words.

Nothing like a fortune in lost diamonds to stop a conversation cold. *And what were they doing in Jack's safe?* Sam ground his teeth. He wasn't big on surprises, and this was a whopper.

He edged closer to Chloe anyhow. That kind of ice on the lam meant danger permeated the air like a fine mist. The scum who'd attacked her would have friends. *The first one who touches her will lose an arm.*

The ferocity of the thought rocked him. He felt far too much for this human woman, but she had been brave, cool-headed despite her obvious distress. He could respect that. And he couldn't deny that she was lovely, even the curve of her cheek showing nature's geometry to perfection. But those weren't good enough reasons to let the weakness of emotions compromise War.

Better to focus on the fact that she was Jack's niece, and alone. Her relatives could not be counted on to keep her safe. They'd be more likely to strip the valuables from her cooling corpse. Therefore, she needed his help. That was acceptable. Best of all, it was a good reason to be near Chloe. Totally legitimate, even for a bloodsucking fiend. From this second on, Sam was the ultimate guard dog, protecting the girl, the diamonds and the dress. He owed it to Jack.

And he owed it to the Princess Amelie, the bride who belonged in that dress. He kicked himself for not realizing it was her gown right away. But then again, he'd never seen it before. And also—even with a connection to the family, why would Jack have the dress of a foreign princess half a world away? That was odd, even for Jack.

Chloe was definitely struggling to stay in the loop. "Lost diamonds?" She scrunched her face in confusion. "What are you talking about?"

"These are the Jewels of Marcari," Kenyon replied.

"Need-to-know," Sam growled in warning. It wasn't the Horsemen's case, but the blanket order to all the Company's agents had been for absolute secrecy about the heist. "We're doing this by the book."

At least that's what Sam would do. Or Winspear. They followed orders. Instead, Kenyon gave him an eye roll.

Sam clenched his teeth harder, sensing chaos about to descend. *Werewolves. Too valuable to strangle. Not valuable enough to lock away for good.* It was the way they'd always worked. Kenyon would push just enough to drive Sam crazy, simply because it was fun.

"You heard about the royal wedding, right?" Kenyon said, addressing Chloe but with a sly look at Sam. "The Prince of Vidon and the Princess of Marcari?"

"Kenyon!"

Chloe shot Sam a startled glance. The look made him feel like a bully.

"The wedding?" she asked tentatively. "Sure, I heard about it. It was in the media for months, especially when

Prince Kyle of Vidon was caught with his hand in the wrong cookie jar."

Sam snorted. The cookie's stage name was Brandi Snap. The wedding was off, but Brandi had a lucrative book deal.

Chloe's eyes narrowed. "So what…?"

Sam folded his arms and interrupted. "It's a long story."

For an instant, Chloe looked hurt again, and then irritation filled her eyes. "Spill. If the diamonds are in my bedroom and bringing out the bad guys, I have a right to the details."

Her voice, normally so low and soft, held an edge. She'd reached the end of her rope.

Sam scowled, torn between duty and a desire to tell her everything because she looked so vulnerable. He opted for a middle ground. "The stones belong to the Royal House of Marcari or of Vidon, depending on which one you ask. The two countries have been at odds since the Crusades. Part of the fight is over these gems."

"The wedding would have resolved it," Kenyon added. "At least in theory. The stones were recut in honor of the occasion. The finest were to form Princess Amelie's dowry."

"I knew that much," Chloe said. "Once the wedding took place, the gems would belong to both countries. End of argument."

Sam shrugged. "Until Prince Charming ended up in the tabloids. Now peace is further away than ever."

Looking pale and shaky, Chloe rose from the bed and crossed to the dress, fingering the elaborately worked bodice. "Then this is Princess Amelie's gown. No wonder the workmanship is so exquisite."

Sam watched her hands, so graceful and precise as they stroked the cloth. He imagined them cooking food, winding a bandage, holding a baby. Things that no longer had a part in his life.

Her voice was wistful. "Speaking as a wedding consultant, putting the diamonds on the dress was a stunning concept. She would have shimmered like star fire. A symbol of peace. Everything a royal bride is supposed to be. What a tragedy it didn't work out."

Chloe turned, her gaze flicking from Sam to Kenyon and back. "So, how did these get stolen? How did Jack get them?"

"Good questions," Sam replied. They were ones Jack would never answer.

"You seem to know a lot about the diamonds."

"Jewelry is a special interest of mine," Kenyon put in, the picture of utter innocence.

Sam wished there was such a thing as a werewolf muzzle. He considered Chloe's doubtful expression. He could literally see her figuring out far too much, the thoughts flying across her face. If this kept up, they would have to wipe her memory.

He hated the idea. Selfishly, he wanted her to remember him saving her. *Why? You can't have her.*

"When did the gems go missing?" she asked.

"Their absence was noted in March. The fact was kept from the media."

"How do you know that?"

"I have friends."

She gave him a dubious look. He held it, giving away nothing even though his hands itched to cup her body and pull her to him. Her anger smelled spicy. She knew he was hiding something. Despite circumstances, the determination in her eyes tantalized.

A contest between them would be interesting. His

strength. Her wits. It would never happen. Their worlds
would intersect for no more than a few days, and then he'd
be gone.

Just as well. War was meant for killing, not affairs of
the heart.

Sam insisted that Chloe move to a different bedroom.
Still spooked, she agreed without a fuss. In her books, Sam
had earned the title of security expert that night, and there
was no way she was getting into that blood-soaked bed
anyway. Once the dress was back in the safe, Sam escorted
her to a room in the south wing, where there were no other
guests to complicate his security plans. He lingered outside
her door until she locked herself in.

Not that she was going to sleep, exhausted or not. Her
thoughts were caught on a carnival wheel, reeling up, down
and occasionally wrong side up. How did Uncle Jack get
mixed up with foreign royalty and diamond thieves? Sure,
he was a man of mystery and all that, but this was—well,
it was pretty out there. But he'd been murdered, so she had
to snap out of the shock and focus on the facts.

Sitting cross-legged on the sea-green counterpane of the
guest room's bed, she switched on her laptop and opened
her spiral-bound journal to a fresh page. If Jack was involved, it might help to reconstruct his movements for the
last few months of his life. A person didn't just happen on
a royal princess's wedding gown, especially one coated in
jewels. It had crossed his path someplace—and not in this
town. Lovely though it was, Wingman County was hardly
James Bond territory.

Chloe handled a few of Jack's private business affairs,
so she usually knew when he went out of town. She clicked
on her electronic calendar and paged back to March, when

the diamonds had apparently gone missing. Nothing of interest. She paged back further.

On February 15, there was a note that Jack asked her to attend a luncheon on his behalf. He had gone to the south of France—an intriguing detail, since it was a short train ride from the Côte d'Azur to Marcari. *Okay, but lots of people go to warm places that time of year. What's to say he wasn't just enjoying the weather?*

When did he come back? She paged forward, landing in April. She'd met him in New York, at a show by the designer Jessica Lark. She was a friend of Jack's, though Chloe didn't know how good a friend. Jack definitely kissed, but he'd seldom told.

Jotting down the dates and places, Chloe stared at the designer's name, remembering her brief meeting with the woman. She'd been about thirty, hauntingly beautiful and a rare talent Chloe had felt privileged to meet. They'd shaken hands, firm and businesslike. No fake little air kisses from Lark.

Recalling that night gave her the shivers. She could hear the clink of glasses, the wash of too many perfumes in the hot room. Chloe remembered the brush of Lark's silk dress against her bare arm, Jack laughing at something she'd said.

An ache in her throat made her shut down the memory. A month later, Jessica Lark had burned to death in a fire that had destroyed her studio. Nothing—and nobody— had survived.

Of the three people in that scene, Chloe was the only one who hadn't been murdered. Yet. *What's the connection?*

The answer was obvious. Jessica Lark was—

Something thumped against her door. Cold terror snaked up her arms, sending her scurrying off the bed. The journal flopped to the floor, making her jump again. She took a breath to cry out, but it died as a chill lump blocked her throat. Memories of the attack came slamming back, pumping adrenaline through her blood. Her hands trembled.

The door had a lock, but no dead bolt. She glanced around for a weapon. Pickings were slim. This wasn't one of the guest suites, just a spare bedroom with nice but functional furniture. No suits of armor with convenient battle-axes. No ancient rifles crisscrossed over the fireplace. Just a bed and a dresser.

She knew where Jack had kept his SIG Sauer, but that was on another floor. *So why didn't I bring that with me?*

Because she wasn't used to actually needing a loaded gun. As a rule, this sort of danger didn't find wedding planners.

Chloe held her frozen position, suffocating with fear, for an entire, eternal minute. She heard nothing but the pounding of her pulse.

Blast! She had to know what she'd heard or she'd stare at the door for the rest of the night, wondering. Guessing. Expecting the worst.

Willing herself to move, she picked up a china shepherdess from the night table and stalked toward the door, moving as quietly as a shadow. She gripped the figure with both hands, the china slick and cold against her palms. As a weapon, it wasn't as hopeless as it looked. Bo Peep and her lambs might be frilly, but they were plenty heavy.

Chloe pressed her ear to the door, holding her breath to listen. Silence. Tentatively, she reached for the knob, balancing Bo Peep in one hand and gripping the cool brass with the other. In one quick move, she popped the lock and pulled it open. With a quick step backward, she grabbed the statue in both hands and hoisted it into the air, ready to bludgeon an intruder.

Sam sat across the hall, his back to the wall, his long legs stretched out. He'd pulled on a plain white T-shirt.

His gun rested beside him, or did in the first fraction of a second that she was opening the door. Then it was in his hand, and he was on his feet.

Her breath stuttered, relief colliding with fresh panic. He wasn't pointing the weapon, just very clearly on the alert, but no one should be able to move that fast.

She slowly lowered the statue. "It's you," she said lamely.

Sam eyed the lump of china. "Is that a sheep?"

"Yeah." She watched, mesmerized by the play of muscles as he relaxed.

"That gives new meaning to offensive weapon."

Chloe cradled it in her arms, feeling weirdly sorry for Bo and her lambs. "It was the best I had. I don't carry a gun."

"You've got me." He took a step closer.

"Yeah, and you wear a gun more often than you seem to wear a shirt, but the rest of us have to improvise once in a while." She wasn't usually this snappish, but the night was catching up with her. Finding anyone, even Sam, lurking outside her door wasn't doing her nerves any good. Neither was the fact that she wanted to move toward him and retreat backward all at once.

"Like I said, you've got me. Until this is all over, I'm your bodyguard."

She was about to retort something about not needing that, but common sense stopped her. Or maybe it was the memory of his gentle hands barely an hour ago, comforting her. Maybe she did need him or maybe she just liked the idea of having someone there, strong and reliable.

Don't get spoiled. He might be Super Sam, but he's only here for a few days.

She stepped back from the doorway, beckoning him into the room. She set the shepherdess back on the nightstand. "I think I've figured out why Jack had the dress."

Sam stopped cold. "You can't be mixed up in this."

Chloe folded her arms, staring into his eyes so that she wasn't gawking at the T-shirt straining over his chest and arms. "Listen to me. We're talking a wedding here. I'm an expert. And I know Jack. You're not going to get past square one without my help."

Chapter 6

"What are you saying?" Sam braced his hands on his waist and glowered down at her.

Okay, maybe she was overstating her case, but she could definitely contribute. Chloe fought the urge to poke him in the stomach just to deflate the arrogant set of his strong body. "I know what I'm talking about."

His brow furrowed. "Oh?"

The single syllable made her vision go scarlet. The tone of it was polite, but beneath the buttering of good manners was doubt. After all, how could she possibly think of something he hadn't already discovered? *Yeah, right. Here comes the ego. The macho guys always have the ego. Next thing he'll pat me on the head...or the backside.* She'd break his arm if he did that, bodyguard or not.

He'd been nearly as bad when they'd talked earlier that day. Trust fund brat? No way. She wasn't an idiot. He had lied. He was some kind of detective. *He thinks I'm an idiot.*

So he'd saved her life. That didn't mean he got to patronize her. "Listen to me, Ralston."

He folded his arms. "I'm listening."

Every angle of his face said he wasn't, not really, but she charged on anyway. "Last April I met Jack at a design show in New York. It was the launch of a new collection by his friend Jessica Lark."

"Mmm-hmm."

"Lark was a designer. One of the most sought-after by a younger segment of the superrich." Chloe sucked in a breath, frustrated. Sam was looking at her as if she was speaking Martian. "Princess Amelie was one of her best clients."

"So?"

Chloe paused. She had theories. Good ones. "This is the fashion world we're talking here."

"Which means what?"

The man was clueless. There was a good chance the princess would have used Lark for the wedding trousseau. Those designs would have set the tone for the fashion industry for seasons to come. A sneak peek at the sketches would have been worth a fortune—but everything had gone up in flames on *almost* the same date that the wedding had been called off. It was as if the whole Brandi Snap fiasco was a distraction from the truly important event—whatever it was that connected the fire, the diamonds and Jack's murder.

And then there was the dress. If Chloe was right, that was Lark's work. Jack had been in Europe at the right time to pick up the diamonds and then take them to New York to be sewn on to the centerpiece of the wedding collection.

Apprehension crowded in on Chloe. She'd meant to blurt all this out, to share her thoughts freely, but Sam had returned to brick wall status. And he was a bored brick wall. This wasn't her wedding business, where people knew she was the expert. In Sam's world, she was just a girl in need of rescue. That look in his eyes was enough to make her rethink.

Chloe clamped her mouth shut. He might be Action Man, but this went beyond physical rough and tumble. Without meaning to, her eyes went back to that muscular chest. *Rough and tumble, huh?*

He raised an eyebrow, still waiting for her response.

She shrugged. "I thought it was interesting that Jack knew someone in the fashion world who was connected with the princess."

His expression said it wasn't very interesting at all. "Jack knew a lot of skinny women with big bank accounts. They were kind of a hobby of his."

Chloe's hand itched to smack him, except that there was a grain of truth in his words. *Thanks, Jack.* "What about the dress? What if Jessica Lark was the one who designed it, diamonds and all?"

"Someone had to. It might have been her."

Do I have to hand this to you garnished with parsley? "She's dead now."

Sam's eyes flickered as if she'd finally said something worth hearing. Chloe felt a tingle of triumph, but it didn't last. His expression returned to neutral almost at once.

"You can't get mixed up in this," Sam said quietly. "I mean it. You don't understand the danger involved. Go to bed. It's going to be dawn soon enough."

Chloe glanced at the china Bo Peep, wondering if Bo's sheep were half as dense as Sam.

"It's not safe to poke around in a murdered man's affairs." Sam touched her arm lightly. "We haven't caught the intruder yet. We will, but in the meantime I don't want you taking any chances."

She could feel a flush of hot blood creeping up her cheeks. All her life she'd been on a need-to-know basis. Her parents had never talked about their work or the strange people who came and went from the house. Same with Uncle Jack. Now they were all dead, and Chloe was left to figure things out without enough information to go on.

And Sam was doing the same thing. Already he was pushing her away, trying to keep her ignorant. "You've got to believe me. I can help you figure this out."

"You can't give anyone reason to think you're still involved." He leaned closer, bringing his lips within inches of her ear. "Think about it. How did the thieves know you had the dress?"

How indeed? Chloe shivered at the thought, but there was an expanse of tight white T-shirt a mere handspan away. It smelled of clean cotton and Sam, and she had a ridiculous urge to wilt against all those hard, warm muscles.

She took a step back, afraid of losing her perspective. They were having a disagreement. Falling into his arms would confuse things. So would admitting that he had a point.

He stepped with her, gracefully mirroring her movement. Chloe felt a finger of unease tickle down her spine. The movement was predatory, a little too smooth, almost catlike. She raised her hand, instinctively pressing her palm against his chest to keep her distance. *What is he doing?*

The distance narrowed without her meaning to let it happen. She looked up, meeting his eyes. In the dim light of the bedside lamp, the gray irises had darkened to black, the pupils disappearing into shadowy pools. He was handsome, the face roughly sculpted with square jaw and high cheekbones, but the mouth—that held a promise of sensuality that made Chloe's chest tighten.

But there was hunger in Sam's gaze that went beyond a man thinking a woman was pretty. Beyond lust or possession or control. It was as if he wanted to devour her.

Chloe's mouth grew thick with yearning mixed with the coppery taste of fear. Sweat prickled the small of her back. She tried to swallow, but her throat wasn't working. Not even her lungs were working right, only pulling in small, shallow gasps of air.

Her fingers began to close on his shirt, gathering up a handful of cotton, fingers sliding over the hard muscle beneath. Her mind flailed, scrambling to make sense of what exactly was going on. He was just standing there, one moment her rescuer, the next…he was something else. For the life of her, she couldn't explain what had changed. It was like he had pulled back a curtain and someone else was looking through his eyes. A man she wasn't sure she could handle. Scratch that. *A man I know is dangerous.*

"Sam," she whispered.

The moment stretched, apprehension chilling her limbs with a strange cocktail of desire and foreboding. Finally, he blinked. The movement, slight as it was, made her start. Sam drew in a breath that was almost a sigh, his chest heaving under her hand.

As quickly as it had come, the moment ended. The shadows seemed to recede to the corners of the room. That electric charge had come and gone without a word spoken, without either of them making a move.

Chloe hesitated, poised between drawing away and drawing near. It was he who stepped back, gently freeing his shirt and leaving her hand hanging in midair. Regret flitted over his face, followed by a flash of…what? Shame? She couldn't place it. Most would never have caught it, but she'd grown up around people with secrets. She knew how to catch these slivers of truth.

She looked away before he noticed her scrutiny.

He was backing toward the door. "Go to bed, Chloe."

"Good night, Sam," she replied, frustrated and relieved when she heard the rattle of the doorknob. Half of her wanted to grab his arm and beg him to stay. But that would be insane. He frightened her.

And yet, she wanted his lips on her, his hands all over her body. That *was* insane. They had the long-term prospects of an ice cream cone in Hades. She wasn't into relationships—however sticky and sweet—that melted away the minute things got hot.

He still hadn't answered. He just hovered in the doorway, his mouth set in a hard line. If she had to guess, she thought he was angry with himself. On some level, he'd slipped. Their eyes met. His were steady, but there were lingering traces of that fierce heat.

"Good night, Chloe." The words were clipped. He turned quickly and slipped out of the room.

She took in a long, shuddering breath. Instinctively, she knew she'd made a lucky escape. She jammed a chair under the knob.

What the hell had he been thinking?

Sam stared at Chloe's door. The corridor was dark, but his enhanced vision made out the grain of the oak. The thick slab of wood would make a racket if he punched his fist through it. Sam growled deep in his chest. Too bad vampires couldn't actually turn to smoke and slip through a keyhole. The base part of his nature wanted back in that bedroom. *Fool.*

He turned away, pacing down the hall and back again, trying to burn off the energy jumping along his nerves.

He'd nearly kissed her. Thank God for that last sliver of self-control. It had been all that kept his beast on a leash. He hadn't fed properly since arriving at Oakwood, relying on the suitcase of bagged blood that was an agent's portable kitchen. It just wasn't the same as the real, live thing. When confronted with Chloe, the combination of hunger and desire gave the world a fuzzy-edged glow, a bit like being drunk. And, like a drunk, he obviously wasn't thinking straight.

He snarled into the darkness. Biting Chloe was the last thing he wanted on his conscience. Heedless, his fangs descended, sharp against his tongue. He wished he'd caught the thief. He would have been enough of a snack to take the edge off.

That last thought burned in his already overheated brain. How by all the dark powers had that thief escaped? The Horsemen never let that happen.

And here Chloe was, digging into the case rather than staying safely away from it. She'd found an interesting connection to Jack's designer friend, but Sam couldn't risk encouraging Chloe in her research. As much as it galled him, the only safe thing to do was shut her down, and as firmly as possible.

He'd seen the hurt in her eyes and hated himself for it.

This ridiculous situation had to end, and that would only happen when the thief was caught. Kenyon might have lost the villain's trail, but Sam hadn't had his turn at playing bloodhound.

He pulled out his cell phone, quickly dialing Kenyon. The connection rang and rang.

"H'lo?" the werewolf grunted when he finally answered.

"Get over here. Guard her," Sam said in a low voice. He didn't bother to identify which "her" he meant. There was only one that mattered.

"Why? Aren't you already there?"

"I'm going outside. I need to know who the intruder was." *I need to put miles between me and her, before I slip from bodyguard to predator.*

"I'm already all over it."

"I need to get out." He couldn't put it any plainer than that. "You know what I mean."

There was a significant pause. "Okay. Get one of Jack's men to babysit."

"I don't trust them like I trust you."

Kenyon grunted with resignation. "I'll be there."

"Now." Sam thumbed off his phone, shoving it back in its belt holster. His shoulders ached from tension, making the movements awkward.

Barely a minute later, an enormous gray wolf came trotting around the corner, tail and ears held high. Kenyon plopped onto his haunches before Sam and lifted his front paws in a classic begging gesture.

Sam stared, huddled in his bad mood. It was hard to keep up in the face of a grinning timber wolf. "Smart-ass. What happens if someone wanders down the hall? I'm tired of bribing animal control officers."

Kenyon flopped down in front of the door, rolling on his back to expose a hairy belly.

"Whatever." Sam gave up and went outside. Annoying or not, Kenyon would keep Chloe safe.

He'd meant what he said about a leak. Someone in the household had tipped off the thieves about the dress. Finding out the traitor's identity was top of his to-do list.

But, right that minute, he needed a break. He was no more domesticated than Kenyon's wolf. There was a reason he steered clear of jobs that forced him to mix among humans. He was the knife in the dark, the menace lurking on a rooftop. A predator. The only reason he was here was out of respect for Jack.

But somehow, Chloe had touched him. She'd seen a glimpse of the beast tonight and hadn't known enough to run for it. He'd seen her face, his own darkness reflected back at him through the desire in her eyes. She wanted all of him, even if she didn't understand what that meant.

That alone meant he owed her protection. He couldn't

articulate why; it was simply a fact. Long ago, when he had been a man, he'd had a wife. He'd adored Amy from childhood, and he kept her memory deep, deep inside where he hid the treasured memories of his human life. But whatever drew him to Chloe was different. It was as primal a response as his hunger for blood.

Sam stood a moment under the night sky, letting the crisp air cool his face. The night smelled of the nearby forest, the scent of pine sharp and clean. Jack's estate covered around two hundred acres, enough room for even a vampire to feel free for a moment.

He set out for the patch of ground beneath the broken window of Chloe's old bedroom, passing a rose garden and a patio set with table and chairs. His gaze swept the ground, hunting the shadows for any sign of the intruder.

He looked up, calculating the distance the intruder had jumped. There was a low roof a story above, then another dozen feet to Chloe's window. A two-part leap to safety—one a trained human could achieve without much trouble. Except this one was wounded. Sam had winged him.

He knelt and examined the grass. This part of the lawn was well trampled. The security guards, once roused, had given enthusiastic chase. Footprints would be hard to track. Blood, however, would not.

Taking a quick look around, he checked to make sure none of the guards still roaming the grounds were in view. Then he crouched until his nose was mere inches from the lawn. A vampire's sense of smell wasn't as good as a werewolf's, but it was better than that of a werewolf stuck in human form. There had been too many people around during the chase for Kenyon to get hairy. Sam might have better luck picking up the trail. Hopefully it wasn't too late to matter.

There. He caught the scent of blood, memorizing its

unique signature. Sam crept forward, following the trace in a diagonal line across the lawn. Now that he knew what he was looking for, the muted glow of lights from the house showed him a particular set of tracks—a medium-sized man wearing soft-soled shoes. Drops of blood dotted the path, keeping the scent strong.

The path led up to a garden wall. It was brick and a good fifteen feet tall. Scuffed dirt at the bottom made it obvious that the intruder had climbed it—no doubt a painful process for a man shot in the shoulder.

Sam took a running step and bounded lightly to the top. He squatted for a moment, scanning the view before dropping to the other side. The wall drew a line between the order of Jack's gardeners and the wild kingdom beyond. Sam landed in a clump of weeds beside a gravel road. Across the road was untamed forest.

He could see where the intruder had stood. Blood had pooled there, but no trail of drops led away. Sam swore. The intruder must have had enough of a head start on his pursuers to risk stopping to bind his wound. Then, he'd splashed whiskey on the ground, drowning what scent there was in a fog of alcohol. Alcohol mixed with something that made Sam's nose numb.

That made Sam's job much, much harder. Was the guy using the smelly substance for disinfectant, or was he expecting tracking dogs? Or did he know there were vampires?

He was willing to bet the latter. Jack's killers had used silver bullets.

Sam walked up and down the road in ever-widening loops, searching for clues. The gravel was hard packed and dry, giving away nothing. Now that he'd left the protected zone of the walled garden, a freshening breeze was sweeping away any lingering scent. Not that Sam could smell much of anything anymore, after encountering that scent bomb the thief had left.

No wonder Kenyon hadn't had any luck. Sam stopped, jamming his hands in his pockets. He was coming up empty, too. *Come on. Everyone makes mistakes. What clue did this guy leave for me to find?*

He had to have escaped somehow. *If I were a villain, which way would I run?* Outside of a few other estates, there was nothing but ocean to the west. Sam followed the road east.

He'd barely gone a quarter mile before he found what he was looking for. A car had been parked by the side of the road—a small compact, judging by the tire treads in the soft shoulder. They weren't deep, and human eyes had missed them. The shadows were dense here at the edge of the forest, so Sam pulled a compact flashlight from his pocket, filtering the bright beam with his fingers and using just enough light to see without wrecking his night vision.

There weren't any obvious clues—no lost buttons or dropped wallets. Just a few spots of blood that probably fell when he climbed into the car.

Sam narrowed his eyes. If he was reading the tracks right, there were two sets of footprints in the soft dirt. It looked as though the intruder got in the passenger side. Had someone been waiting for him?

Instinct made Sam follow the road about a mile to the first bend. The wind was starting to smell damp with a rain that would wash away any remaining clues once it fell. He was running on pure intuition now, all hunter, the beast in him adding its predatory cunning to his human intelligence.

Just around the bend he found the car. It was nose-first into the ditch, the front bumper crunched against a tree. The passenger door was partially open but jammed into the

ground, as if the accident had happened when the door was
ajar. Had someone bailed out partway through the crash?

Sam wrinkled his nose. Despite his deadened senses, a
new banquet of smells, both revolting and enticing, pulled
him toward the scene. He approached cautiously.

The driver was slumped over the wheel, obviously dead.
Air bags hung like deflated balloons. Sam felt a wave of
cold nausea as he circled toward the windshield, peering
through the glass to catch a glimpse of the man's face.

A good deal of the man's head was splattered over the
side window glass. The bullet had come from the passenger seat. Sam mentally reconstructed the events. *Bang, pop
the door, jump out just before the car swerves into the ditch
and smashes the tree.*

Risky, shooting the driver. Then again, he would have
been slowing the car for the turn. A cold, calculated chance.
Not for beginners.

Sam looked long and hard at the ruined face, finally
placing it. One of Jack's security guards. Here, perhaps,
was an answer. Gossip traveled through household staff
like wildfire. News of the dress, however hard they'd tried
to keep it quiet, would have been a particularly juicy tidbit.
If this guard was in league with Jack's killers, that would
explain how he came to be in this car. It also would explain
how the thief got into the house. The question was, who
were his contacts?

Sam circled around to the open door, covering his nose
and mouth with his sleeve to filter the stench of carnage.
Blood was one thing, but there were plenty of substances
inside a human body that should definitely stay inside.

Digging his feet into the soft dirt, he pushed the car
upright enough to free the passenger door. It was a fruit-
less effort; the hinges were bent. Bracing the car with his
shoulder, he gave the door a solid jerk. It came off in his

hands. Sam tossed it into the ditch and let the car settle back into the mud.

Now that he could get inside, he looked for a bullet casing, but found none. Either the shooter had somehow retrieved it or it had flown out of the car during the crash. He searched the glove compartment only to discover the car came from a cheap rental place that specialized in older, practical runabouts. Perfect for getaway cars.

Sam would lay good money the name on the rental papers was fake. Whoever the intruder was, he was an ice-cold professional. He would call Winspear, have him send one of the Company's crime scene experts, but he didn't expect that they'd find much.

Whoever this guy was, he was good.

Sam pulled his head out of the car, sucking in clean, sweet air. His head snapped toward Oakwood, where the lights glinted through the trees. He had found what he could for now. Time to get back. Kenyon was guarding Chloe, but that wasn't enough to stop the tsunami of Sam's protective instincts.

Chloe.

Then, as if on cue, a scream tore the night.

Chapter 7

Vampires moved fast, but at the sound of the scream Sam moved demon-fast, feet barely grazing the ground as he sprinted. The cry had come from the house. No human would have heard it at that distance, but a vampire could—especially one tuned to that particular voice. Within minutes he pushed through the side door of Jack's house.

He skidded to a stop, swearing explosively. The door was unguarded. Sure, the larger part of the security staff was searching the grounds for the thief, but an appropriate number had been assigned to watch the house. Had all of them run off to find the source of the cry? It made no sense. That was a beginner's mistake, and Jack hired only experts. Why would he have idiots watching his back?

He hadn't. This was simple, pure betrayal. Sam growled, remembering the twisted wreck of Jack's car, the attacker in Chloe's bedroom. Who else might be creeping around Oakwood's halls? He cursed again, this time long and low.

Sam bounded up the stairs, feet silent despite his size. He reached the second floor of Jack's house, then the third. As he reached the landing, he froze, listening. *Chloe?* Was that her voice he'd heard? He ghosted forward, eyes searching the shadows for her door. It was shut, but where was Kenyon? *A curse on that flea-ridden mutt!*

After she'd locked Sam out of her bedroom, Chloe had tried to go to sleep. If she'd let herself analyze her thoughts, she would have realized she was too scared to sleep—but she couldn't go there.

If she did, she'd feel like a victim, and she'd felt that too many times before. When her parents died. When she'd been abandoned on what should have been the happiest day of her life—there was a special place in hell for grooms that backed out minutes before it was time to walk down the aisle. No, she wasn't adding this episode to that box of extra-special horrific memories. She flatly refused.

Instead, maybe she'd blame her insomnia on Sam for putting her hormones in overdrive. What girl could sleep after an eyeful of that white T-shirt and all the smoldering manly goodness underneath? And that sculpted mouth… The thought of Sam made her skin feel itchy in that so-good-it-hurt kind of way.

He was just outside, watching over her. He was scary, but he was on her side.

And he was panting. The sound was faint, muffled by the thick door, but in the absolute silence of the middle of the night she heard—something very weird.

What on earth? Chloe sprang off the bed and raced to the door, pressing her ear to the heavy oak panel. She definitely heard heavy breathing, just outside. A chill crept over her skin as her imagination painted bizarre explanations for the sound. The more bizarre the better, because she was full up on real-life horror.

What on earth could make that noise? Sam gasping his last breath as he was strangled by a giant squid? Zombie

Sam slavering at the keyhole, hungry for her brains? *Now I'm never going to sleep. Ever.*

Cautiously, she dragged the chair from under the knob and cracked the door open. She peered into the hallway, but it was too dark to make anything out. This was so weird. No one was watching her door. Irritation niggled around the edges of her fear. Now that she wanted Sam to be lurking outside, where the blazes was he?

"Hello?" she said tentatively, clutching the thick folds of her terry cloth robe around her.

She thought she heard a clicking sound and stared hard at the darkness. There was only one thing that made that sound—animal toenails. Panting plus clicking equaled dog, not squids or zombies. *Boring, but a relief.*

But what dog? Jack had owned many pets over the years, but there were none at Oakwood right now. He'd been gone too much these past few years to look after one. Did the dog belong to the security guys? If so, why hadn't she heard the footsteps of its handler?

Maybe a stray was wandering the halls. After the intruder incident, the security guards were extra-jumpy. If the dog wasn't theirs, they'd probably shoot it on sight. That thought wasn't bearable. She had to be sure the animal was okay.

Chloe quietly thumped her head on the edge of the door. This so wasn't her night.

Silently, not quite sure if she was being bold or stupid, Chloe crept into the hallway and glided for the staircase landing. She flicked on the light switch, the glow from the row of overhead chandeliers banishing the shadows. She looked down the hall, lit by a pool of light every few yards all the way to the end of the corridor. No one—with two or four feet—was in sight.

In the cold, clear sixty-watt light, Chloe felt tired and a

bit ridiculous. She had to be hearing things. Surely, after the attack earlier that night, security had been drawn too tight for a mouse to get through, let alone something big enough to pant like that.

But the guy who jumped you got in. She'd forced the event away from her imagination. Just a tiny bit. Just enough to function. But now the feel of her attacker's hands forcing her into the mattress flooded back to her, and she shuddered violently.

Suddenly, the noise she'd heard seemed far more sinister.

"Sam!" This time she said it with a lot more force. "Sam?"

Silence.

She took a few steps down the hall where she thought she'd heard the clicking toenails. Then she saw it: a gray tail disappearing around the corner. *So there is a dog!* Pulling her robe closer, she hurried after it. It was headed toward one of the big third-floor bathrooms. The good news was, if she managed to herd the dog in there, it should be easy to shut the door and call someone to deal with it.

The bad news was she had left the relative safety of her bedroom behind. Bad guys used animals to lure softhearted victims to their doom.

Shivering, she broke into a trot, wanting to get this over with. She was nearly to the spot where she'd seen the tail disappear. The long terry robe tangled around her ankles, making her stumble. Yelping, she caught herself.

An instant later, a huge, gray head poked out from around the corner. Chloe's brain froze for a microsecond, her face going slack with astonishment. *A wolf?*

But there it was, that creature staring at her with huge yellow eyes, red tongue lolling out from between sharp white teeth. Not a nice dog, but a gigantic, wild *thing*. She screamed for all she was worth. But there was hardly anyone left at Oakwood, and no one sleeping on her side of the building.

There was just her and the great yellow-eyed creature, stuck in a staring contest. The wolf looked more wary than ferocious, but she didn't dare take her eyes off it. The moment went on and on, a stalemate neither was willing to break. Finally, desperate to make the thing back off, she kicked off her mule slipper and slowly, slowly, bent down and picked it up. The wolf watched curiously, but didn't budge. Chloe threw it, but her aim was bad. It bounced off the wall, ricocheting in front of the wolf's nose.

That startled the creature into skittering backward, giving her time to dive for the safety of the first open door. It was the bathroom. She barely reached it before the wolf was already behind her, filling the door frame and blocking any hope of retreat.

Ironic, when her first thought was to trap the wandering dog in the very same room. Now the tables were turned. She scrabbled on the counter for something, anything to defend herself and came up with an aerosol can. She wheeled around, holding it in both hands. "Back off!" she warned. Her tone was clear, even if it wouldn't understand the words.

The wolf didn't come any closer, but it didn't budge. She glanced at the can's label. It was that ghastly hairspray Aunt Mavis used, the kind that could hold a hairdo through a category three hurricane. She'd heard of women using the stuff like Mace. She aimed the nozzle at the wolf.

"Don't come any closer, or I'll shoot."

It was hard to tell, but the beast looked confused. It tilted its head, ears swiveling in her direction.

"Back off!" she snapped again, waving the can in hopes the wolf would get the message.

By this point, her nerves were brittle enough to shatter. She'd nearly been killed once already tonight! Where were all the security guards who were supposed to rush in and save her? Her relatives? She heard conversation, doors shutting, but no one was storming to her rescue. Where was Sam? He'd promised to guard her, but the moment she'd needed him he had vanished.

The wolf sat down, effectively trapping her. Hot, sweaty panic welled up, leaving her sick and shaking. She was in trouble, but no one was here to help her. Claustrophobia squeezed her chest. She had to get out of this bathroom!

"Go away," she shouted.

The wolf barked, making her jump so hard her feet actually left the floor. Reflexively, she squeezed the nozzle of the can, releasing a hissing cloud of perfumed spray. The wolf staggered backward into the corridor with a ragged whine. The chemical reek of the spray clogged Chloe's throat. She covered her nose with her terry-towel sleeve and blinked hard, but for a blessed moment the doorway was clear.

Instinct kicked in. Chloe bolted for freedom, her bare feet hardly touching the floor.

Then she saw security guards ahead, running toward her and raising their guns at the wolf. A few of the other guests were peering around corners, too frightened to come to her aid.

"Don't fire!" she yelped, afraid for herself, the bystanders and the wolf. She glanced behind her.

Like a shaggy nightmare, the creature bounded after her, claws scraping and red tongue lolling. Chloe scrambled, running into the door frame in her haste to retreat. Her feet slithered on the hardwood as she tried to turn and shut the door.

The wolf attempted to stop, all four legs going straight. Its nails skidded on the hardwood floor.

Unsuccessfully. Golden eyes going wide with alarm, it bashed into her, the full weight of it colliding with her legs. Her feet flew out from under her and they both went down in a tangle of fur and terry cloth.

The wolf made a pathetic whimper. Chloe sucked in a shallow breath, terrified that if she moved, if she attracted its attention, it would bite. The stink of hairspray pervaded the air, making her want to sneeze. She froze, fighting the fierce tickling in her nose and throat. A sneeze might startle it.

It was a heavy beast, especially draped over her legs. The thick, coarse fur tickled and was disgustingly sticky with spray. Gingerly, she lifted her head a degree, peering down at it. The thing drooped its ears, giving her a wounded look with its great yellow eyes. Its ruff stuck up at odd angles, as if it was going for a fauxhawk.

"Where did you come from, anyway?" she murmured, forgetting herself.

It whined again, resting its chin on her knee, and gave a tentative tail wag. Apparently, it wasn't going to eat her. Maybe it had eaten someone already. Maybe Aunt Mavis.

At that thought, Chloe experienced a moment of mixed emotions.

Now the security guys were crowding around. Sam burst through them, SIG Sauer drawn and searching out the enemy. When he saw Chloe, he lowered the gun, his gray eyes giving her a look that melted her where she lay. She immediately forgave him for being late.

"You cried out." His voice was thick with concern. With a jerk of his chin, he sent the other men away. Obviously used to his command, they went at once, herding the scatter of bystanders back to their rooms.

Magnificent. It was the only word to describe Sam.

"Are you all right?" he demanded.

But unobservant. "I think so?" she replied from underneath the wolf.

Sam snapped his fingers. The creature rose, shaking itself, and gave Sam a dirty look. Chloe felt tingling through her legs as circulation returned. She struggled to sit up. Sam glowered at the beast.

"Is he yours?" she asked.

"Sadly."

The wolf edged toward Chloe, its tail between its legs. Sam narrowed his eyes. Chloe started to rise, but the wolf leaned into her, burying its head against her shoulder.

"Hey." Startled, Chloe carefully scratched the wolf's ears. "You're a good boy, aren't you? Such a big, handsome boy. I'm sorry I sprayed you, but you scared me."

The wolf wagged its tail, and she started to use both hands.

"Heel," Sam growled.

The wolf gave a start at the sound of Sam's voice, raising its head from Chloe's embrace.

"Now."

The wolf slunk to Sam's side.

"Why haven't I seen him before?" Chloe asked.

Sam's eyes flicked to Chloe's, then away. "I've been keeping him in the garden. I don't know how he got into the house."

Chloe heard the lie, but couldn't make sense of any of it. Her brain was too fogged with fatigue. Too preoccupied with the fact that, if the wolf hadn't been tame, she might have ended up chow.

Why had Sam left her alone and why had he just lied to her about having a pet? Big, strong and protective was great, but reliable and honest counted for plenty.

He noticed her frown. "Chloe?"

She shrugged, suddenly feeling a lot less forgiving. "It's

dangerous to let your furry friend roam. Something could happen to him."

The wolf licked his fur and made a gagging sound.

"He's a big boy. I've been thinking of sending him to obedience classes." Sam offered her his hand.

Chloe took it, letting him pull her to her feet. "That's all you're going to say?"

"What else is there?"

"I thought you were guarding my door."

"I was doing some investigating. I left someone to take my place, but he wandered off without authorization. We're going to have words. Many words." He glared at the wolf again.

The hallway was empty now except for the three of them. Sam held her by her upper arms, so close that her robe brushed against him. "Chloe, I'm sorry."

She could see the darkness in his eyes again, just as it had been during that strangely charged moment in her bedroom. His look was one of possession, fired now by the adrenaline of the moment. He had come to save her—from where, she couldn't say. The damp scent of the night clung to him, enticing in its mystery.

At that moment she realized that she'd leaned into him. Something about the man drew her like a magnet. She tilted her face up, staring into his steel-gray eyes. The need she saw there made her pulse kick up a notch, beating hard and thick in her throat. Suddenly the terry cloth robe was too hot, suffocating instead of cozy. She had a mad urge to peel it off, and then the nightshirt she wore under it, too. It was a fleeting, silly notion but it still wound through her thoughts, tempting her to give in to the demand implicit in that possessive look. Chloe tightened her belt, fighting an aching need to respond. Blood flooded to her face, chased there by the boldness of her thoughts.

A quiver passed over Sam's lips, not humor but another more intense emotion she couldn't read. He brushed the back of his fingers over her cheek, letting them linger there, as if testing the heat of her blush. The touch was cool, yet so light it was no more than the kiss of a wing. The stroke continued, curling around her ear, brushing under her jaw to hover over the pulse beneath her ear. She shivered, nipples suddenly aching. She wanted his cool hands on them. She wanted his wet mouth on them. She wanted him inside her.

In a blink, her whole body was aching and slick with need. This was crazy. She barely knew the man. She scrabbled to pick up the threads of their conversation, to make these insane thoughts disappear beneath the surface of adult conversation. What had he been talking about? Oh, yes.

"Well, did your investigation go anywhere?" Her voice was rough and breathy. She cleared her throat.

He gave her a careful look. "Yes."

"What did you find out?"

Sam did his best impression of a blank wall. Chloe sighed.

"I'm protecting you," he said, voice dropping almost to the range of a growl. "Everything I do is to keep you safe."

"If the dress thief is any indication, ignorance is a lot more dangerous." She pulled the robe tighter around her throat.

"I'm not sure about that."

She shrugged, aching, frustrated and tired of playing games. "Oh, forget it. It doesn't matter."

She threw the statement down like a dare.

Sam watched the shrug do lovely things to the sliver of skin showing at the neck of the white robe. She was trying to hide it, but it still showed like an arrow pointing toward more intimate beauties. Her golden hair hung in glistening waves down her back, much longer than it looked pinned up. All that gold and white softness gave her an angelic air, spiced by the strong scent of her desire. Sam's body tightened, transfixed for a moment by her loveliness, by the promise of pleasure. It was so different from his world of missions and weapons and blood.

He ached with wanting her, a sweet, slow pain filled with yearning and regret. Only part of it was a need of the body. His spirit reached for her, too, somehow knowing that she was a woman who would offer solace and strength. Things War shouldn't need.

She was a good person, and that was exactly why he had to walk away. They had no business being in each other's lives.

Then his brain caught up with what she was saying: "It doesn't matter." The look in her eyes said clearly it did.

But what could he say? That he'd found a dead body? Chloe didn't need one more thing to keep her awake tonight, and knowing the security guards had been compromised wouldn't help one bit. That kind of news could wait until morning.

The moment dragged by like a physical ache. Sam struggled, his instinct to take her then and there warring with the knowledge that whatever might pass between them would end badly. Human women were so sadly vulnerable. He could protect, but he could never *have*.

Then the moment faded, falling in on itself when the moment of burgeoning desire was ignored. Chloe's face grew set, the corners of her mouth pulling down. Sam felt his neck prickle, instincts responding to her darkening mood.

"Where did your pet go?" she asked, a little too crisply. "What's his name, anyway?"

Pet? Scrambling for a reply, Sam looked over to where

Kenyon had been sitting. There was nothing left but a few dog hairs.

Sam cleared his throat. "Fido's shy of people. Some wolf blood, you know."

Her expression said she didn't believe any of that. "He's a marshmallow. I can't believe you didn't mention him before this. Why keep him a secret?"

Sam grunted, knowing he was going to lose if he kept talking. He was the guy who hit things, not the one who provided plausible deniability for werewolves. And something about that fluffy robe was shredding his thought processes. "I've got to go catch him."

"Yeah, there are too many gun-happy guards around." She blinked, her eyes shadowed with fatigue.

"Are you going to get any sleep tonight?"

"I keep trying."

Sam would have liked to personally tuck her in. Maybe she'd stay put this time. Maybe he'd stay there to make sure she stayed put. Yeah, what was that saying about foxes and henhouses?

He had a wolf to catch. "Good night, Chloe."

Her lips curved in a tired smile. "Good night, Sam."

He opened his mouth to keep talking, but she turned away before he could think of anything else to say. *Just as well.* He wanted a few seconds more, but then it would be a few seconds after that, and so on until sunrise.

She turned back, her expression oddly naked. "Are you going to guard my door?"

"Absolutely. Personally."

Her head drooped, not quite a nod. "Thank you."

To his regret and relief, she closed the bedroom door, and the moment passed.

Sam slowly turned to see Kenyon's human shape lurking in the shadows. He'd pulled on sweatpants and a hoodie.

Sam stalked over to him. "What happened?"

Kenyon snorted with disgust. "I heard Chloe moving around and tried to get out of sight before she opened the door. But she saw me. Then she chased me."

Despite himself, Sam chuckled. "*She* chased *you?*"

Kenyon gave a lopsided smile. "What's the point of being a monster unless you can have fun with it?"

Good question. He wouldn't have minded a show of feminine gratitude. After all, the vampires on TV got the beautiful blondes. Not that Sam watched, of course. He yanked his mind back to business. "We've got to call Winspear."

Kenyon ran a hand through his hair, wincing as his fingers caught in clumps of hairspray. "He won't have done the autopsy yet."

Sam recoiled from the image of Jack lying on a cold metal table. That was just so wrong. "Then the doctor had better get busy because I have another customer. I found the thief's getaway car, plus the driver. He was one of the security guards, shot in the head."

Kenyon's eyes widened. "Where? I lost the trail at the edge of the garden."

"A mile up the east road, just around the bend."

"Huh." Kenyon leaned against the wall, his chin sunk on his chest. "I wonder where they were headed?"

"Somewhere to regroup. They didn't get what they wanted, so they'll be back."

"Oh, goody. I can't wait," Kenyon said dryly.

"We'll do some recon. They've got to be hiding out somewhere nearby." The words had no sooner left his mouth than he remembered Chloe. He'd promised to guard her door.

Kenyon caught his look. "You're needed here."

"But nothing will change until we catch the thieves."

For once, the werewolf grew serious. "We have to find

them first, and it's getting close to dawn. I'm your daylight operative, and you know I'm the best when it comes to this kind of detail work. Let me do my job."

It was true. When he put his mind to it, Kenyon could be relentless and methodical. It was one of the things that had made him an excellent jewel thief. "Fine. Report back the moment you find something."

"And when I hit pay dirt?"

Sam gave a grim smile. "Then we'll unleash Armageddon."

"Now we're talking. I'll bring the beer." Kenyon turned as if to go, but then paused. "She likes you, you know."

"Who?"

"Chloe. The way she looks at you. The way she smells around you."

"She doesn't know me. I'm just a hired gun."

"Uh-huh." Kenyon folded his arms, smirking in that irritating way he had. "Just one thing."

"What?"

"I don't remember her writing you a check, so you're not a hired gun. You're here for other reasons. That changes the game."

With that, Kenyon strode down the hall, giving a cheeky backward wave.

Chapter 8

By noon the next day, coffee had moved from beverage to plasma status. Chloe set the delicately fluted china cup on its saucer and rested her head in her hand. She'd drawn the curtains in Uncle Jack's study so that it was still bright but not obscenely sunny. Green-tinted light filtered through the clematis vines circling the window, the shadows of the leaves fluttering on the pale carpet. Like all the rooms in Jack's house, the study was beautifully decorated, the ceiling high, the furnishings classic and tasteful. The orderly atmosphere was soothing as a balm.

She sat at the fruitwood desk, her laptop open in front of her. Across the room, a portrait of a young man in eighteenth-century military uniform stared back at her with a wistful expression, as if he wanted some of the coffee, too.

She'd arisen two more times last night, peeking outside the door to see if Sam was guarding her door as promised. Although she wanted to believe his word—one couldn't be a wedding planner without an essentially optimistic view of human nature—experience had taught her to be cautious.

Both times he'd been there and patiently sent her back to bed. Nevertheless, it had been growing light when her stomach had uncoiled enough for her to relax and fall asleep.

She worked in a pressure-filled industry where a lot could go sideways at any moment, but on top of Jack's mysterious death, the past twenty-four hours had blown her limit for excitement.

It might have also blown her grip on reality. The gardeners had given her blank stares when she'd asked about the wolf Sam Ralston had kept tied up on the grounds. None of the staff had seen so much as a stray Pekinese. She had been sure Sam was lying about his pet, but now she didn't know where truth ended and fantasy began. *Did I make the whole thing up?*

It wasn't a good feeling. In fact, she was feeling very insecure about a long list of things, from the unlikely crash of the Porsche to the wolf to that blasted dress and a bunch of stuff in between—including Sam Ralston.

She opened the desk drawer at the top of the right-hand pedestal of the desk. She felt around, past a stamp box, a squiggly pile of rubber bands and a stapler. At the very back of the drawer was Jack's SIG Sauer. Chloe pulled it forward and lifted it out of the drawer, the cold metal heavy in her hand. Besides sending her to a dojo, Jack had made her learn to shoot. Despite her protests—she was interested in the drama club, not target practice—he was fanatical about making sure she could defend herself. He'd never really say why, any more than he'd say why he kept a gun in his desk drawer when he had full-time security in the house.

She'd assumed he kept the gun around because he was afraid of robbery. Now that he was murdered, she wondered if that were true. After all, no one had tried to take anything but the dress. Something else had caught up with him.

That thought turned her stomach into a cold, hard knot. Carefully, she determined the gun was clean. She hated violence, hated guns, and hated the fact she knew how to use them. That didn't mean she wouldn't defend herself.

There was a box of ammunition, too. She set the gun at the front of the drawer, but left it unloaded and pushed the drawer shut. She wasn't prepared to go full-on paranoid just yet, but she felt better knowing the gun was there and ready for action.

Turning to her computer, she clicked on her calendar to see what the next few days held—thieves, murderers and midnight wolves notwithstanding.

With a sense of surreal horror, she saw an appointment for one o'clock that afternoon. The Fallon-Venuto wedding. She was supposed to meet her clients in the nearby town of Thurston. Chloe squeezed her eyes shut, hoping that would make the bright yellow square of responsibility disappear.

Blast it. She'd booked the appointment before Jack's tragedy and must have missed it when she was clearing her calendar to attend the funeral. She hadn't been able to focus right then.

If she had, she'd have remembered that the bride's beastly mother moved in the same elite social circle as Jack. If Momzilla had had her way, young Elaine Fallon would have been walking down the aisle to become Mrs. Jack and, more important, the new mistress of Oakwood Manor and all of Jack's lovely bank accounts.

Quiet Elaine had dug in her heels and become engaged to her childhood sweetheart, Leo Venuto. Always on the lookout for a good business deal, Jack had charmed Mrs. Fallon into hiring Chloe to design the Fallon-Venuto wedding. It was happy endings galore until the woman had suggested gilding the hooves of the white palfrey Elaine would ride down the aisle.

Elaine had hated the idea. Her mother hadn't cared. Chloe had been caught in the middle—and this had set the pattern for everything that followed.

Mrs. Fallon was the last thing Chloe needed in the aftermath of Jack's death. True, the show had to go on, but it could go on later, like when no one was trying to kill her.

The only reasonable thing to do was to put the appointment off. After checking her notes, Chloe picked up the handset of the massive old rotary telephone on Jack's desk and dialed Elaine's office number. The woman was a mathematics professor at the university and spent a lot of time in the classroom. Luckily, this time she answered on the third ring.

"Hello, Elaine, this is Chloe Anderson. How are you?"

"Chloe!" The woman's soft voice filled with concern. "I was so sorry to hear about your uncle. How are you doing?"

"One day at a time," Chloe answered, concentrating on keeping her voice even. "It was quite a shock."

"I'm sure it was." Elaine fell silent for a long moment. "Um. Listen. I was going to leave this alone, but now that you've called, my mother was bugging me to email the guest list despite everything that's going on with, well, the funeral and everything. I'm really sorry about bothering you right now."

"Don't worry about it. I'm glad you did. It's nice to be talking about a happy event." Chloe quickly toggled to her in-box and quickly scanned her list of unread messages. Elaine's was there. It had arrived about the same time she'd been opening Jack's safe.

"I'm looking at it right now." She double-clicked the attachment. "Oh, wow, six hundred for the reception."

And what a list it was—a who's who of the private jet set. Chloe's lips parted in awe as she read. The bride's family were old money—the kind of folks who endowed everything from animal shelters to public television. Between them, they owned a chunk of every major city on the continent.

The idea that this slice of the social pie would be at a

Chloe's Occasions event—it made her palms sweat with excitement and apprehension. If everything went right, her fledgling business could be picking up referrals for years to come. Her company would have arrived at the big time. Who cared if the bride's mother wanted a gold-hoofed horse?

She tuned back in on Elaine's voice. The young woman sounded even more apologetic. "It was about half of what Mom wanted, but we're trying to be realistic, given the timelines. Oh, I think I forgot to mention in the email that we've finally picked a date."

"That's great to hear. Is it next June?"

She could almost hear Elaine cringe. "In two months. September 15. I'm sorry, didn't your assistant tell you?"

"That's ridiculous." The words were out of her mouth before she could stop herself. *Oh, crumb.*

"Pardon me?"

"I'm sorry, Elaine, but a wedding like yours…" She stopped herself, letting the wave of panic slide through her stomach and out the other side. "I'm sorry if that sounded abrupt, but an event like yours takes a great deal of planning. Two months isn't much time. I haven't even sat down with you and Leo. I've just been dealing with Mrs. Fallon."

"I know. And I'm so grateful that you found a source for those rare orchids she wants for the centerpieces."

"That's just it. I know what she wants, but what do *you* want at your wedding?"

She laughed at that. "I'm the easy part. I just want Leo. He just wants the wedding to be over. But you and I are scheduled to meet, just the two of us. In a few hours, in fact. Or, um, that's what we were planning until things happened."

"But…" Chloe had been calling to put the meeting off. Clearly Elaine would understand if she cancelled.

"But?"

Two months. Now there wasn't time to put Elaine off, and keeping the meeting made sense when she was here, in Wingman County, right now. "I think we should get together anyway."

"Are you sure?"

"Absolutely." She always met privately with her brides, sometimes traveling around the globe to do it. That one-on-one time was the best way to learn a client's true desires. Chloe's Occasions always gave the bride what she really wanted—and they seldom revealed it over the phone.

"I really appreciate this. You see, it's my grandmother," Elaine said softly. "She hasn't got long and she wants to be at the wedding. It forced us to pick something sooner than we would have liked, but making sure Grandma has a front row seat trumps trying to invite everyone that my parents think ought to be included."

Chloe rubbed her forehead. "I understand. There's no problem. I'll arrange an office in town where we can sit down and have a good talk. I'll text you the address."

"Sounds great. Thanks so much, Chloe. See you then."

The call disconnected. Chloe slumped in the desk chair.

They didn't even have a hall booked. A headache clamped her skull. She didn't need this kind of stress. Not now, with wolves and diamonds and thieves in the night to worry about.

"Chloe."

Sam chose that moment to stride into the room, circling close to the bookcases until he reached the windows. He unhooked the heavy velvet curtain from the brass hook that held it in an artful drape. The fabric fell, blocking out every scrap of sun.

Annoyance did a dance with relief. The darkness was kinder to Chloe's aching head, but now she couldn't see properly. She cleared her throat and flicked on the desk lamp, angling the shade to the wall. "Allergic to sunlight?"

"I need more sleep." He looked pale, dark stubble gracing his jaw. The morning-after look suited him. Mind you, he could have dressed as one of Santa's elves and still looked good.

"Coffee?" Chloe waved at the silver service the housekeeper had brought in response to her request for a simple cup of java.

Sam shook his head. "Not unless it's decaf."

"Sorry, it's fully loaded. I needed the jolt after last night." She studied him, enjoying the view for a moment. "How's your wolf?"

"I sent him home."

And where is home? Chloe had a fleeting image of a wolf getting on a Greyhound bus, backpack clenched in its fangs, but let the subject drop. She had enough to worry about.

"I want you to go home, too," he said. "It would be safer."

"I can look after myself." After all, she'd found the gun. She could shoot.

"Against trained hit men?"

Maybe not. "I thought these were thieves."

"I doubt that's all they are."

Chloe crossed her legs and watched him watch her do it. There was definitely a spark of interest between them. She wondered what would happen if she blew on it oh so gently.

Surprised by the bold thought, she pulled the hem of her skirt down. "I'm staying until the guests are gone."

"Your guests have left."

That was true. Half had departed before breakfast, the rest around midmorning. "I guess your pet scared them off."

The corners of Sam's mouth twitched. "Perhaps."

"Wolves rock."

"So, if there are no guests, how come you're not packing?"

She'd felt lighter for a moment, but reality crashed back in. "I have to sell this place, remember? I still have the Realtor to deal with. He called this morning and we're booked for next week. I wanted something sooner, but it's hard to get someone capable of representing a property like this. This guy has contacts in the right circles."

Sam glanced around the room. "Too bad you can't keep Oakwood."

Chloe swallowed hard. "I lived here all through high school. But, even if I could afford the upkeep, I have to divide the estate."

He swore softly. "I wish there was some other way."

"Me, too."

"You shouldn't have to deal with this." His voice was gentle. "Why don't you go home? I'm co-executor. I can deal with the Realtor."

For a moment, she nearly agreed, but she knew better than to believe it when someone said they'd be there for her. That's how a girl got left at the altar. "I don't—"

He held up a silencing hand. "I need to stay here anyway to arrange for the dress to be returned to Marcari. It's too valuable to pop in a box and take down to the FedEx office."

"Wait a minute." Chloe uncrossed her legs, leaning forward across the desk. "You know who to call? You've got the head of the kingdom's security on your speed dial?"

"I have his number, yes."

"Well, I'd already figured out that you know more than your average royalty watcher, but wow." A smidgen of sarcasm crept into her words. "You might have mentioned this last night. Are you, say, on the trail of the diamonds? A special agent on crown-jewels detail?"

"No, not that." He looked down, not quite abashed but

clearly caught wrong-footed. "Actually, Jack worked with me on some security issues. That's my line of work. I didn't know the diamonds were here any more than you did."

She heard the ring of truth. Maybe not the whole truth, but it was progress. Her gaze lingered on Sam's face, the hard angles and strong bones. He looked like an operative of some kind. Stern. Commanding. Bossy. That wasn't always easy to be around. Would Sam be any different?

She picked up a pen, turning it over and over in her fingers. "So, once you call, what then? Does the head of the royal guard show up with a garment bag?"

That shadow of a smile was more pronounced this time. "More or less. Him and a small army of men in black."

"For one dress."

Sam's gray eyes met hers. She caught a glimpse of the predator she'd seen last night. Her skin prickled, as if she were a fraction too close to a fire.

"For the diamonds," he corrected her. "And it's not just jewel thieves they're worried about. There's more than money at stake. There are their old enemies, the Vidonese, to consider. If they're involved, the game is for blood and honor, as well."

Chloe leaned back in the leather desk chair, no longer tired. "So how come the two countries both think the diamonds belong to them?"

Sam paced to the window, staying in the shadows but gazing out through a chink in the curtains. The gesture reminded her of a dog pining to go outside. "It's a long story, and I don't know all of it."

"Then tell me what you do know."

"You're changing the subject."

"I love stories."

"This one doesn't have an end."

"The best ones don't."

He didn't reply, but kept looking out the window, his back to her.

Chloe watched the set of his shoulders. He was tense, maybe even angry, but she wasn't going to give in and go home like an obedient dog. Or wolf. "I suppose it starts something like 'A long time ago, in a galaxy far, far away...'"

She heard a low reluctant chuckle, and then he began. "A long, long time ago, just after the fall of Rome, the Kingdoms of Vidon and Marcari were one."

Chloe visualized the map of the Mediterranean. The two tiny kingdoms sat next to each other on the north edge of the sea. "Okay."

"During the time of the Crusades, the land was divided equally between two warring brothers."

Sam turned from the window, blinking as if that tiny amount of sunlight had hurt his eyes. Chloe waited while he sank into the chair opposite the desk, stretching out his long legs. For a moment, he looked lost in thought, his big, strong body in perfect repose. "The eldest brother, Vidon, pursued dreams of wealth and military conquest. Marcari, the younger, followed the path of books and knowledge. Both were power-hungry and a fierce rivalry grew between them."

He sat forward, and Chloe was caught for a moment by his intense gray gaze. It was hypnotic, almost invasive. Her mouth went dry, a sweet ache starting low in her belly. His very presence made her feel as if she were dissolving into a puddle of need, and she couldn't begin to explain why. It wasn't any one thing he did. It was just...Sam. Gorgeous and utterly wrong for her.

He was looking at her as if she were the last chocolate brownie on the planet.

He leaned forward another degree. She struggled to take

in what he was saying, and then struggled again to make sense of it. "Then their youngest brother returned from the Holy Land with a great fortune in gems, thinking to share it with his brothers, for his heart was more generous by far. Tempted by the beautiful stones, the kings of Vidon and Marcari each separately schemed to cheat his siblings of the glittering prize. Unexpectedly—or perhaps not—the youngest brother was assassinated as he slept. Though the true killer was never discovered, Vidon and Marcari quickly accused one another. At once a huge battle raged between them, and the kingdoms have been at war ever since. The Kingdoms of Vidon and Marcari have fought so long that some factions cannot accept the possibility of peace. Their pride forbids it. The Knights of Vidon have made it clear that they will not permit a union between the two kingdoms."

Forcing herself to look away, Chloe poured more coffee out of the pot. She didn't want it, but she had to break the spell he had over her. Her heart was beating fast, her hands slippery with perspiration. "You mean a marriage. The war would have ended with the wedding."

Sam smiled, just a faint curl of the lower lip. She would have bet good money he was aware of the effect he'd just had on her. "The wedding. Yes, peace was the plan. Finally, the wealth would have been shared as was the intention of the youngest brother, Armand Silverhand, almost a thousand years ago. Keep in mind the diamonds form only a small part of the treasure."

That made Chloe blink. "Really?"

"There are far more valuable pieces in the collection—which Marcari has in its treasury, by the way. They beat Vidon in that first terrible fight for possession of the jewels."

"More valuable than what's on that dress?"

"Absolutely. Emeralds, rubies, topazes, moonstones. All specimens of the first quality, all of exceptional size and beauty. I don't know what battles Silverhand fought during the Crusades, but I have a feeling he hit a treasury somewhere along the route."

"And people are still robbing to capture the same prize." For a second, she could feel her attacker's breath on her neck, and she shivered.

Sam saw it. "Which is why I'd rather you were miles away from that dress."

Chloe shook her head.

He frowned at that. "What's so important that you're willing to risk your safety?"

"I have a business to run, for starters. I'm not blowing off a client like this one."

Exasperation brought a hint of color to his cheekbones. "Fine."

"Right. And on top of that, this is my uncle Jack's estate, which I'm responsible—"

"Half-responsible."

"Okay, half-responsible for. Furthermore, your case is about a wedding, which is my professional area of interest. I could be of help. And, on top of all that, I was the one who was attacked last night. This is my inheritance they're after. I know you don't want me involved, but I already am."

She paused for breath, watching Sam's face. He'd gone into brick-wall mode. Irritation threw cold water on her hormones. She swore under her breath. If she didn't stand her ground, he would steamroll right over her. The next words came out in soft, precise syllables. "Being rescued is very much appreciated, believe me. I would have died last night but for you. However, I'm intelligent, not reckless. I don't need to go down the basement stairs to confront the monster. If kept informed, I can take reasonable precautions."

Sam's eyebrows lifted. His expression said he was letting her win. "Very well, but I have rules."

"Good for you. Your rules are not mine."

"They are now."

They locked gazes, neither giving an inch. Chloe could sense his impatience, but she wasn't backing down. If she did, she would disappear from view, another problem tagged, bagged and forgotten.

Perversely, as much as she wanted to prove she could look after herself, she wanted very much to remain Sam Ralston's problem. Was that what was making her so stubborn?

"What?" she finally snapped. "What are your rules?"

"You don't go anywhere without a bodyguard. That's me, Winspear or Kenyon."

"You can't enforce that."

"I found one of the security guards shot dead last night."

Chloe felt her breath stick like a barb in her throat. "Who?"

"A guy named Will Tyler. Did you know him?"

Chloe shook her head. "Just the name and face. He was new."

"It looks like he was the getaway driver."

Not sure what to say, Chloe picked up her coffee, staring into the cup. It was bad enough that someone had attacked her. Now a man was *dead*. An awful numbness crept up her body. *Am I really so tough? Should I just leave?*

"Chloe?" Sam prompted.

She cleared her throat, fighting back a prick of tears. "I can't believe Jack's staff would turn against him. Or me. He treated them like family."

"The diamonds represent a lot of money. He could have been a plant, Chloe." He shrugged, just a slight lift of the shoulder. "Plus, there are all the political implications of the royal marriage. Not everyone wants peace."

She swallowed hard. "That's crazy."

"That's why you don't set foot out the door without one of us. I'm not joking. From now on, I'm your shadow."

Perhaps she'd hit her limit for dread, or maybe it was the lack of sleep, but his statement struck her as funny. She gave a short laugh. "Is that why you always avoid the sun?"

He looked at her sharply. "What do you mean?"

"Aren't shadows made of darkness?"

His smile was wry, but there was something softer in it, too. "Darkness still needs light to define us."

Us? Chloe wondered, but her thoughts scattered as Sam put his hand over hers, his thumb caressing her wrist. The cool, steady touch swept logic aside and, along with that, all her defenses. She let herself ride the swell of feeling. *My shadow. The darkness that is always with me.* That would always be touching her, because that was the way nature had made it.

Then he lifted her hand, as he had done last night, and brushed his lips against her fingers. Chloe's heart stuttered, a flame in a new and unfamiliar breeze.

He hadn't simply told her a fairy tale of gems and kings of old. He'd walked straight out of one.

Chapter 9

Later that afternoon, Chloe's fairy tale mood crumbled to despair.

I'll never sell happily ever after. Not here. Not unless someone is marrying their gun.

She'd never been to Jack's offices in town. They didn't resemble his house in the least. The sign on the door of the top floor suite said Gravesend Security. The decor was all hard steel edges and industrial grays. The pictures on the waiting room walls were hung with artful portraits of motorized vehicles designed to vaporize small towns. If Chloe's business represented Venus, this was definitely Mars's clubhouse.

Chloe knew where she could rent a perfectly nice meeting room just blocks away, but the large windows and street level entrance hadn't met Sam's security requirements. Instead, he'd insisted they come here, where the offices occupied the top floor. It made sense, he'd said, because the admin offices of Gravesend would be empty on the weekend and he had to pick up some files there anyway. He could combine business with the infinite pleasure of being her bodyguard. After a brief protest, and possibly because of that kiss to her fingertips, she'd given in.

To find herself in the least romantic office space on the planet. Just to make matters worse, Sam had dressed in head-to-toe black Grim Reaper chic. With pitch-black sunglasses. Indoors. *He looks like a GQ undertaker.* Handsome as sin, but he didn't fit with the happy, friendly Chloe's Occasions image.

As soon as they'd reached the suite of offices, Sam had prowled from room to room, checking for intruders. Any that did venture into Gravesend would have had to be brave with so much testosterone oozing from the walls.

"It's clear," Sam announced, relaxing an infinitesimal degree.

"Great," Chloe replied, taking her armload of bridal magazines to the small conference room and dumping them on the table. Sam followed with her briefcase, setting it down while she sighed at the bland walls. "I wish I'd thought to bring some flowers."

Sam whipped out his cell, hitting a speed-dial number.

"Who are you calling?"

Sam gave a brisk smile. "This whole building is Gravesend Security. There are people in the operations center monitoring surveillance equipment. There's always a gofer for coffee runs, things like that."

His focus shifted to a voice on the phone. "Hello, Ralston here. We need flowers on twelve." He looked up from his call. "Type and quantity?"

Chloe waved her hands in the air. "Mix bouquet about so big? In a vase?"

"Mixed bouquet. Container. Floral estimate forty-five centimeters across. Stat. Clients are incoming at fifteen hundred hours." He thumbed off the phone, looking pleased with himself.

"Thank you," she replied, struggling to wrap her mind

around the conversation. Who said "stat" when ordering a bouquet?

She fanned the magazines on the table, made coffee and tried to soften the look of the place as best she could. There weren't any knickknacks around and, while opening the blinds would have made the place brighter, Sam probably wouldn't have liked it. For all her efforts, the place still had as much personality as the inside of a metal filing cabinet.

Elaine Fallon arrived ten minutes early. Despite her monied background, she was simply dressed in slacks and a sweater, her soft brown hair pulled back in a messy ponytail. She looked every inch the overworked professor, down to the courier bag stuffed with what looked like exam booklets waiting to be marked.

"Do you mind?" Elaine asked, pulling out a plastic container of salad and a fork. "It's the only chance I'm going to get for lunch."

"Not at all." Chloe had the feeling the woman was so busy she lived by a rigorously planned schedule.

"Thanks. So where do you want to start?"

"Have you decided on where you're going for your honeymoon? Last time we talked, that was still up in the air." That choice often gave Chloe a good clue to what they considered fun. That was an excellent building block of information to work from.

"Cancún," she replied between bites of spinach. "There's a Fibonacci Group conference on integers right around that time. I'm presenting the keynote."

A math conference? On her honeymoon? "And Leo?"

"He likes the beach." Elaine smiled, and there was a hint of mischief there. "We'll lie in the sun and pretend we're not going home ever again. After so many years in school and then working toward a tenured position, I'm not sure I remember what sun looks like."

Chloe heard Sam stir and realized he was standing by the door. "Lying on the beach sounds fabulous."

"I'm overdue. Leo is, too. He's put in a lot of eighty-hour weeks lately." Elaine looked around at the putty-colored walls. "So this place is some kind of military thing?"

"No, it was my uncle's private security firm." Chloe smiled apologetically. "I borrowed the space for today. The atmosphere is a bit more severe than my own offices."

Elaine's eyes softened at the mention of Jack. "It really was good of you to meet with me today given everything going on in your life."

"Thank you, but it's okay. As I said, weddings are something to look forward to. This will cheer me up."

"As long as you're sure." Elaine murmured, her gaze lingering apprehensively on Sam. He was standing with his arms folded, a perfectly neutral expression around the black lenses of his shades. He looked like a man in need of a martini—shaken, not stirred—or a kneecap to break. "Does he come with the place?"

"Sam, uh, provides advice on security arrangements for my wedding guests," Chloe improvised. "You know, when there are celebrities."

"Really?" Elaine raised an eyebrow. "Pity the paparazzi."

"Never," Sam said in a voice like the slamming of a tomb door.

It was only one word, but it left a chill on Chloe's skin. Elaine paled and set down her salad, still half uneaten.

Chloe seized the moment and began fanning out brochures. "Now, we have your guest list, which is great. Then, whether we're talking indoor or outdoor venues…"

They spent the next fifteen minutes going through the pros and cons of half a dozen sites. She'd found the places with an opening on the right date and put the trendiest sites at the top of the pile.

"I love the look of Philip's," Elaine said, folding out the brochure for the oceanfront dance club. More bohemian than most of the places Chloe had queried, it had an "it" factor that put it in very high demand. "Can't you see the reception here? There's a huge dance floor, and look at the views."

Chloe heard a note of longing that said Elaine was far gone in her fantasy, even before they'd visited the place. "It has a more relaxed atmosphere than many venues of its size."

"I know. I'm sure my mom will hate it."

"She has more traditional tastes."

"I know." Elaine made a face. "It's all white linen and tiaras. No way she'd go for, say, a theme park or waterslides."

Chloe caught the remark. *Waterslides.* This was the sort of information she'd been waiting for. As usual, it was hiding in an offhand remark. "Do you like water sports?"

Elaine smiled ruefully. "I want to have fun. I don't mind the whole princess bridal fantasy thing Mom's after, but I wish we could have foam rubber swords and a toy dragon to go with it. Maybe soaker guns. I think hard enough at work. A wedding should be a party."

"Why not go for it?" Chloe said.

Elaine shrugged. "There's my mom and six hundred of her nearest and dearest to consider."

She picked up a brochure for the golf club. "If I'm honest with myself, this is way more boring but much more appropriate. It's bigger and the parking would be better. And look, there are luxury guest suites right on-site."

Chloe could see the struggle between "want" and "should" in Elaine's eyes. It was her job to find a way her bride could have the best of both. "But..."

"Both Philip's and the club are outdoor venues. I would advise an indoor function," Sam put in, his voice still the monotone he seemed to use when in his bodyguard persona. "But, if you must be outside, the golf club is superior."

Chloe was startled. *Since when are you the wedding expert?* "What makes you say that?"

Sam turned in Elaine's direction, inscrutable behind his sunglasses. "I assume most of those on the guest list could be considered affluent?"

"Yes." Elaine's brow furrowed. "Some are highly placed executives with international corporations. Mom thought the club would be good because many of them play golf."

"It is also less exposed to the public. Philip's wine bar reception area backs onto the esplanade. Although the event would be roped off, it is hard to limit access to the public and, with them, pickpockets, unauthorized photographers and drive-by gunmen."

"Drive-by gunmen!" Elaine exclaimed, her eyes round and huge. "What are you talking about?"

Chloe sensed her client growing increasingly tense. She touched Elaine's arm gently. "It's just a worst-case scenario."

"I don't do worst-case," Elaine said sharply. "I do mathematics, the more abstract the better. Nobody is going to shoot anybody at my wedding, okay?"

"Of course not." Chloe couldn't resist aiming a furious look at her soon-to-be-ex bodyguard. "Why don't we talk about the church for a while? There are *no security risks* in the church."

Sam opened his mouth, but must have caught her eye. He closed it again.

"My grandmother is going to be there, you know." Elaine was staring at Sam again with the look of a cornered rabbit. Chloe could almost see her nose twitching with anxiety. *This is a freaking disaster.*

"We'll take every precaution," Sam said helpfully.

Great. Now even Chloe was imagining mobster-movie massacres.

The door flew open, making everyone except Sam jump.

A man in a security uniform thrust a vase of flowers at Sam. The man gave a smart salute, wheeled and made his exit, pulling the door shut as he left.

An awkward silence hung in the room. Sam neatly positioned the vase on the conference table and retreated to his patch of wall. For a moment it was so quiet that Chloe could almost hear the dust settling on the industrial gray carpet.

Chloe studied the flowers, trying to understand exactly why no one was talking. The lovely bouquet of roses and baby's breath looked utterly out of place. It underscored how completely she'd wandered into the wrong world—Sam's world, where putty-gray walls were normal and of course you considered whether people could drive by and murder your guests. You'd be an inconsiderate host if you skipped that little detail.

No, this wasn't the safe, sunny fairyland Chloe conjured for her brides. She wasn't mistress of this realm. Her wedding fantasy magic wasn't effective here at all, and her client could feel it. Elaine looked, well, appalled. *Bridal fail.*

She cleared her throat and looked at her watch. "Uh, Chloe, I'm afraid I've got a class to teach. I have to go."

She heard the lie in Elaine's voice and couldn't even blame her. "I completely understand. Why don't I call you later to go over a few details? We are very, very short of time."

The woman nodded quickly, gathered her things and nearly bolted from the room. Sam let her out, locking the door after she left. Finally, in the windowless waiting room, he pulled off his shades. Chloe watched him, catching what might have been a disappointed sigh.

"She's not coming back, is she?"

"I don't know," she said bluntly, giving vent to a tiny burst of anger. It was a mere puff of smoke from the volcano she could feel brewing underneath. "I always address security issues, but I'm very careful how I handle it. Brides are typically stressed, always imagining the worst things are going to happen. In fact, they're usually a little bit crazy. I have to make them relax and believe their day will be happy and perfect."

His face tightened. "I shouldn't have said anything."

You should have listened to me. You should have let me use the nice offices. But…what could she do now? Water under the bridge.

A raging torrent sweeping my career under the waves and about to knock over said bridge. Chloe took a long breath, fighting for her poise. *Surely I can fix this. They've only got two months. They need me.*

Or I could just grab one of these weapons out of Uncle Jack's display cases and thump Sam over the head with it!

The slight slump of Sam's shoulders said more about his distress than a litany of excuses. He rubbed his forehead. "I'm very sorry. I'm not good with the hearts and flowers. It's just not in me. To be honest, I'm a monster."

Chloe caught her breath, recognizing the raw honesty beneath the words. *Wow. That's how he sees himself. A monster.* "No, you're not."

Most people passed her over without ever sharing that much truth. Few guys had the honesty to face their own shortcomings. Maybe there was more to him than she had assumed.

He quirked a quizzical eyebrow. "You're going to argue about this?"

For a moment, she actually felt sorry for him. "Monsters don't care. You got the flowers. You found a safe place. You listened to what Elaine was planning and gave her the benefit of your experience. I can tell that you care."

Regret flickered through his eyes, followed by a deeper sadness. There was more here than Elaine and an ugly office. The whole monster comment resonated far beyond today's problems. Something had happened that had made him doubt himself, and she knew with every instinct that would be unbearable for a man like Sam Ralston. What on earth had happened? But he spoke again before she could chase that thought any further.

"I am sorry," he said. "If I'd found a better place…"

She sliced a hand through the air, on the edge of too much emotion. "It's not up to you to anticipate absolutely everything. Sure, I know you're the guy with the gun who's going to save the planet, but you don't know my business like I do."

He opened his mouth and then closed it, head tilting as his eyes searched her face. He was looking at her, really looking at her, as if she were the newest wonder of the world.

She couldn't wipe away the smile tugging at her lips. "Thanks for being more than just a suit with a sidearm. Maybe next time you'll listen to me about the kind of office I need for my clients?"

He nodded. "You know your business. Got it."

"Fair enough." Chloe raised up on her toes and kissed him on the cheek. His skin was cool but already roughening with the shadow of his beard.

"Don't." The word cut through the air.

Faster than she could follow, he turned to her, grasping both her arms with his large, square hands. He wasn't hurting her, but there was no way she was going anywhere. Faint color rose to his face, his steel-gray eyes wide and intense.

She grabbed a surprised breath. If she'd wanted honesty, it was there in his gaze. He wanted her, no question. The idea of it hit her bloodstream like strong liquor. "Don't?"

"Kissing me might be a door you don't want to open."

And yet, he'd kissed her. Or her hand. Twice. And perhaps she did want to open that door. If he could be vulnerable, maybe it was worth getting to know him after all. "Oh?"

The single syllable seemed to rob him of his will. "Chloe, be careful what you start. I'm the one in the shadows, remember?"

"No, you're *my* shadow. There's a difference." Chloe raised her hands, breaking his hold. He didn't resist, or try to stop her when she rested her hands on his shoulders. Automatically, he reached for her waist, almost as if they meant to dance.

Perhaps they did. As if by unspoken consent, he bent down and she reached up, their lips meeting at a perfect midpoint.

His lips were softer than she expected, as if every part of Sam Ralston capable of tenderness had been distilled for the purpose of kissing. An electric current seemed to rise from beneath the soles of Chloe's feet and rush to her head, leaving her dizzy but connected with some primal, earthy power. She leaned into him, relishing the hardness of his muscles beneath the crisp white shirt. He smelled of soap and man and something darkly spicy she couldn't place. Not cologne, but some element of him that was unique.

Her heart sped as Sam pulled her closer, his strong grip against her back. She ran her fingers around the back of his neck, burrowing through his thick, dark hair. It was like silk. Another softness she hadn't expected.

She opened her mouth to him, tasting as they explored each other. His mouth trailed down her jaw to her collarbone, his breath coming soft in a sigh that was all lust. She nearly crumbled where she stood, burned to ash by the searing heat of sensation.

"Sam," she whispered. She had no idea what she'd say next. She was lost in the moment and loving it.

But he pulled away. She looked up into his face and saw her own desires reflected in the drowning darkness of his eyes. And then, slowly, his fascination sank into regret.

"This isn't the time or place," he murmured, pushing a strand of hair out of her eyes. "Before you ask why not, there are surveillance cameras everywhere in here."

Chloe froze. Slowly, her fingers rose to check her buttons. Mercifully, he'd left them all in place. She fell back a step, putting air between them. She didn't know what to say.

When would be the right time and place? Her whole body ached to ask the question, but who was listening? A building full of her uncle's security guys?

Chloe raised her chin, not sure if she wanted to kiss Sam again or kick him in the shins for leaving her all revved up with no way to follow through. "You should have warned me."

"Back at you." Sam's smile was slight but full of mischief. "We should go."

"Fine," she grumped.

"Don't forget your roses." He returned to the conference room and came back a moment later with the bouquet.

"They really are lovely," she said, taking them from him.

He gave a slight bow. "Probably the prettiest things to see the inside of Jack's offices, present company excepted."

"How very gallant."

"Kind of you to say so. I'm sadly out of practice."

Because something made you think you're a monster, and you gave up on important parts of yourself. Chloe wanted to say it but didn't dare. She knew she didn't have the whole picture. "You should practice more."

He slipped his sunglasses back on, but she could still read his expression. He actually looked happy. "We shadows need light to give us purpose, Miss Chloe. Shine on."

Chapter 10

"How can I make this up to you?" Sam asked.

"Don't worry about it."

They were back in the car, which now smelled like the roses in the backseat. Chloe was staring out the window at the summer afternoon. Even through the heavily tinted glass of Sam's car, she could tell the sky was a brilliant blue, wild poppies a riot of orange in the grass.

The car was a bright red gull-wing Mercedes-Benz SLS AMG. What was it with the men in Jack's crowd and their cars? Every time she took a ride with one of them she half expected to find herself in an aftershave commercial.

Sam was silent. Telephone poles whizzed by. Chloe felt the weight of his regret, although none of it showed on his face. He needn't have worried about the unfortunate encounter with Elaine. She had let him off the hook, mostly. That kiss had bought a lot of forgiveness.

She summoned her no-problem voice. "I'll figure out a way to bring Elaine around. The Fallons are on a tight timeline, so they're not going to want to start over with someone else. Besides, Mrs. F. has decided she wants Jack Anderson's niece at her beck and call. Iris Fallon doesn't change her mind easily." *And, since she is the biggest client I've ever had, all that had better be true.*

Turning away from the hypnotic view of the roadside, she smiled sweetly. She felt, rather than saw, Sam relax a degree.

"I could take you to a late lunch," he suggested.

A pleasant twinge of surprise made Chloe smile for real. "I could accept. Unfortunately, there isn't a lot around here, unless you count roadside vegetable stands."

"I know a place."

"Where? I grew up here. If there was a place, I'd know."

"I have my ways."

"Oh, that's right. You're an international man of mystery. You have ways."

Sam made a most un-Samlike snort, and signaled to change lanes. "Jack and I went for dinner a few months ago. He wanted to show me one of his new business ventures. This place hasn't been open very long."

He took an exit that forked away from the main highway and wound toward the coast. The land was uneven, cloaks of grass and wildflowers thrown over jagged slabs of rock. Chloe could see swatches of ocean between the jutting boulders.

"Jack did like to play angel."

Sam gave her a sideways look. Sunglasses hid his eyes, but she could see the amusement at the corners of his mouth. "You mean financially?"

Chloe laughed, but it twisted inside her. "Yes, in the angel investor sense. I'm not sure he would have volunteered for wings and a harp. Sitting on a cloud all day wasn't his style."

"No." The amusement was suddenly gone, replaced by the tight grief Jack's friends had worn ever since they'd arrived.

Chloe looked out her window, fighting back a sudden wave of loneliness. She had friends, but Jack had been the only family left who'd really cared for her. His death had left her disconnected, an oddment like a stray button that got pushed to the back of the drawer because it went with nothing else.

Sam reached over, putting his hand over hers for a moment. Chloe barely had time to form a thought before his hand was back on the steering wheel. She blinked quickly, banishing the tears the unexpected gesture had summoned.

Neither of them spoke. Sam turned onto a steep incline that crawled up a winding lane between tall stands of pine and cedar. It was like plunging into a primeval forest.

She cleared her throat. "How does anyone find this place?"

"It's meant for a select clientele. There's a helicopter pad for those who don't care for the drive."

She could see the appeal for Jack. He worked every hour of every day, but he liked his luxuries. "Who owns this? It wasn't listed anywhere in his estate."

"The Hope family. The place is called Hope's Reach. And I don't think he ever made a formal agreement. He took risks once in a while, but people always paid him back eventually. These folks did."

Chloe could see the Reach's sign now, arching over the narrow roadway. As they drove beneath it the trees opened up into a wide clearing at the top of the hill. Ahead stretched an unobstructed vista of ocean, only a pair of eagles interrupting the view. *Breathtaking.*

The drive circled around a broad lawn set with a stone fountain. The main building was four stories and curved around the north side of the grass. Smaller structures that might have been private cabins were scattered farther away beneath the trees.

Sam pulled up in front of the main entrance, the Mercedes humming to a final cadence. The butterfly doors lifted gracefully. By the time Chloe picked up her handbag, Sam was at her side of the car to offer her his hand.

"A man of mystery *and* style," she said.

"There's no point to a poor effort."

The only sign of tension was a crease between his brows, and she realized this was perhaps the first time she'd seen him standing in full sun. The contrast between his dark hair and pale skin was striking enough that she had to force herself not to stare. It took him beyond handsome to something exotic.

The moment didn't last long. Valets ran forward, vying for the privilege of parking Sam's car. He tossed the keys to the fastest, and quickly escorted Chloe beneath the glass-and-fieldstone facade of the main building.

Inside it was dim and cool, all the light coming from floor-to-ceiling glass windows that were shaded by the dogwood and arbutus trees outside. With the rough rock walls carried through to the interior, it felt a bit like walking through an upscale cave.

"The dining room is this way." Sam led her up a short flight of steps that opened to a shady patio.

The hostess was a pretty brunette. "Welcome back, Mr. Ralston."

"Fay," he said cordially. "How are you?"

The woman dimpled in a way that made Chloe itch. How well did these two know each other, anyway? *Don't be ridiculous. He's being polite.*

But Fay brightened under his pleasantry. "I'm very well, thank you. The corner table is free, if you would like that."

"Please."

She led them to a space that was sheltered from the ocean breeze, but still had a view. From this side of the hill, a steep cliff descended to the beach. Chloe could see a boardwalk and pier far below. The scene was utterly peaceful. Sailboats, some with white sails, some with brilliant reds and blues, floated on a silver sea. Sam held her chair, and then took the seat in the deepest shadow.

Chloe couldn't help herself. "You must come here often, if you know the staff's names."

"Fay is one of the owners. As I said, I came here with Jack when they first opened." He gave her a slight smile, just a twitch of the lips. "There are three Hope daughters, all young, beautiful and unmarried."

"No wonder my uncle invested."

"I didn't inquire about Jack's methods for testing the assets."

Chloe closed her eyes. "I'm not touching that statement with a ten-foot pole."

"Good. Just so we're clear, I came here for the wine list." He glanced over the top of his sunglasses. "Though I hear the spa offers an amazing hot rock treatment."

"Thanks for the tip, but I'm very selective about hot rocks and who is offering them."

"I'm relieved to hear it."

Fay returned. Chloe ordered seafood salad; he asked for the bisque.

"I've never seen you eat much," she said. "If you don't mind my mentioning it."

He answered with the air of someone used to the question. "My job requires rigorous physical training. That means following a very restricted dietary plan."

"And yet you drink."

"It's a failing. I'm not a saint."

"Fair enough." The wine Sam ordered came and Chloe sipped it. A Mondeuse blanche. Her tastebuds tingled at the citrus taste. "Not an everyday choice. I appreciate someone who knows their vintages."

"You apparently do, as well."

She shrugged. "I have to for my business. I have a lot of food and wine experts on speed dial. You never know what someone is going to ask for."

"What made you choose to spend your time arranging other people's weddings?"

She felt a twinge, like an old injury. "My own."

Sam frowned. "You are—or were—married?" He sounded shocked.

"Almost." She took another mouthful of wine. The memory of Neil was enough to drive her to drink. "My college sweetheart. It never happened."

"Why not?"

Chloe hesitated. "It's a long story."

Sam played with the spoon resting on his napkin, seemed to catch himself, and put it down. "Something must have made you decide against it." He was clearly curious.

She smiled, a bit wryly. "Actually, it was the other way around. He backed out the morning I was to walk down the aisle. Another hour and I would have literally been left at the altar."

Sam pulled off his sunglasses. "That's not possible." He said it quietly.

"I beg to differ. I was there." *And people wonder why I have abandonment issues.*

"What reason could he have?"

"There was another female in the picture. He wasn't up to sharing that tidbit of information until the last possible moment. Either I was blind or he hid it very well." She remembered the world dropping out from beneath her, the rage born of fear. Fear that she couldn't navigate a world where the one person she loved best could make such a fool of her. Fear that she couldn't trust anyone ever again.

Sam was studying her face, as if he could see her memories there. "He is fortunate I don't know his name."

"Jack made his feelings clear. Neil left the state after that."

Sam gave an unpleasant smile. It was enough to make a girl adore him.

Chloe gave a short laugh. "I guess when it comes to lovers, what you don't know can actually hurt you."

Sam had been reaching across the table to touch her but withdrew his hand. She pretended not to notice.

Time to change the subject. "The good part of it all was that I found out how much I liked weddings—the pageantry and celebration, the decorations, everything. I'd organized my own event pretty much by myself and had a blast doing it. So I thought, why not plan weddings for a living? I had just finished a fine arts degree in set design. There weren't too many jobs around in literal theaters, but with weddings the stage is wherever the bride and groom want it to be. It's one of the few moments in life where everyday people are the stars. I'm there to make it a hit production just for them, and it feels wonderful."

Sam nodded, his slow smile igniting something deep in her belly. "Good for you. Good for turning the situation around."

"I consider my own experience a fortunate escape. That doesn't mean I think a happy ever after is impossible."

He raised his glass. "To an eternity of happiness, Chloe Anderson. May you be your own most successful client."

The food came, and there were many pleasant things to contemplate. Sam sipping his wine. The delicious food. The glorious day. Sam offering her a taste of his soup, then stealing a pecan from her salad. She'd never been tempted to gaze at a man for hours on end, but he was handsome enough. And interesting. Without showing off, Sam seemed to know something about every subject under the sun.

They talked lazily, drifting in and out of subjects the way the eagles overhead banked from one air current to the next. There was still the underlying tension of newness between them, like glue that hadn't yet set. A slip could still make everything come unstuck. And yet there was also an instant comfort, as if they'd known each other long before.

Sam had a confidence she normally saw in someone far more mature. It wasn't cockiness. To her it felt more like the ease of experience. He didn't have to impress. He just knew who he was. His sureness made her relax.

"Are you sure you won't try dessert?" he asked. "I understand their pastry chef is extraordinary."

"I wish I could, but that was a huge salad, and it was so good that I ate every bite."

"Coward." He smiled, and this time it was wide enough that she could see his strong, white teeth. Not that he'd used them much at this meal. He had only eaten about half his soup. How could anyone survive on so little food? She wondered if she looked in the backseat if she'd find a secret stash of fast-food wrappers.

"So tell me something about your work. What kind of security jobs did you do for Uncle Jack? Was it just bodyguard work?"

She regretted her words as soon as she spoke. He sat back, pushing the sunglasses back on. It was obviously not a welcome question.

"There's more to it than being a bodyguard, though that's mostly what I do."

"I see."

She had time to pour cream into her coffee before he spoke again. When he did, he looked away, as though he was talking more to himself than to her. "Being a body-guard isn't as easy as it sounds. Sometimes things go wrong and innocent people die. Then you wonder if you were to blame."

The way he said it resonated with memory. Whatever had happened still stung, but he said nothing more. He was apparently done sharing for the day.

Was this the source of the "monster" comment? What was so awful that he couldn't tell her?

Chloe tasted the coffee, but the pleasure of it didn't reach beyond her tongue. Neil had kept secrets, but they were the simple kind. Another woman. A fickle heart. Unkind, but hardly lethal. She'd survived him. But Sam?

She watched him cautiously. There was nothing fickle about the set of his jaw or the square strength of his shoulders. And yet, she was willing to bet his secrets were far, far bigger than a second girlfriend. Even more disturbing, if she let herself fall for him, she wouldn't get over it so easily. Their kiss had told her that much. He would be the lover that destroyed her for anyone else.

The warm summer afternoon lost its charm. She set down the coffee cup, no longer thirsty.

Sam's dark black sunglasses were aimed her way, but they gave away nothing. The perfectly sculptured mouth—the one that had kissed her so beautifully—clamped into a hard line. "My work isn't as pretty as setting the stage for a wedding."

"No." What was she supposed to say?

"Does that frighten you?"

"What I don't know about you frightens me more."

He folded his napkin, setting it on the table. "Good call."

Chapter 11

Sam drove down the dark highway, wishing he could just keep going and leave Oakwood in his taillights for good.

There is a reason that vampires don't date, Sam told himself. It was confusing. Chloe wanted him, and that was natural. Vampires seduced; it was part of their hunting behavior. Their legendary attractiveness was no more than survival skills with a few pheromones thrown in. After all, what was courtship but a mild version of the predator's dance with its prey? That much Sam understood.

But there was more between them than that. Chloe had looked at him as if she actually saw who he was. Not the monster, but the man. The Sam he'd been long ago. And, more than anything, he'd wanted to believe what she saw was true.

But that was impossible. He'd barely caught himself before he surrendered to the lie. He was a vampire. As War, he battled with murderers, thieves and abominations worse than himself. By nature, he was a killer surrounded by death. *Women like her die around creatures like you.*

Moreover, any kind of a relationship could get truly awkward. It would be impossible to explain who he was. There was no good way to raise the topic of sucking blood.

No, it was far less complicated to be the superhero in the background, protecting the golden-haired maid from the dark forces of villainy. That, at least, had dignity.

"What are you brooding about?" Kenyon asked from the passenger seat.

"I'm not brooding."

"Yes, you are. Your eyebrows get all wrinkly."

He cursed. "I'm planning how we're going to find the dress thief in this dive."

"If they're still around," said Kenyon darkly. "This neck of the woods is big on hunting and fishing. There've been a surprising number of guests in and out in the last couple of days, and it's not like we had a good description to go on. Just another bunch of guys with knapsacks and equipment."

"They'll be there. They didn't get what they wanted. They're too professional to give up just like that." At least that's what Sam was counting on. Kenyon had spent the entire day roaming the area in search of a lead.

And, although he'd said nothing to Chloe, the files Sam had searched out at Gravesend Security had been Jack's detailed notes on local tourist businesses. It seemed the Salmon Tail Hotel and Saloon had a reputation for renting rooms to scum.

Sam slowed as the sign for the Salmon Tail—missing a few of the old neon letters—came into view. He took a right into the gravel parking lot, parking the Ford Super Duty right in front of the saloon-door entrance. He'd borrowed the truck from Jack's garage. His own ride would have stuck out like a Thoroughbred among a herd of goats.

"Like I said, there's no other hotels or motels close by," Kenyon said. "It's a reasonable theory."

Sam grunted agreement. The Salmon Tail occupied a gray area between functional drinking establishment and dump. Sam noticed a dent in the siding where someone with a skinful had driven right into the west corner of the building. Another, smaller neon sign hung over the front window, representing a heifer doing a jerky cancan and holding a tray of burgers.

They got out of the truck, Sam's muscles grateful for the chance to stretch. He looked around. The town was tiny, no streetlights bleaching the velvety black night. Frogs chirped a counterpoint to the country music spilling from the bar.

Kenyon folded his arms, scowling at the ramshackle building. Sam ignored him, instead giving the parking lot a critical review. No vehicles he recognized. Not that he had really expected any. Kenyon took a step toward the door. Sam caught his arm. "Be careful."

"I'm new. I'm not brain damaged."

Sam dropped his voice to a murmur. "The thief who attacked Chloe was a professional, and that means subtle. We don't know who we're looking for."

"I thought you said it was the Knights of Vidon."

"That's my theory. They would be more likely than most to know about the gems. They're human, but they use silver bullets. And they hate the idea of an alliance between Vidon and Marcari. Covert ops is their specialty. Plus, they were always after Jack and had the guts to take him on."

"So they fit the profile. That's good, right? We've fought them and won before."

"Not like this. The Knights are at their deadliest when they're operating in secret."

Kenyon drew his eyebrows together, his expression a mix of sympathy and irritation. "Like I say, I may be fuzzy, but I'm not fuzzy-headed."

All the members of the Company had experienced a run-in with the slayers, but in the time-honored code of men they never openly spoke of it.

"I'll mind my manners," Kenyon said quietly. "But you know I could bend, fold and spindle any of them."

"Maybe one at a time. No one can take them all."

Kenyon gave Sam a toothy smile. "I wouldn't want to be greedy."

"I wouldn't let you." Sam jerked his head toward the door. "Let's go find Winspear."

Jack's autopsy would be done by now. Not that they wanted to think about that. Sam pushed through the double doors without another word. Kenyon followed a pace behind.

A sour fog of noise and slopped beer engulfed Sam the moment his boots hit the bar's wooden floor. The place was stereotypical enough for a movie set: dark, down-at-heel, complete with pool tables, rickety stools and strings of lights shaped like tiny chili peppers.

The atmosphere itself didn't bother Sam, whose first alcoholic experiments had taken place in a shack in the woods. One of his father's tenants had come by a recipe for home brew and, well, it had been a wonder any of them still had internal organs. Compared to that, this place was upmarket.

What bothered him was not knowing which of the blue-jeaned, flannel-shirted patrons were slayers in disguise. Sam let his gaze touch each person, assessing body language, posture, scent. No one stood out. Then again, they never did.

Eventually, his scrutiny fell on a lone dark-haired figure at a corner table, long legs stretched out and crossed at the ankles. Winspear. Sam and Kenyon navigated the room, skirting the pool table and a cluster of barely legals playing darts. Winspear straightened to a sitting position as they grabbed chairs.

Kenyon picked up the beer bottle sitting in front of the

doctor. His eyebrows lowered. "Since when do you guys drink plain old pilsner? I thought you were all, like, Chateau Frou-frou Chardonnay types."

Winspear raised an eyebrow. "After a day in the morgue, my only criterion is that it's not formaldehyde."

"Another myth shattered." Kenyon set the bottle down.

While vampires had little appetite for food and drink, at times the ritual was comforting—but empty. Scratch the surface and the blood hunger bubbled up, poisoning everything.

Sam rubbed his eyes, suddenly exhausted in spirit if not in body. *Why did I let Chloe kiss me?* Actually, there hadn't been much "let" involved. She was hard to stop once she focused on something.

He'd nearly drowned in her eyes back there in Jack's old office. She'd had that hopeful look, the one that said you might be worth a woman's time and energy.

He wasn't. He was a monster. He'd flat-out told her so. And for someone who claimed no one ever told her anything, she was very good at ignoring his warnings. *Impossible woman.* Chloe Anderson was everything he didn't deserve, could not have and absolutely craved. Worse, he was on the brink of giving in to his desire for her and didn't know if he could stop himself. If he wanted to. *Monster.*

The beer came and Sam grabbed his bottle as if it was a comfort object. The cold, sweaty glass felt good against his palm.

Nine hells, what was he thinking? He was a vampire! It would end up in some B-movie moment with Chloe in a white nightgown on a parapet and him with his fangs sticking out—hoping to get them stuck in her.

Sam frowned. That image was so wrong in so many ways. Did Jack's house even have a parapet?

"Something bothering you?" Winspear asked.

Sam snapped back to the present, irritated at losing his focus. "No."

There was no point in even apologizing for how phony his answer sounded.

"Then maybe we can get down to business."

Sam caught Winspear's impatient tone and lifted his gaze from the tabletop. The doctor's dark eyes were filled with a cold anger.

"What?" Sam demanded.

Winspear lowered his voice so that his words wouldn't be overheard. "You wanted an autopsy report. Here it is: The only thing I can say for sure about the body we pulled from the Jag is that it belonged to a vampire. I can't tell you anything else."

Kenyon looked sick. "Seriously? It was that messed up?"

Winspear leaned forward, lowering his voice yet further. "Vampires burn extremely well, and the fire from the crash was fierce. I'd hoped to get some viable samples for testing, but almost everything useful was consumed."

"I thought one of the servants identified…him." Sam couldn't bring himself to say Jack's name.

"There were personal effects. A watch, some jewelry. The physical build was right."

"Dental records?" Kenyon asked.

"We don't get cavities," Sam put in. "All vampires have perfect teeth."

"We do, however, have full body X-rays on file with the Company," Winspear continued. "Bone formation, skull shape, healed fractures and so on provide enough individual differences to identify a vampire. I took a set of films and sent them in for comparison. That should at least give us a positive ID."

Kenyon looked confused. "There's doubt that it was Jack in the car?"

The corners of Winspear's mouth twitched downward. "I'm a scientist. I require objective proof before I commit one way or the other."

Sam's stomach squeezed painfully. Given what little Sam knew of the doctor's history, Winspear didn't like or trust many people—okay, anybody—but he had respected Jack. He would feel his loss keenly. "Jack's gone, Mark."

A savage look flashed through the doctor's eyes. "I don't have to believe that yet. When the Company phones and tells me it's a match, then I shall mourn for him."

Sam looked away, trying not to react to Winspear's vehemence. Some vampires went feral as they aged, ran for the wild and ended their days like savage beasts. There had been whispers that Plague was headed that way. He was certainly centuries older than Sam. How many horrors had Winspear seen in all those years?

Sam shoved the beer bottle aside.

"So the autopsy is a dead end for now." He winced at the unintended pun. "What else have we got?"

"I checked the guest register," Kenyon volunteered. "I didn't recognize any names, but that's no real surprise."

"What about the bed-and-breakfasts in the area?"

"Nada," Kenyon said with exaggerated patience. "I also checked the trailer park, campgrounds, and looked through the community paper for short-term rentals. This is our best bet. If our visitors are still around, they're here somewhere, hiding in plain sight."

Sam took a quick glance around the room, wondering if Chloe's thief was in the crowd. Was it one of the college students? One of the men leaning on the bar? He considered each figure, assigning a level of probable threat to each. The Horsemen could have met somewhere else, somewhere more secure, but this felt right. War didn't hide.

Plus, Sam wanted this confrontation over with. It was

so much faster when the battle came to you. Never mind what he said to Kenyon, he wanted to see just how many of the enemy he could take down. Those were the moments when it was good to be a monster.

"I'm happy to know you spent your day in constructive endeavors," Winspear observed.

Kenyon folded his arms. "Glad somebody noticed. All that legwork makes me want another beer."

"Fill your boots," Winspear muttered, pulling out his phone to check it. "Be your friendly self and soon the locals will tell you their every secret."

"Thanks, old-timer." Kenyon rose and sauntered straight toward the auburn-haired bombshell tending bar. He always went for the redheads.

Turning to watch the werewolf go, Sam watched with amused disgust. Then he stiffened. He knew the figure staring at him from the shadows of the doorway. The man was dressed as one of the locals, drawing no attention.

Sam stared at the vampire who had made him. The wave of recognition brought a complicated tangle of affection and resentment, but then it always did. More important, why had his sire come unannounced?

Dismay fingered the back of Sam's neck as his maker gestured for silence, and then vanished from sight.

Chapter 12

Chloe sat on her bed, too wound up to go to sleep.

She'd spent an hour on the phone with Elaine smoothing everything over after the disastrous appointment that afternoon. Okay, disastrous from a business perspective. She wasn't going to regret anything about that kiss with Sam. It had been far, far too long since she'd had that kind of a tingle in all the right places.

Not since Neil, and that was a pale shadow compared to what Sam inspired.

Odd that she'd thought about her ex-fiancé twice in one day. She'd blocked him out of her mind as much as was humanly possible. As Uncle Jack had put it, unfortunately some water under the bridge came straight from the sewers.

When bad memories bubbled up, good friends and chocolate were the only answers. She'd already eaten half a bar of dark Belgian supreme.

With a glance at her bedside clock, Chloe picked up her cell phone and thumbed in a number. It was eleven o'clock. That meant it would be eight in the morning in Vienna, which was early for Lexie but not indecent. After a long pause, she heard a ring.

"Alexis Haven."

The sound of her best friend's voice gave her a surge of comfort. "It's Chloe."

"Hey!" Her friend's husky voice suddenly brightened. "Are you back at work? Are you through sorting out the estate? What's going on?"

The warmth in Lexie's tone made her smile. "I'm back at work, more or less. In fact, I need you to photograph a couple of weddings, but that's not why I'm calling."

"What's up?"

Chloe paused a moment, not sure where to begin. "Some odd things have happened over this estate. I just sent a picture to your email. Don't laugh. I'm not a photographer like you."

"Hang on." She heard the distinctive sound of a Mac computer coming out of sleep mode, then a keyboard clicking. "Okay, got it. What is it?"

"I think it's a designer's signature." Chloe had taken the wedding dress out of the safe just long enough to search the garment for anything like a maker's mark. She'd found a tiny patch of embroidery along the hem, stitched in thread that matched the cloth.

"It looks like a bird."

"It might be. I have a dress on my hands and I want to know who designed it. You're working for that woman who organizes all the big shows, right?"

"Anastasia?" Of course she would be on a first-name basis with one of Europe's fashion queens. Although modest among friends, Lexie was an up-and-coming runway photographer just on the edge of being outright famous. It was a mark of their friendship that Lexie still made herself available to Chloe's Occasions.

And, at the moment, Lexie was Chloe's source for the info she needed. "Do you think she would know whose label this is?"

"Maybe. Do you have a theory?"

"I think it's Jessica Lark's, but I can't find anything online."

"Cool. I'll ask."

"Thanks."

"Where did you get the dress? Lark originals are hard to get."

"It was part of Uncle Jack's estate." Which was true, just not the whole truth. She'd tell her the rest later, when they could talk face-to-face.

"Huh. Interesting. I'll get Anastasia to email you directly." Chloe heard typing. Lexie was probably forwarding the JPEG as they spoke. "So you said something odd was going on. There's got to be more than just that, right?"

"Yeah, well, it's Uncle Jack's friends. You know he was in the security business, right? Among other things?"

"Sure."

"A handful of these G-man types showed up at the funeral. The one who's the other executor, Sam, is—I don't know how to describe him."

Lexie chuckled. "In a good way or a bad way?"

"More good than bad."

"You mean he's hot? Available? Tall, dark and handsome?"

"Sure, but—that's not it."

A dramatic sigh gusted halfway around the world. "How can that not be it? That's everything."

"He's different."

"Like how? Eats with a fork? Speaks in complete sentences? Chloe, you've had a dry spell the size of the Sahara. Count your blessings."

"He's a bit like a Swiss Army knife."

"Oh, baby!"

"Not like that."

"I like the corkscrew best."

"No, really. He's been with me through some real emergencies. Big ones. But you know how this always ends for me, Lexie."

Lexie caught the tone of her voice and sobered. "I know your history, and I get why you would worry about ending up with another Neil."

"Maybe I'm not being fair. Sam's been the only bright light in this whole mess."

"How serious a mess, Chlo? What exactly has been happening?"

"What would you say if I said I'd been attacked in my own bed by thieves, suddenly acquired a pair of bodyguards and found a wolf running up and down the hallways in the dead of night?"

She heard Lexie's intake of breath. "A wolf?"

"The attack part was worse. The wolf was kind of a sweetie."

For a moment, all Chloe heard was the crackle on the line.

"Chlo, what in blazes is going on?"

She gripped the phone, as if it could bring her physically closer to her friend. "I don't know, Lexie. And if I'm totally honest with myself, I'm a little bit scared."

Suddenly the shadows in the room seemed darker. Chloe pulled an afghan around her shoulders, burrowing into the crocheted softness.

"Who did you say this Sam guy is again?" Lexie asked.

"One of Uncle Jack's friends. There were three who showed up for the funeral. One left but the other two are still staying here. Sam and his friend, Faran Kenyon."

Chloe felt her friend's shock, even though there wasn't a sound on the line.

"Faran?" Lexie's voice smoked with ire. "You're not serious?"

Whoa! That was full-on Lexie temper. "You know him?"

"Only the most arrogant, pigheaded…"

Chloe suddenly smiled. "Is he that ex you always go on about?"

She remembered there had been an unnamed boyfriend when Lexie was in Cannes—an affair as passionate as it had been brief.

Lexie made a sound that would have done the wolf credit. "That's only half of it, Chloe."

Chloe sat up. "What do you mean?"

"How much do you know about these guys?"

She felt a niggle of alarm. "Sam saved my life. These are good people."

"*People* being a subjective term," Lexie muttered.

"What do you mean by that?"

Lexie sighed, her breath loud in Chloe's ear. "I can't explain. At least, not on the phone. Listen, I'm done here in Austria. I'm catching the first plane I can. It sounds like you need a friend. In the meantime, I wouldn't be going on any moonlit walks with your Swiss Army knife."

"How serious are you about that?"

"More than I like. I would be supercareful. Think about it. I don't do careful."

Sam was staring at the spot where his maker had been a second before. His vanishing act had been too fast for human eyes, but Sam saw the blur streaking out the door. Only ancient vampires could move quite that quickly. *What in the nine hells is going on?*

A moment later, Sam's pocket vibrated. He pulled out his phone. A text message was up on the screen. All it said was Parking lot. Code Gray.

Gray meant official business in Company-speak. Official as in need-to-know, supersecret, grab your decoder ring and eat this message if it doesn't self-destruct first. Combined with his maker's mysterious behavior, this could not be good news.

According to protocol, Code Gray meant he should go alone, mentioning the message to no one. Sam looked up. *That ship has sailed.* The werewolf had returned with his fresh brew and both Winspear and Kenyon were watching him stare at his phone, curiosity rampant on their faces.

Sam looked from one to the other. These were his brothers-in-arms. They might lack a lot of things, like a regular heartbeat, but they were loyal. *And there is something amiss.* He had a profound sense he was going to need his friends.

He rose, the legs of his chair scraping on the wood floor. "I have to take a walk."

Winspear gave a cool nod, checking his watch. "You're sure?"

"I promise to look both ways before crossing the street."

The doctor shrugged, eyeing Sam's cell phone. "Then go. I'll finish my beer just in time to come save your backside. You're not ending up on my examination table."

"What he said." The werewolf was peering down the neck of the beer bottle as if expecting to see a tiny Moby Dick breaching the suds.

The tension in Sam's chest eased. There was no question they'd be watching him every step of the way. Protocol meant he couldn't tell them anything, but there was more than one way to ask for backup. Jack had done the same thing plenty of times. A Horseman was brave, but he wasn't stupid.

Pushing through the steadily growing crowd at the bar, Sam shouldered his way to the door. For a dive in the middle of no place, it was hopping. Outside, the summer night was deliciously cool.

He paused, waiting for the latest arrivals to head inside the Salmon Tail. Then he circled the parking lot, the soles of his boots silent on the gravel. Wind ruffled the trees, drowning out the constant chirruping of frogs.

Finally, he sensed his maker. When he spoke, his voice was conversational. "Hello, Carter. What's going on?"

A match flared from the darkness of the woods, stinking of sulphur. It was an old-fashioned lucifer, struck against the bark of a tree. The scent of old Virginia tobacco followed, and Sam wondered where Carter got it. Most modern cigars didn't smell like they had in the old days. Too many pesticides, he supposed.

The scent triggered a flood of memory. The first time he'd encountered that blend of tobacco was a century and a half ago. Then the sweet smoke had been mixed with the stink of his blood and bile. December 1862, near the Rappahannock River. Reflexively, Sam put a hand to his stomach, where he'd been gutshot. A wound to the belly is a long, painful way to die. Carter had saved him from the agony.

Sam turned to see his maker a few yards away, leaning against one of the Douglas firs that ringed the parking lot. Carter wasn't an especially tall man, but he was solidly built with a mane of gray-streaked hair and ice-blue eyes. He'd been in his middle years when he'd become a vampire, but he moved with the quick energy of a young man.

Sam's shoulders tightened, memories coming too thick and fast for comfort. He'd begged for a quick death. He'd been an officer in the Army of the Potomac, proud of his command, prouder still of his honor. He hadn't asked to live.

But instead of granting him peace, Carter had made him War.

"My boy." His maker took a puff on the cigar. The end glowed like a blazing firefly in the darkness.

"What are you doing here?" Sam kept his voice neutral.

"I thought you would be glad to see me." Carter's smile was half a challenge.

"I am." It was true, and not. However mixed his feelings, Sam knew Carter was the Company's best agent. "I just didn't expect to see the director of the Company in the parking lot of a backwater bar."

Carter flicked his ash. "A good man's dead, Sam. One of the best. It was time for me to stir my old bones."

"I'm not going to refuse help. Jack was murdered. We don't have a lot to go on."

"I know."

Sam closed the distance between them, feeling the years fall away with every step. There was no denying the pull of nostalgia. They'd fought together, watched nations rise and fall. Time and shared enemies formed a bond. He respected the man and regarded him as a second father, almost. If only he could forgive Carter for making him what he was, they might have been friends.

Families, especially vampire families, were ever complicated.

A little unwillingly, Sam dragged himself back to the present. "The Knights of Vidon are involved. I'm sure of it."

Carter's bushy eyebrows shot up. "What makes you say that?"

"You wouldn't be here if you hadn't read my report. They're after the diamonds."

"Are you so sure it's the Knights?" Carter gave him that familiar smile of his—half teasing, half fatherly. "There are plenty of thieves in the world."

"Who else would know the dress was in Jack's safe?"

"Whom did Jack trust?"

It was a good question. "The Company, of course."

"Not all the Company."

Sam frowned. Whom would Jack have distrusted? "Is that why you used Code Gray?"

"Did he trust the Horsemen?"

"Certainly, but we didn't know what was in the safe."

Carter's look was significant. "All we know for sure is that you didn't."

"But…" His words ground to a halt. "Are you saying Kenyon and Winspear knew Jack had the diamonds?"

He spoke the last in a low voice, suddenly aware that the other Horsemen were no doubt watching his every gesture. He'd broken protocol because he trusted them.

Carter nodded. "Keep an open mind. Someone had to get the stones from the castle vault to the dressmaker. The dressmaker had to give the gown to Jack. There were a lot of steps involving a lot of people. A jewel thief could have taken interest at any point along the way."

Sam remembered what Chloe had said. Jessica Lark was dead. Jack knew her. He'd never mentioned her murder, or the dress, or the diamonds. Sam suddenly felt a gulf between himself and the Horsemen's dead leader. "But why would Jack confide in Winspear and Kenyon and not me?"

A gust of wind stirred the trees while Carter framed an answer. "Walk with me awhile."

Sam fell into step beside his maker. They moved slowly, ambling like men out to enjoy the air. Nonetheless, Sam felt the creep up his spine that said they were being watched.

Now he wondered if he should have been more secretive. *But they're my comrades. Jack trusted them and so do I.*

Carter puffed his cigar for a moment. "You're a straight arrow, Sam, and everyone respects that. Jack, on the other hand, was coloring a long way outside of the lines."

"Why do you say that?"

The older vampire ran a hand over his face. "The king never authorized the removal of the diamonds. They're stolen goods."

Sam looked at him sharply. He knew that already, so there must be more to Carter's point. "Are you saying that Jack stole them?"

"If he hadn't, wouldn't he have simply handed them back once they came into his possession?"

"Could it be that he was curious to see who turned up looking for the diamonds?"

Carter raised his eyebrows. "You mean Jack set a trap?"

Sam shrugged. "Just a theory. It would be like him to wait and see what fish would show up to take the bait."

"That makes good sense. More than you know." Carter kicked a rock from his path, sending it bouncing into the roadside scrub. "I need your help."

"What do you want me to do?"

"Three things. First, you need to assume command of the Horsemen."

"Pardon me?" He stopped in his tracks.

"Jack formed the unit because the Company needed a crack team. We still do. You were his second-in-command and, truth be told, the best soldier. You're War."

Pride shot through Sam, but not happiness. A promotion was good, but having Jack back would be better. "It was his team. He handpicked us."

"Now it's yours." Carter gripped his shoulder. "You were an officer. You enjoyed command, as I recall. The Company can't have a leaderless unit."

That made sense. It was only a matter of time before someone was appointed. It might as well be him. *But it makes Jack's death too real.*

Carter started walking again, Sam falling into place beside him.

"What's the second thing you need from me?"

"Turn the dress over to me. Quietly."

"You?"

"I'll take it back to Marcari while attracting as little attention as possible. That should throw the thieves off its scent until the diamonds are safely back in the palace vault. If we can pull this off, the king has agreed to keep Jack's theft out of the official record. No stain on his name."

Sam nodded. That appealed to him. "Do you need an escort?"

"No. Fewer people, less attention."

That made Sam curious. In his view, it was an unnecessary risk, one Carter would not usually take. "And third?"

"Watch your men closely. Like I said, Jack trusted them, and now he's dead."

Sam's jaw tightened, but he kept his voice calm. "What do you mean by that?"

Carter clasped his hands behind his back, head bowed. "Now, I just stated two demonstrable facts. It's the connection between the two that you're refusing to see."

"With good reason. I trust the Horsemen with my life."

"With your existence. Your life was over when I found you praying for death because your guts were spilling on the ground."

Sam didn't reply. Even now, the memory was still too vivid for comfort.

Carter gave him a searching look. "Sam, listen to me. Winspear's as socialized as a jaguar. He's got his own rules. He's a doctor now, but don't forget he spent the first few hundred years of his life as an assassin. Kenyon is a werewolf. He's not even one of us. And what else? Oh, right, Jack might have taken the boy in hand once he was all but grown, but Kenyon spent his adolescence crawling through windows for a team of international jewel thieves."

Sam stopped again. Like a kaleidoscope, all the pieces of his world were shifting into a new and uncomfortable pattern. "They are proven men."

Carter waved an impatient hand. "And you're a good friend. How nice."

Anger flared, and now Sam didn't care if Carter saw it. "The Horsemen are a team."

His maker's face sagged into regretful lines. "I'm not saying this lightly. Follow the facts. What two crimes do we know for sure happened? A jewel theft and an assassination. Who are your teammates? A jewel thief and an assassin. Give me a straight edge and a pencil, and I'll connect the dots for you."

Stunned, Sam was silent.

"I'm sorry." Carter put a hand on his shoulder. "We're vampires. You know all too well what that means. We may believe in loyalty and render great service to our king, but that impulse for good is a shaky thing. I've faced my true nature, mastered my base instincts. I've been the iron hand of the Company that keeps the vampires in check. Scratch the surface of any of us, and the pus of pure evil will come bubbling out. It's a fact of nature, as surely as the cock crows at sunrise."

Speechless, Sam could only stare. It didn't help that he'd been thinking the same thing only minutes before Carter had appeared.

Carter went on. "But none of this is news to you."

"No," he finally replied.

Chapter 13

If I survive this, I deserve my own reality show.

Chloe spent the morning in Uncle Jack's study pulling miracles out of her hat. Or, to make the metaphor more appropriate, her bridal veil. She'd booked the golf club. She'd found an orchestra and a DJ. She'd nailed the church. She'd got her staff started on finding limousines.

Oddly, working was doing her good. She was in a fairly good mood by the time Sam made his daily invasion into her territory. Today he looked more serious. Lines of fatigue etched deep into his face, as if he'd spent the night worrying. With everything going on, she'd be surprised if he hadn't. Still, she tried to ignore just how good he looked in his perfectly tailored suit. If she got sidetracked, she'd fall even further behind.

"What are you doing?" he asked when he saw her typing madly on her laptop.

"Working on Elaine and Leo's wedding."

Surprise flickered over his features. "I thought…"

"Yesterday was just a temporary setback. After all, there aren't that many wedding planners available and willing to work this quickly. At least, not with my contacts." Chloe let a note of defiant pride into her voice. "This is what I'm good at. And this is the agreement with the catering company."

She hit Send and barely resisted the urge to pump her fist in the air. Okay, she was overtired.

"Are you meeting Elaine in Thurston again?"

"Yes, at the nice offices I wanted to rent last time. From now on, I'm doing this my way."

Sam scowled.

Chloe scowled back but couldn't keep it up. "Body-guards and bridal bouquets don't mix. I'll figure out some way to manage things sensibly. I have a friend coming back from Europe. I know she won't mind going with me to these appointments, just so that I'm not alone."

"Is she a weapons expert?"

"She's a photographer. I'm asking her to do the wedding shoot."

"A camera's not going to help if someone jumps you."

"I dunno. My friend's a redhead. I wouldn't try it."

"I'm serious."

"So am I." Chloe closed her laptop. She wanted Sam to feel appreciated, but this was her livelihood. "Everything has to go right this time. I appreciate your concern, but I can't afford to alienate my clients. They want sunshine and puppies, not a private army."

Sam folded his arms. "Kenyon and I are going with you."

"Sorry, I can't have you guys standing around brooding like angels of doom."

He winced. "I'll stay in the background. Everyone likes Kenyon. He can be the good cop."

Remembering Lexie's odd reaction when Faran Kenyon's name came up, Chloe balked. She still didn't know what to make of that conversation, but Lexie would be in town soon enough and could explain. In the meantime, she wasn't risking another disaster with Elaine. "No. I'll go by myself. Bridal talk is a girly thing. You're not girls."

"Chloe," he said, his voice close to a warning growl.

"Don't 'Chloe' me. I appreciate everything you've done, but I'm in charge of my own business appointments."

She felt his displeasure like a physical wall. Too bad. He was pushing her in a way that set her alarm bells ringing. And it set her imagination racing, taking that moment and painting it large. If she gave in now, what would happen down the road?

It was easy to guess. If she didn't stand up to him, he would take over everything, an inch at a time. And, sooner or later, he would leave—maybe not as dramatically as Neil, but men like Sam didn't do the domestic scene. Then she would have to pick up whatever pieces he dropped— even if that included pieces of her heart. Better to stand her ground now.

She took a deep breath, trying to sort fact from fear. This would be so much easier if she was more willing to trust. *And what if I am taking a stupid risk? He knows more about this security stuff than I do.*

She rose, drifting around the desk and crossing the thick Oriental carpet to the window. Sam had left the drapes alone this time, so she could look out at the garden. Not that she cared what was outside, but it gave her a moment to gather her wits.

It was gray out, raining lightly. She was wearing nothing but slacks and a sleeveless blouse, and the air near the French doors was cool. She rubbed her bare arms.

He finally spoke. "Chloe, with luck, this will all be over soon."

"What do you mean?"

"Things will go back to normal. The dress will go back to the princess. You'll go back to your home."

"And you'll go back to *your* home, wherever that is." She said it flatly. The implication that they'd soon be out of each other's lives was all too clear.

"Wherever. I have several addresses."

He said it inconsequentially, but the statement made her turn around. "That sounds—" She started, then stopped. "That sounds like a logistical nightmare, actually. I can barely keep track of my cable bill as it is."

He chuckled, a surprisingly warm sound for a man who didn't seem to get much practice. "You never say what I expect you to."

Chloe took a step toward him, feeling the cold from the window on her back. "It's a flaw of mine. I think I'm checking to see if anyone is paying attention."

"Who wouldn't?" His smile was filled with male appreciation. Unexpectedly, everything seemed to shift, the mood in the room lightening.

"Why do you have addresses and not a home?"

He shrugged. "I work here and there. I'm never in one place very long."

"Does that bother you?"

He touched her arm, just a light brush of the fingertips. "Honestly, yes. Sometimes I long for a real place, just so I know where I'm going to come back to."

Both his touch and his words made her shiver. Neither was an overt come-on, but she suddenly wondered if there was a possibility for something between them. It was an odd thought—a complete reversal—given their tense conversation a moment ago, but it wasn't completely unthinkable, either. She could feel his interest like an electrical field, invisible but still crackling along her skin. *I'd like to come back to you,* it seemed to say.

Get real. He has one foot out the door. He's just said

as much. But maybe he wouldn't go if there was a reason to stay.

Her heart sped for a moment. Sam raised his head as if he could hear it. *Trust Sam,* Jack had said. On the other hand, Lexie had told her to run for the hills. The choice was wide-open.

"Now let me ask you something," he said. "Why are you so determined to put yourself in danger by going to Thurston by yourself? I promise Kenyon and I will be very, very good."

She stiffened. "You know why."

"You think we'll be in the way."

"Yes. Maybe. You scared Elaine half to death. And I have to look after myself. We all do."

"When it makes sense." Sam's hand traveled to his gun. "When it doesn't, I'm there."

Until you're not. Chloe dreaded having this conversation with anyone. It always sounded crazy. "I can't leave it up to you."

"Why not? Why not let me take care of you? It's what I'm good at."

"I'll try to explain."

"Good." His gaze held hers, but this time the gray wasn't like steel. It was like a far-off storm, dark and heavy with power.

"It's an old thing with me. My parents were scientists working on something supersecret."

"You said they died."

"When I was a teenager they were murdered in a home invasion. All I ever found out was that it had to do with their work. I still don't know what that work involved."

Sam didn't say anything for a moment, just frowned. "You were very young."

She folded her arms protectively across her chest. The

atmosphere in the room was softened by the clouds out-side, the jewel tones of the carpet and drapes washed with gray. "The worst part of their death has always been never knowing why it happened. Was there something I could have done to take precautions? Sure, I was only fourteen, but I still wonder. Had I said the wrong thing to a random stranger? Did I leave a door unlocked? Give away our phone number when I shouldn't have? Will whoever killed them ever come looking for me?"

Sam shifted, moving a fraction closer. "Unlikely. That was a long time ago."

"But I don't know because I have no idea what any of it was about. It's left me with doubts for the rest of my life."

Sam leaned against the bookcase, a boneless motion that reminded her of a big cat. It put his face only inches from hers. "And the point of this is that you see lack of in-formation as a threat."

"Yes, that's part of it." Chloe exhaled. So few people understood, but Sam was keeping up.

He studied her, his expression intent. "Your uncle was full of secrets, too."

"He was."

"How did you feel about that?"

Gently, he traced a finger down her cheek. She shivered slightly, but was too mesmerized to pull away.

"Not great. And now look where that's got us. I adored Uncle Jack, but a safe full of hot diamonds? Not a great goodbye present. And yet, without telling me anything about what's going on, he leaves me a note asking me to do the right thing. How should I know what that is?"

"You think he abandoned you with a mess. That you'd learned to count on him and then suddenly he wasn't there."

"Yes."

His finger came to rest on her lips and hovered there,

light as a bee, before pulling away. "Just like your fiancé and your parents."

Chloe nodded, a little amazed. No one had ever grasped what she felt that quickly. "It's not completely fair to them, is it? People don't mean to die."

He gave a lopsided smile. "Feelings and logic don't always go together."

"Nonetheless, I don't like counting on people. It makes me feel safer to stand on my own two feet."

"There's nothing wrong with being independent." Sam put a hand on her waist, stroking her ribs lightly with his thumb. "But don't think your parents didn't want to be there for you. And I don't know if Jack could have done anything different. He was my friend and we worked closely together, but there are a lot of things about him that I'm just finding out."

"Are you trying to say Jack's secrecy was nothing personal?" The feel of his hand made her want to curl into him. Her thoughts struggled to stay with the conversation.

"I'm sure of it in your case. I'm still trying to decide that in mine." Disappointment colored his expression. "He trusted you to do the right thing. Hang on to that."

"He trusted you, too."

He gave her an odd look. "I hope so."

"Have you found anything out about the thief? Or his murder?"

For once, he didn't shy away from answering. "I can tell you that there are no guests registered in the area who are likely suspects. Kenyon and I have been going through the names."

"Is that all?"

"So far."

"I don't want to be shut out."

"I get that." His hand slid to the small of her back. "I'm on your side, remember?"

She swayed into him and he reciprocated, letting the hard length of him brush against her hip. Suddenly everything felt so right. *Trust Sam.*

She ran her hands over his shoulders, enjoying their massive strength beneath the fine wool of his jacket. He was giving her his signature smile, the barest hint of amusement curling the corners of his mouth. His gaze roved over her in a way that brought heat to her skin, setting every nerve tingling.

Her touch strayed from his shoulders, trailing down his arms. They were thick with muscle, strong in a way that appealed to the most primitive part of her brain. The fact that she was holding him like this, her fingers spanning this much pure male power, sent a ripple of need low in her body. If he had taken her then and there, she would have been ready.

His eyes darkened, as if he sensed the change in her.

Impulsively, she put one hand on either side of his face, caressing the hard, strong bones of his cheek and jaw. His cheeks felt rough with beard against her palms. She pulled his head down to press her lips against his. Firm and swift, she caught him before he could resist.

And gave a cry when something sharp poked her lip. She broke the kiss. "Ow!"

A salty, metallic taste teased her tongue. *Blood.*

Instantly, Sam turned away.

Ugh. Embarrassing. "I'm sorry, honestly. Too much enthusiasm."

Much more slowly, Sam turned back to her, his color high. He had one hand to his mouth, as though she'd bruised him. "It's okay."

The words came out in a mumble. His eyes were nearly

black, as if the pupil had expanded to fill the steel-gray irises. The room was dim, but she could see hunger in those black depths. Chloe shivered, falling back a step. There was a look men got when they wanted a woman. This was it to the umpteenth power.

"Okay, then," she breathed, her stomach going cold with unease and then melty with the need to answer that look.

Then, quick as if he'd flipped a switch, the look was gone, the emotion behind it locked away behind the wall of his self-control. Chloe blinked, wondering if she had seen it at all.

Tentatively, she reached out. She had to apologize to know what he was thinking.

It wasn't to be. He flinched away as if her fingers burned white-hot. Without another word, Sam walked out of the room, his shoulders hunched and his hand still over his mouth.

Embarrassment twisted through her, sending heat flaring up her cheeks. She could run after him, or she could stay frozen in abject humiliation. But what would she say when she caught up to him? *Sorry I knocked out a tooth, but it means I like you?*

Feeling twelve, she stayed put, as if her feet were nailed to the carpet. What *was* that look? Had it really been there? Had she ruined everything?

Chloe fell onto the library's leather couch and breathed a curse to the rain outside. She touched her lip. It felt hot and sore, but there was no more blood. It had barely been a scratch, but obviously Sam was hurt.

How humiliating. She should have agreed to go home when this whole mess had first started. She buried her face in her hands.

Now she'd be known by all the Men in Black as the little wedding planner who kissed like a battering ram.

Chapter 14

It wasn't exactly news that he was a slavering beast. Sam just considered it a private matter. One didn't let *those* hang out in public.

Humiliating. Sam stomped down the basement stairs of Jack's mansion, feeling like Dracula returning to his lair. Cue the spooky organ music.

The problem with pretty girls was that, in their warm, soft way, they brought out a vampire's fangs. As if men didn't have enough involuntary physical reactions to deal with. Usually Sam's control was much, much better, but Chloe was in a league of temptation all her own.

As if things weren't already complicated enough. Sam slammed the door to Jack's office. His real office, not the study Chloe was using. This room wasn't all fine furniture and frilly china. This had a plain desk, several computers and not much else. All business. The door, hidden in the mansion's vault of a basement, was coded to chip cards only Jack and Sam possessed.

He flung himself into the squeaky desk chair. He wanted to break something. Assert his will. Prove that he had force and power. He was War. He wasn't a teenaged boy awkwardly asking for his first dance.

Cursing, he poked the desktop monitor to life. A log-in box popped up. While Sam typed in his Company email ID and password, his thoughts returned to Chloe. They'd done that every five seconds or so since the first moment he'd met her.

He had to make a decision. Not that there were any real options, of course, but just *pretending* that it would be okay to have an affair with a human woman—and Jack's niece to boot... Even wanting it seemed like folly.

Pre-vampire Sam had carried on functional relationships. Post-vampire War had lovers, but not women he loved. He'd learned the hard way to steer clear of such weakness. Until Chloe. For her, he could see staying in one place, going to bed with her every day, guarding her through the journey of her life.

Clearly he was losing his mind. If he took one of those magazine tests to find out who his ideal mate might be, Sam Ralston should be sending flowers to a wolverine. He was a predator with healthy self-esteem and a triple-A-plus alpha rating.

Which was all true, except when it wasn't. Part of him was still just Sam, terrified of what he'd become and afraid he was going to hurt someone he loved.

Disgusted with himself, he two-finger typed his way to his email. There was a message from Winspear. It was typically brief. "Death's medical file predates skeletal identification program. No comparison films on record."

So, Jack never got around to doing the full-body X-rays. Sam shut the email with a curse. *It was just an X-ray, Jack. Couldn't you have done that much for us?* But no, that would have been too much like paperwork. Not Jack's thing. Neither, apparently, was turning in the crown jewels when they found their way into his personal safe.

Was Sam the only one who ever followed the rules? Who did his job because he'd taken an oath to say that he would?

A memory surged up of a crowded dance floor. Girls in scraps of dresses, Sam assigned to watch over them. It hadn't been his comfort zone. Parachute him into a jungle, give him a mountain to climb, and he was in heaven. But this time the jungle cats wore human faces. He was trained to spot the enemy, but it was harder when they looked exactly the same as the victims—kids on a dance floor, having fun.

He had been Princess Amelie's bodyguard. The shooter who had tried to kill her—and ended up killing the princess's friend instead—had been little more than a boy.

The kid had looked utterly blank, as if he'd just happened to be holding the gun at the time. Sam hadn't hesitated to bring him down, but he'd still been too late. Despite metal detectors and pat-downs, the guards had somehow let the boy into the club with a weapon.

Sam had been uneasy that night and had wanted to put his own men on the doors. But he hadn't because Carter had specifically told him to leave the usual security in place. War followed orders, especially Carter's orders. He was the weapon, not the hand that wielded it. *And didn't that work out well?* he mused bitterly. The guards had turned out to be traitors. The boy had claimed he had no recollection of the incident—almost like he'd been the victim of vampire mind control.

Impossible, of course. Why would any of the vampires hurt the princess?

That was just one more good question to tighten the knot in Sam's stomach. The incident had shaken his faith in those around him. Sam had started thinking a little harder about his orders since that night, an unease that had haunted him since.

He was thinking about his orders now.

So what was Carter's point about the other Horsemen? Kenyon and Winspear made good suspects. As well as having the right skills, they were close to the victim and involved in the investigation. Absolutely true. But Carter had no proof. *Why sow distrust without something to back up those accusations?*

He turned the question around. Why would Carter, iron hand of the Company's vampires, want Sam to believe his friends were traitors? Good question. Carter considered himself a one-person crusade against vampire-kind's vile instincts. Fierce discipline alone made these mad dogs into obedient warriors for good. Sam had always believed him.

Yet Chloe insisted that Sam wasn't a monster. She contradicted Carter's pus-and-evil assessment of true vampire nature. She had no idea he was the walking dead, but otherwise she was pretty perceptive. Sam didn't want to dismiss her opinion out of hand.

Then again, Carter should know how bloodsuckers thought. He'd been undead longer than any of them, except maybe Winspear. Had one of the Company's vampires suddenly lost their scruples and decided to steal the diamonds?

"No," Sam said out loud. "I don't buy it." If it had been outright theft, why sew them onto a dress? That made no sense.

This is what Chloe meant when she said lack of information makes her nervous. Sam felt a surge of sympathy for her. Unfortunately, she had to be kept in the dark. Everything about this case—about Sam—was a secret. If she found out what he was, he would have to make sure her memories were erased. If it ever got out that Sam had revealed what he was and let her walk away, it could mean death for them both. Carter's rules.

A sick feeling invaded Sam's gut, as if something noxious was seeping upward from the floor. He had to let Chloe go. Anything else was unfair to both of them—but he couldn't walk away until she was safe. That meant getting the dress back to the palace as soon as possible.

Carter was waiting in the wings to do just that. But, good Company soldier or not, Sam wasn't ready to hand it over. With Chloe involved, he wasn't taking any chances until he was absolutely sure of what was going on. He'd made the mistake of going against his gut instincts that night in the dance club, and right now there were far too many unanswered questions.

Speaking of which...

He logged in to a restricted part of the Company's security system, then another, passing through firewall after firewall to access the database that listed agents. Sam had higher clearance than most.

He typed in the name "Jessica Lark" and then hit Search.

The database returned a terse message: Deceased. Special division.

So she was an agent! It had been a wild guess, but he'd been right. A tingle of satisfaction passed through him. He was finally getting somewhere.

There was a picture. It wasn't a portrait, but a candid shot taken in front of the Algonquin Hotel in New York City. Jessica Lark had been a beautiful woman. *I should have listened to Chloe. She hit on the truth when she couldn't even understand what it meant.* The woman's instincts were downright scary.

He stared at the monitor, his world doing that kaleidoscope shift all over again. Lark wasn't the only person in the picture. Between one cursor blink and the next, he thought he understood what was going on. Horror turned him cold, and for a brief instant he prayed he had it all wrong.

Chapter 15

Not long after, Sam tracked Chloe to the garden. He had two purposes in mind. The first was to listen again to what she knew about Jessica Lark. The second was to persuade her to accept a security detail for her afternoon appointment. Simply announcing that it was going to happen had brought out her difficult side, blast it. He had to regroup and try a gentler tone. That was going to take some imagination on his part. War wasn't used to saying "please."

She was walking slowly under the twisting branches of the Garry oaks, her head bent in thought. He studied her, squinting against the sun despite his sunglasses and the overcast sky. The sun hurt him, a hot pressure against his skin, sharp knives to his sensitive eyes. Still, if the outdoors was where Chloe was to be found, that was where he would go.

She'd slipped a loose sweater over her blouse and wore low-heeled canvas shoes with a pattern of pink and green flowers. Sam thought he could see glimpses of the girl she had been when Jack had brought her, an orphan, into his house.

He cursed whoever had killed her parents. When he was done with this case, he would look at their file. He couldn't bring them back, but perhaps he could offer Chloe some justice.

He liked that idea. A lot. "Chloe."

She looked up, surprise lighting her face. "I'm sorry. I hope your tooth is okay."

Sam's step hitched. For a blessed moment, he'd forgotten about the dental incident. "I'll survive."

Her cheeks flushed a delicate pink. In the hazy gray of the overcast afternoon, her skin was a shade of tawny pearl, lightly freckled where the sun had touched it. Sam's fingers yearned to tame the wisps of hair blowing across her cheeks. He dared not risk it. He wanted her so badly that touching her invited his beast. He could at least begin the conversation minus the slavering fangs.

"I don't usually kiss like it's a contact sport," she grumbled.

"The idea has interesting possibilities. I'm curious about penalty shots."

That earned him a dark look. "Really, I'm better than that."

"I know."

He could feel his resolve crumbling. Her essence was more powerful than all of War's arsenal of strength and speed. The most he could do was try to stick to business.

He had to. What he'd realized when he'd opened Lark's file—or as much of it as his clearance allowed—had him worried. It confirmed his decision to keep the dress until he absolutely understood what was going on.

"Tell me again about Jessica Lark," he said, moving to the shadier side of the path.

"I don't know much more than what I already told you. One thing, though. I found her signature on the wedding gown." Chloe folded her arms, hugging herself. "I emailed a picture to someone who knows the designers.

She wrote back this morning and confirmed it was Lark's. That means, even without the jewels, that dress is worth a small fortune."

Sam digested that. "How did Jack say he knew Lark?"

Chloe shrugged. "He knew all kinds of people."

The walk curved around a pond bordered by trailing willows. Ducks paddled across the surface, chuckling softly amongst themselves. Chloe stopped, pulling off one of her flats to empty out a stone. Her toenails were painted a pale pink.

Sam watched the play of bones and tendons in her slender foot. He had been born in a time when women hid their ankles. He suddenly understood why. They could be incredibly erotic. His blood stirred in an extremely unhelpful way. "Maybe one of Jack's girlfriends knew Lark? Bought from her collection?"

"No. I remember now." Her voice gained energy as she spoke. "It had something to do with old books. Jack was a collector. So was she. They met at an auction."

She smiled up at him, obviously pleased to be helpful. It was adorable.

It was also useful information. If Lark was an undercover agent, she would have needed a reason to publicly associate with Jack. That, in turn, might give a clue as to what she was involved with. "Any particular area of interest?"

Chloe pulled her shoe back on, wriggling her heel into place. "Occult stuff. Jack has some odd manuscripts. He let me look at them whenever I liked."

Sam looked at her sharply. "Really?"

"He had a thing about vampires."

Shock slammed into him, his chest squeezing with alarm. "What?" *Had Jack lost his mind?* Vampires never showed an open interest in the occult, in case it raised questions.

Chloe turned, walking backward a few steps while she studied his face. She'd seen that moment of astonishment. "Yeah. He was an avid collector. Everything from Renaissance books of magic down to plastic teeth. It was his main hobby."

Sam took a deep breath, trying to still his churning stomach. "Why do you think he was so interested?"

"Maybe it was because he lived like a creature of the night. Up all hours. Bad diet. Coming and going without warning. Went through women like snack food. He was a great uncle, but he had his quirks."

The way she said it, so offhand, softened Sam's sense of alarm. "Did you talk about it much?"

"Some. He loved sharing his collection with a few people he liked. He didn't talk about it much otherwise."

In a roundabout way, Jack had been letting Chloe know who he was, telling her without telling her. If any of the Company—like Sam—had known, they would have panicked. But, as always, Jack had gone his own way. Sadness flooded Sam for his friend, and for all the secrets they had to keep.

As if sensing his melancholy, Chloe took his hand. "The books are still here, if you want to see them."

Her slender fingers were lost in his. All of her seemed fragile compared to the masculine world of his existence. Irrationally, he felt afraid to close his own fingers lest he crush her bones.

Sam swallowed hard. "No, that's okay. I just keep trying to figure out Jack's connection to Lark and the dress."

They walked a few paces, Sam tucking her hand into the crook of his elbow. Leaves rustled on a thyme-scented breeze. It was hard to believe this was the same route Sam had followed, chasing the blood trail of Chloe's attacker. In the gentle afternoon light, the garden was a haven.

Chloe pushed a strand of hair behind her ear. "My guess is Lark trusted him enough to give him the dress for safe-keeping. Maybe she knew something was up. And if a friend asked Jack to do something, he'd do it." She gave Sam a shrewd look. "Maybe Jack was just holding it for her, and then she was killed."

"Maybe. It's a good explanation, especially if his intention was to eventually return the dress to Marcari."

Chloe's blue gaze was steady. "Jack wasn't a thief."

"No, he wasn't." Sam felt the truth of her words, sharp and clean as a sword. She could see to the heart of people, and it made far more sense than Carter's dark view of the vampires.

Chloe's fingers squeezed his arm as they walked, the heat of her like life itself. Her lips quirked. "So now you know Jack's deep, dark secret."

"That he collected Count Chocula bobblehead dolls?"

She laughed softly. "I'm not sure there is such a thing."

"We all have something we'd rather not share."

"How about you?"

"Pardon?"

"Don't shy away now. Fair is fair. We shouldn't get to pick on Jack unless we confess our own peculiarities."

"I have Fido."

"He's just a pet."

You have no idea. "What are yours?"

"Isn't spending my life playing with balloons and confetti enough?"

"That's just a job."

Chloe ducked her head, obviously thinking of something but too embarrassed to say it. Sam grinned. "Okay, I'll go first."

She looked up. "What?"

"I'm a Civil War fanatic."

"What, with little armies covering the dining room table, or are you one of those guys who goes out to fight Gettysburg once a year?"

"I did Fredericksburg. Never made it to Gettysburg."

"Still, that's pretty hard-core."

"Now it's your turn."

She turned that rosy pink again. "I never threw out my collection of stuffed ponies. I still have them all in my bedroom."

He smiled. He couldn't help it. He had a ridiculous mental image of the Four Horsemen done in pastel plush. "Is this part of the same fantasy that requires a gold-hoofed palfrey for Elaine to ride down the aisle?"

"That's not my idea, Elaine's mom came up with that. But, yeah, I understand the fantasy appeal."

They'd reached the end of the path. Behind Chloe, delphiniums fountained in blue spires, matching the color of her eyes.

Without even knowing what he was going to do, Sam kissed her. It happened too quickly for second thoughts. She was suddenly in his arms, his fingers folded in the soft fabric of her sweater.

There was no straight line of reason in Sam's mind, just a burning need to do this right. Just once, he needed to approach Chloe as a man. A man who wanted her more than anything.

He began kissing her slowly, first the top lip, then the bottom, teasing until her body began melting into his, her weight sinking against his chest. Her fair hair tumbled over his dark jacket, reminding him of gold turning to molten liquid in a crucible. Gold, the one element that was incorruptible.

He was a creature of darkness, but she drew him into the light. The part of him that was still a man, the lost part, the lonely part, craved it the way a man abandoned in the desert for years craved cool, clear water.

Sam stroked her arm, the feel of the soft, plush sweater against his palm strangely arousing. Her fingers touched his neck, featherlight brushes. As her breath exhaled against his lips, his ears, he could feel her pulling him down to her, yearning to be closer. He drank in the warmth of her skin through his lips. She smelled golden, like the sun shining through a kitchen window. She tasted like everything he missed.

Sam ached through his whole being. Like an endless wellspring, there was ever more begging for his touch, no matter how much of her loveliness he claimed with mouth and hands.

His hand traveled up her spine, from the sway of her back and along the arc of her ribs. He found the warm fullness of her breasts, surprising in a woman so slender. She shivered under the pressure of his fingers, but it was in anticipation. He kneaded her gently, feeling her nipples grow hard and ready for pleasure.

The thought intoxicated him, drew him further into the moment. Chloe broke away, her lips lingering near his before they returned, soft and warm, to kiss him back.

And this time he kept his fangs to himself. Everything was perfect.

Chapter 16

It was no great mystery how Sam eventually talked her into accepting his protection that afternoon. When she thought about it, Chloe felt sheepish. As much as she had tried, she was no match for his masculine wiles.

Happily, Faran readily agreed to go, as well. Cheerful and client-friendly, he would cover the interior of the small, pretty business center in the Eldon Hotel. Sam would watch the exterior. Two bodyguards seemed absolute overkill to Chloe, but she wasn't going to argue anymore. Maybe she was being naive. After all, she had limited experience with crazed jewel thieves, and Sam seemed to feel his presence was a necessary precaution. As long as he didn't talk to the clients, Chloe was okay with that. And he did kiss so very, very well.

However, she remembered Lexie's warning about falling for her Swiss Army knife the moment she got to the meeting room and pulled out her phone. There was a voice message from her friend. Chloe waited to play it until Faran had deposited her binders of photos and samples and went to park the car. Sam, of course, assumed his guard dog post outside the door.

Lexie had booked her flight from Austria for that day.

She'd also booked into the Eldon, adamant that she would not stay in the same house as her former boyfriend. A quarter hour later, Elaine arrived along with Iris Fallon, the mother of the bride. Chloe summoned her brightest smile. "Lovely to see you again, Mrs. Fallon."

The straight-backed, trim woman had a firm handshake and a brisk, no-nonsense snap to her words. "I came along to make sure things don't run off the rails."

"Of course," Chloe replied, doing her best not to be offended.

It probably would have made no difference if she were. Iris didn't look the sensitive type. One might have broken china against that no-hair-out-of-place helmet of iron-gray waves.

"Please don't take this personally, but I don't trust anyone who doesn't come from within our circle to strike just the right chord." She gave Chloe an assessing look, as if deciding whether or not Jack Anderson's niece counted. "Speaking of which, I insist upon a harpist for the reception."

"I'm sure we'll all appreciate your insights," Chloe replied.

"I should say so, since I'm paying your bill."

They settled into chairs.

Chloe offered her sweetest smile, glad she'd decided to start with something easy. "I thought perhaps we could look at some cake designs, just to get a sense of what appeals. Then we can think about doing some tasting. I have an excellent dessert chef who will deliver anywhere we like."

"Did somebody say cake?" Faran entered the room carrying a tray laden with coffee and cookies.

Chloe mentally crossed her fingers, hoping Bodyguard 2.0 would hit the right chord with Elaine. "This is Faran Kenyon, who will be assisting me today."

She needn't have worried. Faran gave a sunny smile and waved a hand at the tray. "The coffee shop had vanilla-hazelnut blend. It smelled so good, I couldn't resist. How do you take your coffee? Cream? Sugar?"

Elaine gave him a huge smile. "Cream and sugar, please."

Perfect. Chloe could see shoulders relaxing, spines curving into the soft and welcoming furniture. Within seconds, she saw Faran knew how to work a crowd.

Only Iris seemed reluctant to thaw. With a chilly smile, she flipped the pages of the photo album with an audible snap.

"So what kind of cakes are these?" Iris sniffed. "They're not that cardboard flummery you put out for show? I want the real thing under the icing."

"I assure you, those are real cakes." Chloe watched them speed by under the woman's rough fingers. There were the traditional tiered cakes, but also castles and ships, a huge sheet cake decorated like a football field. She'd been proud of every one.

"If I may." Faran pulled up an armchair and sat down. "What kind of cake batter you use is sometimes dependent on the style of the cake. It has to be firm enough to support the design."

Iris gave him a sharp look. "How would a young man like yourself know about that?"

Chloe wondered, too. Last thing she'd heard, he was a spy with an unsettling interest in other people's jewelry. And she didn't need another Man in Black ruining her appointments.

But Faran just gave a pleasant smile. "I have my chef's papers, ma'am. Desserts aren't my specialty, but I know one or two things about cake design."

Elaine spoke up. "Chloe, you know some very interesting people."

"Elaine," Iris snapped, using her daughter's name like a reproach. "You can't believe every bit of nonsense a pretty boy tells you, and you'd be better off if you'd paid attention to that fact long before this circus came to town."

Chloe narrowed her eyes. She'd had enough. Weddings belonged to the bride and groom, and Elaine wasn't being heard. "Excuse me, Mrs. Fallon. I completely understand how you want everything to be perfect. That's why I'm here to help you." Gently, Chloe pulled the book of photographs from Iris's hands and set it on the table. "As you know, we settled on the medieval theme as a compromise between elegance and a sense of fairy tale wonder."

"Yes." Elaine said. "It was the one theme we all could live with."

"All right." Step one, get everyone back to a place of consensus. Step two, work out from there. "So our cake has to be in keeping with the medieval theme. What would be perfect for our fairy tale kingdom?"

"A castle," Elaine said, suddenly enthused. "We could have a cake that looked like a castle."

"A white castle with shining turrets," Iris added. "With pennants fluttering from the towers."

Chloe smiled warmly. "What an excellent idea."

Never mind she'd already thought of it. The castle itself could be fruitcake, the surrounding forest, moat and drawbridge could be spun sugar on a softer cake base. That way both bride and mom could have something they wanted. She didn't know the exact engineering required—her culinary experience barely stretched to scrambled eggs—but her dessert chef was a genius at these things.

Unfortunately, Elaine was looking a little glum again. Shining turrets were good, but not perfect. *Needs to be more playful.* "What does everyone think of adding a dragon?" Chloe asked.

"Oh, yes!" Elaine brightened at once. "A castle has to have a dragon."

Iris looked less convinced. "Maybe a small one."

"I'll see what the chef can do." She gave Elaine a wink. The woman smiled, ducking her head. "I'll have some samples sent for our next appointment. Maybe Leo would like to come to the tasting?"

Faran had moved to stand by the credenza where he'd left the coffee tray, out of everyone's line of sight but Chloe's. He made a thumbs-up gesture. Chloe tried not to watch him, keeping her face serious.

"He must send samples within twenty-four hours," Iris demanded. "Since the wedding will be next week."

"Next week?" Chloe squeaked. "You said it was in two months!"

Elaine looked abashed. "I'm so sorry, but that was before Grandma Fallon's last appointment. She's not going to last until late summer."

"You neglected to mention the new timeline?" Iris asked her daughter in freezing tones. But Chloe had noticed the flinch when Grandma Fallon was mentioned. Iris was covering up a lot of sadness.

Elaine closed her eyes. "I forgot. I think I remembered to forget. This is too fast. We can't ask Chloe to do it."

"Next week." Chloe's voice sounded weak in her own ears. Her head felt inflated, as it might float off her shoulders at any moment. "I can try, but I have no idea what to do about a reception hall on such short notice. They're booked months in advance, sometimes years."

Iris's thinly plucked brows drew together. "Well, this isn't the kind of service I expected. What kind of a wedding planner can't provide a reception hall?"

One with insane clients! Chloe longed to scream it as she lunged across the coffee table to throttle the woman, but no one hired a planner with a record of strangling her customers.

"I have an idea," Faran broke in.

Everyone turned to look at him.

"What about Jack's place? It's big enough for two weddings this size."

Chloe sat back, feeling dizzy with relief and dread. Faran was right. It had everything that she needed: parking, gardens, reception rooms, guest accommodations, kitchens and staff.

And thieves. If Sam was right, assassins.

"That's Oakwood Manor, isn't it?" Iris purred. "What a splendid idea."

Be careful, Chloe thought. *You might get the wedding you deserve.*

Chapter 17

The humans and Kenyon were eating their dinner downstairs. Sam was upstairs, pacing the hallway. He wasn't in the mood to pretend. He'd heard the whole wedding-at-Oakwood discussion through the meeting room door. Part of him wanted to say it was a terrible idea—a security nightmare—that should be squashed immediately. On the other hand, that amount of chaos would surely tempt his adversaries to make their move. In a perverse way, the Fallon–Venuto wedding would give Sam the opportunity to choose his battleground and he knew Oakwood inside out.

Sam wandered into one of the empty bedrooms on the third floor. It had the feel of an abandoned place, a little too cold, a tiny bit dusty. Still, it was a perfectly good place to make a private phone call. He pushed the door shut.

Sam was ready to deal with villains popping out of the woodwork, but there were three other things to consider before he invited them to come get the diamonds. First was the shooting in the nightclub. The second was what he had learned about Jessica Lark. Last, there was Carter.

The shooter in the nightclub had always bothered him. Although an assassination would have furthered the agenda of fanatical elements invested in conflict between Marcari and Vidon—such as the Knights of Vidon—the shooter had no known political affiliations. In fact, the boy had seemed in a trance, almost as if he had no idea what he was doing. *Mind control.* Some vampires had the ability. Sam wasn't one of them, but both Carter and Winspear were. Both had been there that night. Both were here now. So were the Knights. Coincidence or connection? It was hard to tell.

And then there was Jessica Lark. From what he could tell from her records, Lark was not a vampire, but she wasn't human, either. Sam's guess was that the designer had fey blood. As a rule, the fey had their own agenda and weren't to be trusted, but the Company dealt with a few in a limited capacity. Only those agents with the very highest clearance went near the seductive, unpredictable creatures. The fact that Jack had been her contact made sense. He was an old and trusted agent of the Company. But why was Mark Winspear, a newcomer, the one in the photo with Jessica Lark?

And why was Carter really here? The Company's director didn't make pickup runs, no matter how important the cargo. Was he here only because he suspected Winspear and Kenyon to be traitors? He'd said as much, but Sam didn't buy it—no matter how sound Carter's reasoning. There had to be more to it.

He sat on the edge of the bed and pulled out his cell phone. *Do I really want to do this?* Once he dialed, once he set things in motion, he would have to accept the results, whatever those turned out to be. Even if his friends were in fact revealed as thieves and murderers.

But was that really a possibility? Kenyon had been devoted to Jack, who had pulled him out of the gutter and turned his life around. Kenyon wasn't an innocent, but he had his own code. A heist for old time's sake? Maybe. Anything more than that? Sam's gut said not—to the point where he hadn't hesitated to ask him along as Chloe's bodyguard. Sam didn't think Winspear would kill Jack, either, and he'd sooner pull out his own fangs than work with the Knights of Vidon. So what was his involvement?

This was all wrong. Sam had always trusted his maker completely, but the Horsemen were closer than brothers. That changed everything.

He dialed Carter's number on his cell. Much would depend on how his maker responded to Sam's plan.

"Sam, my boy," said the familiar gruff voice.

"Carter." Sam got up from the bed and began pacing to the window and back. "The only way to end this is to take the bull by the horns. Why don't we flush out whoever it is who wants this dress?"

Carter hesitated for a long, long moment. "Very well," he said at last. "That could put a lot of doubts to rest. I know all this suspicion must be killing a straight arrow like you."

Relief surged through Sam's tight muscles. Carter was absolutely right. Certainty was the first thing he wanted. The rest would follow.

The only real remedy for Chloe's headache would be to lock Mrs. Fallon away for a week or two. Once Leo and Elaine were safely out of the country, she could release the mother of the bride and present her with a bill.

She'd barely tasted dinner. After thanking Faran for his help one more time—somehow he'd been roped into helping with the reception menu—she retreated to her bedroom and kicked off her shoes. She could almost feel the blood rushing back into her toes. She wanted an aspirin, a hot bath and fleecy pj's. It was all of eight o'clock. The meeting had lasted hours. It had felt like days.

What Mrs. Fallon wanted, besides Jack's house and the blasted gold-hoofed horse, included real cannons, flocks of doves, and coffee beans that had been ingested and then pooped out by an Indonesian civet cat. Kopi Luwak was the most expensive coffee in the world and thankfully Faran thought he knew where he could get some.

This is insane. Chloe lay on her bed, fully clothed, too tired to change. The only thing that made the stress worthwhile was that pulling off this impossible wedding would make her career. People who mattered would know Chloe's Occasions.

According to Iris, between three and four hundred guests would rearrange their schedules in order to attend. It was going to be a security nightmare. *Poor Sam.*

Chloe sat up, feeling bad. He really was being a sport about moving the wedding to Oakwood. She wondered whether he was really okay with the extra workload.

The only way to ease her conscience was to talk to him. She got up and located kinder shoes.

Walking down the hall, she thought she heard his voice. It was coming from one of the empty guest bedrooms, but that door was closed. Not so empty, then. She stepped closer, listening to see if she was right.

Yes, it was Sam. The conversation sounded one-sided, like he was on the phone, and he sounded tense. To interrupt or not? She was just tired enough to be rude. Softly, she knocked.

Sam's words stopped abruptly, and then he said, "I'll call you back."

A moment later the door opened. He lifted one eyebrow. "I was wondering how long you were going to hover out there."

The man had to have the ears of a bat. She folded her arms. "The wedding's going to be here next week."

Sam stared at her blankly. "Yes, I know."

Nerves skittered through her stomach. She hadn't realized how worried she was about his goodwill until now. "I really, really hope you're okay with me having it here."

He stood with one hand on the doorknob, his big body blocking the doorway. "Is that what you came here to ask?"

This wasn't how she wanted the conversation to go. She wanted him to tell her everything was okay, and then they'd kiss again like they had in the garden that afternoon. He didn't appear to be in a comforting mood, though. She was going to have to help this along.

"Yes, well, I know there are a million reasons not to have it here." She pushed past him into the bedroom. "Not the least of which is that we won't get a break from wedding madness for days."

The muscles in his jaw flickered, as if he were clenching his teeth. His reply came out with a light dusting of sarcasm. "There are a few other reasons. Thieves. A man tried to kill you. Don't forget two people are already dead."

"I know, but maybe having more people around will actually make it safer."

His face said he didn't think much of that. "What are the reasons in favor of having it here?"

Chloe faced him, barely a foot of carpet between their toes. She could tell he was preoccupied with something that wasn't making him happy. His posture was stiff as steel. There was a perfectly good bed right next to them, and a closed door, but the timing just wasn't right for what should have been obvious next steps. The tension just made her more nervous.

She put a hand on his arm and tried to pull the frantic jitters from her own voice. "I can pull it off. If I'm on location 24/7 between now and the I-dos, I think I can make this work. It's very important to me, Sam. I need to make it happen for my career and, well, if I have to sell Jack's house, isn't a huge party the perfect way to bid it farewell?"

Something flickered behind his cool gray eyes. The line of his mouth softened. "Then we'll do it."

She wanted to give him a hug, but right now the line of his body wasn't inviting that. The shield he kept around his emotions was snapped shut.

"Thank you," she said, squeezing his arm. "And if it's important to me, just think how Leo and Elaine feel."

A smile flickered at the corners of his mouth. "No doubt like the center act in a three-ring circus."

"I'll have you know I run a very good circus." Chloe took a step back, remembering he had been in the middle of a phone call. Was that what his bad mood was all about?

He narrowed his eyes. "How many times have you planned this wedding?"

"First it was going to be next summer. Then in two months. Now it's Saturday."

"I thought so. If they get any closer, we can do it over breakfast." Sam smiled, but it didn't reach his eyes. "Doing everything this quickly is pretty unusual, isn't it?"

"I think it's safe to say it's unheard of."

"Don't worry. It'll all work out."

She prayed he was right. "One other thing."

"What?"

She rose on her toes and kissed him lightly on the cheek. Nothing intrusive. Just a reminder that he was more than just her security guy. Sam replied by kissing her lightly on the mouth, but that was it.

Chloe made her goodbyes and left the bedroom, closing the door behind her. She stood for a moment, her hand still on the door. What was wrong with him? Had something happened? *It had to do with that phone call. Is he going to call whoever it was back?*

Curiosity prodded her, but it was none of her business. *Yes, it is. I distinctly heard him say something about the dress. Whoever wants the dress.* She'd totally skipped over that in her anxiety about moving the wedding.

She had to know what the conversation was about. Unfortunately, Sam had that irritating talent Uncle Jack had possessed. He seemed to be able to see through doors. So, she walked away, making sure her footfalls were loud enough to hear.

And then crept back in stocking feet, holding her breath. It had worked with her uncle, sometimes. Tonight, it worked with Sam. She hovered near the door, careful not to bump against the wall.

"I'll have the dress. Can you come tonight?"

Chloe felt her cheeks grow hot. Sam had no right to give the gown to anybody without talking to her first.

"That's right," Sam said after a pause. "It'll be like throwing down raw meat. Let's see what animals show up to take a bite."

There was another long pause.

"In the garden, where Jack had that card party. Nine is too early. Make it eleven. That gives enough time to be sure the grapevine knows the details. I'll call a guy who'll tell his friends. We'll see who shows up."

Who was he talking to? The Men in Black with a garment bag? Chloe's temper was stirring. *Raw meat? Take a bite?*

It didn't sound as if he was returning a precious object to its rightful home. This sounded like a secret meeting after dark. Chloe leaned closer to the door, straining for every word.

"I haven't said anything," Sam went on. "Getting it will be easy. Knowing who's after it will be worth the risk."

Chloe's pulse pounded in her throat. Sam was doing the one thing she couldn't stand. He was leaving her out of the loop. *And he's using the dress Jack left in my care for bait!*

Chapter 18

How dare he!

Chloe silently slipped down the hall, eager to put distance between her and Sam. She really, really hadn't seen this coming. Sam was one of the good guys, or so she'd thought. It was bad enough that he was treating the dress as if he had a right to it—Uncle Jack had entrusted it to *her,* thank you very much—but Sam was keeping her utterly in the dark.

What was he about to do that he couldn't share with her? Nothing that would make her happy. Otherwise, why the secrets?

She was skilled at reading people, but never the men she liked. As usual, she'd totally misjudged the one person who counted the most. Chloe descended the stairs, only half aware of where she was going. For once, she was grateful Jack's house was so huge.

She couldn't let Sam shut her out. She had a huge stake in all this, too. She might not have the skills to take down the bad guys herself, but she had a right to know what Sam was planning.

Chloe slipped back into her old bedroom. Flicking on the overhead, she paused by the door. The bloody bedcovers had been stripped from her mattress, leaving it looking oddly naked. Reluctantly, Chloe closed the door behind her, shutting herself in with the memories of being forced to the bed. *All the more reason to hurry.* The faster she moved, the shorter time she had to stay there.

Quickly, she crossed the room. She pulled open the drawers of the tall dresser, relieved to see her old clothes from college were still neatly folded inside. Emotion made her fingers tremble, but she cut herself no slack. A quick rummage produced an old black T-shirt, running shoes and a thick fleece jacket. She'd packed jeans when she came but didn't have anything else casual enough for what she wanted to do.

In the back of the bottom drawer she found an ankle sheath and knife Jack had given her. If she'd insisted on jogging on campus, he'd insisted she know how to keep herself safe. She'd hated the idea, but now she was glad she'd let him teach her a few things. Finally, she found her old camera. Lexie had given it to her years ago when they'd both been in a nature photography club, and it was far better for taking pictures in the dark than the point-and-shoot she carried now. She stuffed it in her pocket, just in case.

Chloe took everything back to her room and changed. Strapping on Jack's SIG Sauer, she did what she could to adjust his shoulder holster. It had definitely not been made for a girl. She finally got it into an acceptable position and then slid the fleece jacket over top. It felt bulky, but then again guns always felt too large to her. Thanks to Jack, she knew how to use them and wasn't afraid to shoot if she had to. She just prayed it wouldn't come to that. She was gathering information, nothing more.

Keeping out of sight, she crept down the stairs, stopping in the room where the security guys kept their stuff and scrounged a pair of night vision goggles. Then she went in search of Sam. He had to be around somewhere. He wasn't meeting whoever-it-was until eleven.

A search of the house took her downstairs and eventually outdoors. The night was clean, washed by a drizzle that had quieted to a hazy, starless night. Chloe made a circuit of the house, looking in the windows for signs of Sam.

It wasn't until she reached the side yard that she spotted him through the laundry room window. He stood next to a rack of clothes that had been returned from the dry cleaners. To her utter mystification, Sam tore the plastic off a pale dinner gown forgotten by someone who had come to stay for one of Jack's dinner parties. Normally, the staff would ship it on to the owner, but Sam apparently had other ideas. He was stuffing it into a gym bag, mashing the yards and yards of expensive antique white silk into its bulging maw and struggling with the zipper. *What the...?* And then it twigged with an electric tingle of amazement.

The dress was nearly the same shade of antique-white as the wedding gown. Sam wasn't taking the real wedding dress. Relief made her legs rubbery.

As soon as she recovered her wits, she ghosted away from the window. Sam was a professional security guy and, like Jack, seemed to have amazing senses. She didn't think Sam would find her snooping around endearing. He'd be more likely to lock her in with the dryer sheets and scrub brushes.

Sam emerged through the mudroom door, barely making a sound as he moved. Chloe squished herself into the deep shadows of the wall, holding her breath so that he couldn't even hear her intake of air. She needn't have worried. He barely paused to pull the door shut before he was walking through the garden at a brisk clip, the gym bag in one hand.

Chloe hesitated, counting the reasons to go back to her room. She was inexperienced and Sam seemed to hear everything. One mistake and he'd know she was there. And now she knew at least he wasn't stealing the dress.

But none of that changed her purpose. She needed to see who showed up every bit as much as Sam. From what she'd heard, whoever it was on the phone didn't know it was a substitute gown. Sam was playing an interesting game. And whoever fell for his bait was probably connected to Uncle Jack's murder.

A wave of pain and anger welled up inside her. She needed to know who had robbed her of her only real family. That was non-negotiable.

Moving as quietly as she could, she detached herself from the wall and crept to the head of the path Sam had used to disappear into the still darkness. If she squinted, she could just make out his form, a dim patch of black moving ahead. *He's headed toward the gazebo.* That made sense, given what Sam had said to the person on the phone. Jack had held plenty of card parties there.

With a rush of hard, cold satisfaction, Chloe set out along a separate path, planning to loop around and observe Sam's rendezvous from an entirely different vantage point, well away from any action. From there she would see everything, but not be seen. *It's okay. Uncle Jack taught you enough to handle this much.*

And Sam wouldn't have anything to complain about if he never knew she was there.

Set flush with the rock face of a small hill, the gazebo was one of the property's main features. Covered with wisteria, it was a large wood-and-wrought-iron structure big enough to house a table for eight.

Sam stood with his back to the structure, listening hard. At first there was nothing—no footsteps, not even a rustle of wind. The rain had stopped, leaving the air not only clean and cool but also washed of scent. He remained perfectly still, needing to hear whoever approached. He had told the regular security to vacate the gardens that night. He didn't want any unexpected incidents. Still, there were a few people scattered through the grounds.

The lights from the mansion glowed to his left, giving just enough illumination to see the figure silhouetted under the trees. The shadowy form crept closer, darting between the concealing bulk of the bushes and trees. He—for the figure moved like a man—was of medium height and build, and definitely human. Sam waited until the man was almost to the steps, and then stepped forward to grab his arm.

The figure made a surprised cry as Sam wrenched him around and slammed him against the gazebo's wooden porch. As he moved, Sam dropped the bag with the fake dress to the grass.

Like a striking hawk, another man swooped from the darkness to snatch it up, vampire-fast. Startled, Sam nearly let his prisoner slip from his grasp. *Didn't see that one coming.*

With a curse, Sam slammed the human to the ground, pinning him. The man whimpered, but Sam doubted he was doing any real damage. Then he saw the bandage above the man's collar, and recognized him as Chloe's attacker.

"Now I've got you," he snarled.

"Not before my friend gets you," the human replied.

Sam glanced up at the vampire, who was lingering a few yards away. The vampire's face was hidden beneath a hood, but Sam could see his Smith & Wesson clearly enough. "What are you hanging around for?" Sam snarled at Hood Guy. "You've got what you came for."

The only reply came when the vampire jacked a bullet into the chamber of his weapon. At the same moment, Sam

became aware of someone moving along the rocky hill behind the gazebo. He caught the scent of lemon perfume.

Nine hells! Chloe! His gut seemed to make a corkscrew move, twisting until he thought he'd be sick. *What
the blazes is she doing here?* Anger warred with panic. He
absolutely couldn't let her be hurt. There were too many
guns, too many possibilities for a stray bullet. He had to
end this fast.

He didn't want to let his captive go, but he needed
his hands free. Sam jumped to his feet, raising his gun
in answer to the vampire's Smith & Wesson. The human
scrambled upright and bolted, as Sam knew he would—but
guarding Chloe came first.

"Your friend's free, now what do you want?" Sam
snarled. "Get out of here."

The S&W fired, sending a bullet inches from Sam's
cheek. A warning shot, but it was enough to make Sam
flinch. A split second later, a muzzle flash flared from
above the gazebo, and the vampire spun to his right, cursing
with pain. Regular bullets couldn't kill, but they sure hurt.

"Chloe, duck!" Sam cried, dropping to one knee and
sending three neatly clustered rounds Hood Guy's way.

The vampire dodged, but still managed to send a shot
toward Chloe's hiding place. Chips flew from the wood
and the bullet ricocheted from the wrought iron frame, rattling into the bushes.

Sam swore, emptying his clip. But when his sight cleared
from the flare of the gunfire, his opponent had dissolved
into the night.

Sam clamped down on his emotions, forcing his head to
stay clear, and slammed another clip into his gun. "Chloe,
are you all right?"

"Yes." Chloe's voice sounded small, but he smelled no
human blood.

The moment she spoke, another shot spurted from the dark, aiming for the gazebo roof. Forgetting to play human for Chloe's benefit, Sam launched himself after the enemy, letting his feet fly over the rain-dampened grass. Wind rushed in his ears and stung his eyes, robbing every sense but that of smell. The vampire had come this way.

And then he realized he recognized the scent. The height and build were right, too, but he still didn't want to believe it.

Mark Winspear! Against all Sam's instincts, Carter had been correct. *But why is he doing this?*

Chapter 19

Chloe clung to the rock, fingers cold and stiff. It had been easy enough to get to this vantage point. She'd figured out how to get up here during her teens, when she needed a place to get away from adult supervision. Then, she'd been looking for trouble. Now, she'd found it.

She lowered the night vision goggles, letting them dangle around her neck. Their greenish glow was making her feel slightly sick, and she felt plenty nauseous already.

She'd shot someone. It had barely snagged his attention, but still. *She'd shot someone.* Hot tears spilled down her cheeks, her stomach roiling every time her mind replayed the moment.

A cold, practical part of her brain had taken charge and done the necessary thing. No hesitation. But all the training in the world couldn't prepare a person for the reality of that moment. It terrified her. She terrified herself.

And now Sam was charging through the darkness after the two men, faster than she'd believed it possible to move. Would he stay safe? If she could pull a trigger, so could anyone else.

Her heart sped, racing on adrenaline until her head felt too light. *Please, please be okay.*

Night sounds seemed strange and muffled—her ears were still ringing from the sound of the gun. Chloe shivered, tightening her grip as she slid from the rock to the cedar shingles covering the gazebo roof. She'd picked this vantage point to take photos. She'd snapped just one before she'd drawn her gun instead. Now no one was around to shoot, in any sense of the word.

Time to get down. She inched over the shingles, hearing one crack as she wriggled to one of the corner posts. The gazebo had an ornamental facade that jutted above the roofline by just enough to give her a footrest. From there, she swung her legs over and crawled down its trellised side.

A body slammed into her the moment her feet touched the ground. She fell hard, her elbow landing on the edge of the gazebo's concrete foundation. Chloe yelped, her gun arm dissolving into tingling pain, utterly useless. Her weapon fell to the ground with a thud.

Hands grabbed her, dragging her upright. "I should have killed you in your bed."

Chloe's spine slammed against the iron post of the gazebo. The back of her skull smacked metal, leaving her dancing on the edge of nausea. When her eyes finally focused, she saw a man looming over her, pushing his face close to hers. She tried to turn away, getting only an impression of a closely trimmed beard and stale fish breath.

"Did you miss me?" Crushing her into the iron post, he managed a full-body grope. He was taller, so his crotch ground against her belly. "I nearly had you, little princess."

Sam shot you that night. Next time it'll be me, and I'll finish the job. Chloe clung to the thought, but her whole body broke into a trembling sweat.

He'd pinned her hands behind her, between her back and the post. *Helpless.* Or not. She had a knife in her ankle sheath. *How do I get it into his ribs?*

"Your friend has the dress. What do you want with me?" She forced the words to snarl, using anger to stave off tears.

"Guess." He yanked open the zipper of her fleece jacket and grabbed for a breast. He squeezed hard enough to make her give a sharp cry. "That's more like it," he said in a hiss that was half a purr.

She took sideways glances at him, dodging his face as he thrust his just inches away from hers. Yet every time she moved, so did he, their noses nearly touching. "Get away from me!" she snapped.

"Baby, I'm the last thing you'll ever see."

Like hell. Her one advantage was the wound in his shoulder, where Sam's bullet had struck. She could see the bandages showing above the collar of his sweatshirt. They were stained with fresh blood—all this running around must have opened the wound. Good to know. He favored that arm as he moved. His left side was weaker.

He was using his weight to pin her, which put him off-balance. He also assumed she was too petrified to fight back.

Try again. She hooked a foot around his ankle and swiveled her shoulder to his left, using the post behind her for leverage. When he tried to step back, he fell.

She scooped up her gun, gripping it with both hands. Her elbow still hurt, but her fingers worked again. Chloe turned, pointing her weapon at the man who had tried to smother her in her own bed.

An arm grabbed her from behind. "Not so fast, little girl."

This was someone new. She couldn't see his face, but he had a long, shining bowie knife.

Chloe screamed, letting her voice rip through the darkness. Then she swiveled the muzzle of the SIG Sauer down and shot him in the foot. With a surprised yell, he flung her forward.

It wasn't like the first guy knocking her down. This time Chloe flew through the air, as if an immense tennis racket was vaulting her forward. Instinct made her cover her face. Training made her bring her knees up, so that she landed in a roll.

It was not a good landing. It was hard and graceless and it hurt. The air left her lungs in a rush, but she managed to keep rolling until she slammed into a tree.

But she was alive.

Get up! Her mind screamed at her, urging her to run.

She couldn't. Sick and dizzy and aching, Chloe couldn't make her limbs obey.

Her eyes would only open to slits. The one who'd thrown her was braced against the gazebo, cursing and bleeding. The other was picking himself up off the ground. In about five seconds one of them would decide to finish her off.

"Kill her," the second man commanded.

Sam was in a maelstrom of rage. Winspear had escaped. Sam knew he was faster, but Plague was resourceful and clever.

Leaping over a fallen tree, he scrambled up the next rise of ground, searching the darkness for any sign of the doctor. There was nothing. *If he'd really wanted me dead, he wouldn't have missed that shot to my head.* Whatever his plan, Winspear was playing a longer game than just a diamond heist. Killing Sam and Chloe tonight wasn't part of his script.

There were worse things a centuries-old assassin-turned-physician could do. Already, he'd effectively separated Sam from Chloe by making himself too immediate a threat for Sam to ignore.

Sam's greatest fear was that Winspear had somehow doubled back to find her. He'd barely admitted this to himself when he had heard Chloe cry out. When he broke through the trees he could smell blood, both human and undead, but no one was in sight. Without breaking stride, he leaped to the top of the octagonal gazebo, landing silently on all fours.

He could see much of the garden, the winding paths like pale gray tracery through the dark lawns. He could smell vampire blood but couldn't see one anywhere. Whoever was bleeding had left or was hiding. And where was Chloe? His gaze tracked in a slow arc, searching every shadow.

Then he spotted her, huddled under the low branches of a rhododendron. A man was reaching down as if to drag her to her feet. The same man who had nearly killed her in her bed.

Fury swept through Sam, a white-hot need to defend. It wasn't just chivalry. There was a territorial edge to the impulse that sprang from his primal core. Baring his fangs, he surged into the air.

Bullets flew from west of the building, skimming the skin from Sam's back. Pain licked past his spine, but was forgotten the instant he grappled with Chloe's attacker. Momentum carried them into the bushes. Sam grabbed the human in one hand, tossing him back onto the paving stones as if he were no more than a sack of oatmeal.

Incredibly, the man rolled to his feet, lurching into a run. Sam sprang after him. The man was quick, charging up the side of the rocky hill, but Sam bounded upward, caught his ankle and yanked him back to the earth. The man landed with a hollow thump.

Sam's first instinct was to bite, but Chloe was there, her eyes already wide with fright. Instead, he pounded his fist into the man's face. Again. And again. He could have broken his neck, snapped it with one blow, but Chloe was watching. Muted violence would have to do.

Sam finally planted his boot on the man's chest, pinning him to the ground. "Where did the vampire go? The one who's hurt?"

"He's gone," the man croaked.

"He can't have gone far. Someone shot at me just now, and it wasn't you."

"You'll get nothing from me."

"We'll see about that." Sam bent, grabbing the front of the man's shirt. He gave a hard, sharp jerk that made the man grunt with pain. The cloth ripped, baring the man's chest. There, just below the notch of his collarbone, was a tattoo of two blades crossed over a twining serpent.

The mark of the Knights of Vidon. *Winspear is working with the Knights?* It still seemed impossible. No one on the planet loathed the vampire slayers more. Sam swore under his breath. Whatever was going on, he was going to get to the bottom of it.

The man was watching Sam's face, reading every expression. "I'm not telling you anything."

"Oh, you will." Sam knelt, leaning forward. He felt a cold smile curl his lips as his rage found a target. "Let me introduce myself. They call me War."

Chapter 20

But Chloe was Sam's first priority. His prisoner could wait. Within seconds, Sam had zip ties around the man's wrists and ankles, then gagged him with a strip of his own shirt.

Chloe was sitting under the bushes, her face smeared with dirt. He knelt beside her, pushing a lock of hair from her eyes. "Are you hurt?"

"I'm a little banged up, but nothing's broken." Her voice sounded detached, as if she were shell-shocked. Her fingers were shaking as the adrenaline left her system. "I dropped my gun."

Sam rose to his feet and looked around, found it within moments and put the safety on. He handed it back to her, his chest tight. She didn't look good. "Are you sure you're not injured?"

"Thanks." With slow, awkward movements, she took the SIG Sauer and holstered it. "Uncle Jack said you should always know where your weapons are."

In an almost unconscious gesture, her fingers went to an ankle sheath, and Sam saw the hilt of a respectably sized knife. He noticed she had night vision goggles, too, hanging from a strap around her neck. She'd come prepared. He had to admire that much, but by the nine hells this was no fight for a civilian.

Sam gave in to the impulse to check every inch of her for broken bones. He dropped to his knees beside her, checking along her arms and legs for bumps or tender spots, every sense tuned for the faintest whiff of blood. The feel of her soft, warm form under his hands roused his protective instincts. She'd risked herself. It was unthinkable. He wasn't sure if he wanted to kiss her or shake her until her teeth rattled. "What did you think you were doing?"

Chloe's eyes snapped into focus. "I told you I need to know what's going on. I told you that just hours ago, but apparently that doesn't matter to you one little bit."

Sam felt an answering spike of anger, struggled to bite it back. "If I didn't tell you, there was a good reason." He found the camera in her pocket and pulled it out. "Did you take any pictures?"

"One."

He stuffed it in his own jacket, then zipped the pocket shut.

"Hey!" She grabbed for it. "That's mine!"

He caught her hand. "Stop it. Just. Stop. Now."

Her anger spiced the air. She was clearly furious, the pulse in her wrist pounding against his fingers. Guilt raked him, but he knew his reasons were good.

Sam sucked in a deep breath, reminding himself that yelling wouldn't help. "You want information? How about this—if I'd been a minute later, I don't know if you would still be alive."

"And I shot the guy pointing a gun at your head, remember?"

Sam had to give her that. "Good shot, too, but that's not the point." With a slow sense of wonder, he realized this frail mortal woman had tried to save his life. *She* had done her best to save *him*. An uncharacteristic feeling of humility besieged him. "Thanks for that, all the same."

All the tension went out of her, her forehead sinking to rest on her knees. "I've never shot a man before."

He'd won their argument, but it didn't solve a thing. Sam released her hand, tucking the whole of her under his arm instead. "Sucks."

"Yeah." She was softly crying.

Sam squeezed his eyes shut, feeling her pain all the way to his own heart. "I'm sorry."

She leaned into him, the silk of her hair under his chin. He wished there was something he could do, but once a person pulled the trigger at another being, there was no going back. He kissed the top of her hair, smelling the sweetness of her shampoo.

"Following you was the stupidest stunt I've every pulled," she muttered.

"Not that I'm encouraging you, but I've seen rookies do worse."

"I thought I'd be safe."

He heard the anger in her voice. Anger at herself. He knew she prided herself on being sensible, but she'd taken a bigger risk than she'd anticipated. He'd seen it before, people caught up in the heat of the moment. An unfamiliar queasiness passed through him when he imagined what might have happened.

But he kept that to himself. "You're safe now."

He shifted uncomfortably, adrenaline and his protective instincts colliding with a sudden wave of pure, primitive lust. Her breasts pressed into him, soft and warm, her pulse throbbing in her throat. Her top had pulled up, leaving a strip of bare, silken skin free to brush his wrist. The next kiss he gave her was on her lips. He shifted, knowing he had to end this. His fangs itched to come out.

There were too many primal emotions ricocheting through his blood to make holding her a good idea. Any moment, the hunger for her blood would blossom from a dull ache to an unbearable thirst.

He broke the kiss. She looked up at him, her eyes unfocused. Her small, pink tongue darted around her lips. They were swollen, glistening like ripe berries in the uncertain light.

The only thing that pulled him back to the present was the stirring prisoner. Sam sucked in a deep breath, clearing the confusion from his lust-addled brain.

"I get it. You'd be stupid not to wonder what was going on. But this goes far beyond a regular crime," he said softly. "I can't tell you much. I wasn't briefed myself. I don't have that clearance."

"I get it," she mumbled. "I think."

"Good." But if he held her much longer, he'd confess whatever she wanted to know. Nine hells, he'd make a story up if she just kept looking at him like that. "You need to get back to the house. And I've got to get this guy into custody."

Chloe lifted her head, turning to look at him. Tears had made trails through the dirt on her face. He kissed the tears, tasting the salty echo of her blood. By the gods, she was sweet. Her lips found his, forgiving him, begging him to get closer.

He wanted her. By the changing scent of her skin, she wanted him, as well. Chloe's lips were flushed, her eyes dark with desire. Sam felt his self-control slithering away like a soft, silken robe falling to the floor.

"Sam," she murmured.

He teetered on the brink of losing himself utterly. He ached with a primitive need to take her right there on the dew-spangled grass. *Mine. Now.*

He cursed silently, struggling as a last vestige of good

sense prevailed. Setting her aside gently, he moved before their prisoner got far more of a show than he'd bargained for. Chloe sank back on her heels, looking up at him as he rose. The dirt stains and disheveled hair made her look like an urchin, both innocent and wise beyond her years.

"There were more than just the man you caught," she said. "There were two that found me."

Sam frowned. "Our friend there said the other guy ran away. Did you see him?"

She shook her head. "He attacked me from behind. He was horribly strong. He threw me like I was no more than a dishrag."

Winspear. Sam felt a grim foreboding. "I'll kill him for that."

Chloe blinked. "You literally mean that, don't you?"

Sam didn't answer, not trusting himself to sound like a mere human right then. *Of course I mean it. You matter too much to make empty threats.*

Chloe trailed a step behind as they returned to the house, Sam carrying the man over his shoulder like a sack of potatoes. Sam's face darkened with every step. He was obviously unhappy that she was anywhere near his prisoner, but he hadn't been prepared to let her walk back to the house on her own. When they approached the door to the laundry room, she ran ahead to open it. Sam's burden was awake and starting to struggle.

"Get me something to tie him up with." Sam's tone was harder than Chloe had ever heard coming out of his mouth. It startled her enough that it took a moment to obey.

"Now!"

The man thrashed in Sam's hands. Sam thrust him into a folding chair beside one of the dryers. The chair's aluminum legs skidded across the tile floor with a squeak.

Chloe looked around desperately, then tore down a length of laundry line that had been strung from the ceiling. It was too long, but Sam used it anyway, winding it around the prisoner several times before knotting it behind the chair.

Chloe stared first at the battered face, then at the tattoo on the man's chest, half-hidden in the blood from his re-opened wound. "What's that?"

Sam hesitated a moment, but then answered her. "His—I guess you could call them a gang—all wear that mark. If you see someone with it, run."

Chloe looked again, memorizing the design. She edged toward the man, at least until Sam put out a hand to keep her from getting too close.

"It's not a gang," the man said, bloody lips curling away from his teeth. "We are the Knights of Vidon."

"Be quiet," Sam ordered. "I'll let you know when it's time for you to speak."

Chloe narrowed her eyes, taking in every detail of the tattoo, the clothing. If this was the enemy, she wanted to know how to recognize their kind. In return, the prisoner gave her a long, long look that lingered on her skin like rancid oil.

She felt her cheeks heating. "What's your problem?"

"You keep staring at me." He had an accent. Not Italian, but not entirely unlike that, either. "You like what you see?"

"You almost killed me in my own bed. I'm trying to see that in your face."

He gave a bark of laughter. "Every one of us is a killer. Every face is a killer's face."

"I don't believe that."

"Then you haven't suffered enough."

A flash of rage curled her fingers into fists. "I've never done anything to you!"

"You're with *them*. That is enough." The look he gave

Sam dripped with loathing so virulent that Chloe instinctively reached for the butt of her gun. He was tied up, but that much hate had power.

Sam had gone pale. "Chloe, you should leave."

"Why?"

"You don't need to hear his nonsense."

"How do I know it's nonsense?" Her voice was bitter.

The man in the chair laughed. "She has no idea what she might learn, does she?"

Sam glanced at her quickly, not taking his eyes off the prisoner for more than a second. "Trust me. Let me handle him. I've done this before."

"I haven't," Chloe said. "But if he killed Jack, I'll hold him down for you while you ask questions."

The man stopped laughing. A sick satisfaction shot through her. She had spoiled his mockery. Or had she? A sly look came over his face.

"You don't know what he is, do you?" The words were for Chloe, but he looked at Sam as he said it.

Sam's fists balled tight. "Silence!"

"He's the one who saved my life," Chloe said quietly.

"For now. It won't last. Sooner or later, they always show their true faces. Killer faces."

Sam's hand moved too fast to see. He struck openhandedly, the crack of skin on skin echoing in the small room. The man's head snapped to the side, the chair rocking with the momentum.

"Sam!" Chloe gasped, then felt foolish.

Sam had slapped him. It was nothing, given that the man had tried to kill her. But that didn't make it any easier to watch.

"What's your name?" Sam demanded.

"Pietro." He spit blood to the floor, missing Chloe's shoes by inches.

She felt sick, a hot wave of dizziness rolling through her. "Pietro what?"

He closed his eyes, swallowing hard. "We perform our mission to keep the throne of Vidon free of the Devil's influence." The toneless statement sounded like the equivalent of name, rank and serial number.

"Then why are you in league with Winspear?" Sam snarled, clearly struggling for control of his temper.

"Winspear?" Chloe backed away. "What are you talking about?"

Sam gave her a pained glance. "He was the one who took the dress."

Chloe reeled. She'd hardly spoken to the doctor. He'd been too solemn, too withdrawn to invite even casual interaction, but he hadn't seemed treacherous. *Every face is a killer's face.* Could that be true?

She didn't know because she hadn't seen her attacker's face. She'd exchanged so few words with Mark Winspear that she wouldn't recognize his voice. But the doctor wasn't as big as Sam, and whoever had thrown her had been incredibly strong.

Sam grabbed the man's jaw, forcing him to look straight into Sam's eyes. "How is Winspear involved?"

"I don't know what you're talking about." The words were distorted by Sam's hand.

Chloe watched Sam's expression. There was deep sadness in his face. Her chest ached for him. "Are you sure that was Dr. Winspear? I couldn't see his face."

Sam gave a single nod. "I'm sure."

Chloe took a step back. She tried to picture the doctor shooting at Sam, and it just didn't fit.

"How did you know the diamonds were here?" Sam asked Pietro, removing his hand from the man's face.

Pietro worked his jaw as if it hurt. "Little birds listen at keyholes. For a price, they may open the door."

"Will Tyler?" Sam named the security guard who had become the getaway driver, and then had become dead.

Pietro's head was hanging forward, his chin on his chest. He looked up, moving only his eyes.

Sweat trickled down Chloe's sides, slithering over her ribs. Had Tyler known Pietro would try to kill her?

The prisoner laughed. "That kind always wants more than they have. For a price they'll leave the door unlocked." His gaze slid toward her. "But believe me, sweet girl, that's not the worst of your problems. This movie is far from over."

The words made Chloe draw in a quick breath that caught Sam's attention. He took her hand, pulling her to his side. It was a wordless gesture of comfort, putting her securely in the circle of safety he offered. She locked her fingers through his.

Sam pulled out his phone and thumbed a key. Chloe heard someone pick up and thought she recognized Faran's voice. "I'm in the laundry room, with Chloe. Where are you?"

Chloe locked eyes with Pietro, trying to read his face. All she could see was spite. She couldn't trust a thing that came out of his mouth.

Sam was still talking. "Then get down here. I've got a package." He put the phone away.

Package? She wasn't sure if she should laugh or shudder at the innocent-sounding phrase. She turned to Sam. "What happens now?"

Sam leaned against the dryer. "Now? Now Kenyon comes."

"He's not...like the doctor." She remembered Lexie's warnings about Faran.

"No," Sam replied. "He'll take you back to your room."

"Does he know about any of this?"

Sam frowned. Thoughts she couldn't read flitted across his features. "Don't say a word about what you've seen here. Not even to him or to your photographer friend. Anything you might say puts them deeper into danger."

Chloe's skin went cold. "Okay."

The prisoner gave a derisive snort.

Chloe's eyes narrowed. "Are you going to go on questioning him?"

Pietro tried hard not to look up at Sam, tried to pull his chin down and stare at the floor some more, but fear won out. Sam continued to lean, looking almost bored.

"I'll find out who killed Jack. I'll give you their heads on a platter."

The way he said it make Chloe shiver. "Where do the police come into this?"

Sam looked at her, his face like stone. "I am the police."

"What?" She pulled away, tingling with surprise. "I thought you worked security for Uncle Jack."

"Call the FBI or the CIA. Ask for someone who deals with international crimes. Mentioning Jack's name should get you someone in charge. They'll confirm that I have authority to handle this."

That shocked her. "Seriously? Jack never said anything about ties to those agencies."

"Because you aren't supposed to know. It's that simple."

Chloe swore under her breath. That explained so much—Jack's secrecy, his obsession with weapons, and his connection to men like Sam. *And I've been trying to spy on these guys?* A sudden wave of embarrassment heated her cheeks.

Sam straightened, scowling down at the man tied to the chair. "Chloe, the business with the diamonds is the tip of an iceberg. There's a lot more underneath."

The prisoner tilted his head back to look Sam full in the face. "Good luck figuring it out."

Sam smiled. "I have all night."

Unfortunately, Sam's night got more complicated.

Kenyon came, clearly curious, but took Chloe back to her bedroom. Moments later, Carter arrived.

Sam's maker strolled around the laundry room, hands behind his back. He was hiding a slight limp, but Sam knew Carter well enough to see it. An injury? Unusual, for a fast-healing vampire. One might say a coincidence.

Ugly suspicions fluttered through Sam's mind.

"So, you've got yourself a plaything, my boy," said Sam's sire. "Do you think he will be tasty?"

"Knights never stay with me. I'll want another in half an hour."

"Perhaps we can arrange something." Carter paused to consider Pietro as if he were a steak on the grill.

The prisoner was starting to look less defiant and more fearful. He tracked Carter's every move.

"So your ruse with the wedding dress worked?" Carter asked.

"Yes. And you were right," Sam replied, keeping his voice controlled and even. "Winspear took it."

"Did he now?" Carter's thick eyebrows drew together. "I'm sorry to hear that. He was a good agent until this. A bit fond of having his own way, but he always got the job done in the end."

"I thought he was my friend."

Carter shook his head. "Since when do monsters have friends? We have honor. We have duty. The rest is only memory of what we were."

"This one has a ladylove, boss man," Pietro said, sneering. "She doesn't know what he is."

"Be quiet!" Sam snarled.

Carter gave both of them a sharp look, but settled his piercing eyes on the prisoner. "I would hold your tongue until we ask you to speak. You'll be singing soon enough."

But Pietro was done with obedience. He returned Carter's gaze, eyes wild with fear and hatred. "You're going to kill me anyhow, right? I may as well ask a few questions of my own. Who is this Winspear? What's he got to do with anything?"

"You think he'd give you his real name, you clot?" Carter rested a hand on the man's head and looked up at Sam. "So who is the woman?"

"I've been keeping an eye on Jack's niece."

"You know the rules."

"I do. There is nothing between us."

"You've always been a terrible liar."

Pietro sniggered. "But that's what you're all best at, isn't it? Everything about you is a lie. Isn't that right, boss?"

"I wish you would be quiet," Carter sighed, and snapped the man's neck.

The sudden *pop* startled Sam. "I needed to question him!"

Carter gave a faint smile. "He didn't seem the helpful type."

Sam stared at the limp body, slumped against his bonds. "As you say." He had the sudden conviction that Pietro, helpful or not, knew far more than Carter had liked.

Sam was going to have to play this carefully. Carter was old and wily and knew him far too well.

"About that dress," Carter said, wiping his hands on the thick twill fabric of his pants. "I could take it now if you like."

"I don't have the combination to the safe," Sam replied. "Only Jack's niece has that."

He couldn't have been that bad a liar, because Carter bought it.

Chapter 21

Chloe didn't know what to think.

Last night had been something of a turning point, or maybe it was simply a realization.

Sam wasn't just a bodyguard, a security expert. He was something more. Incredibly dangerous, for a start, with the blessing of some of the most powerful crime-fighting agencies in the world. Being close to him was, as the old saying went, like having a tiger by the tail. It was a wild, perilous ride.

Who is Sam, really? That was the question of the hour.

Restless, Chloe picked up her laptop and wandered through the house, looking for someplace that didn't remind her of darkness and danger. She drifted until she found the breakfast room. It was more a glassed-in porch than a proper room, filled with plants and light. Chloe sat down at the wicker table, enjoying the warmth of a sunbeam on her back. A window was open, and she smelled the clean, fresh scent of greenery as the wind ruffled the curtains.

It was exactly what she needed. Chloe closed her eyes and pressed her fingers to her eyelids, trying to stave off the headache threatening to invade. Her head still hurt from whacking it against the iron post of the gazebo.

"Hey," said a husky female voice.

Chloe looked up at the sound, blinking the room back into focus. Alexis Haven stood in the doorway, holding a cup of coffee. Chloe started in surprise.

A grin spread over her friend's face. "Gotcha."

"Lexie!"

"Live and in person. How are you doing, Chlo?"

Chloe jumped up with a whoop, throwing her arms around her friend and just about spilling the coffee. "I'm so glad to see you!"

"Right back at you!"

Chloe released her friend, holding her at arm's length for a good look. The photographer was tall and slender to the point of skinny. It wasn't from dieting so much as moving too fast for any ordinary metabolism to keep up. She had bright hazel-green eyes and a fall of dark red hair that swept her hips. With the artless grace of the true bohemian, she wore no makeup, a shapeless khaki tunic dress and hiking boots that laced up to her knees—and somehow managed to make it look fabulous.

"How are you?" Chloe asked, giving her another hug before she let her go. "How was your flight?"

"I'm fine." Lexie's smile was crooked. "I tried to call last night, but kept getting your voice mail."

"Sorry, I was out."

They sat at the table.

"Good time?" Lexie asked.

"Hard to say. I don't remember a lot of what happened."

In truth, her memory was fine until she got to the part where she was on top of the gazebo shooting at Jack's so-called friend who had turned out to be one of the villains. Then it just seemed like a bad dream. *Mark Winspear? How is that even possible?* She was usually better at reading people. The doctor was a bit scary, but he hadn't struck her as evil. Somehow his betrayal had made more sense last night, when she wasn't sitting in a sunny, bright room.

"Sam and I were chasing bad guys last night."

"Whoa!" Lexie set down her coffee and scrunched her eyebrows together. "You and Sam, huh?"

"Yes." Chloe waved her hands helplessly. "I don't want it to be real. I don't do that kind of thing. I'm the girl who spends hours worrying about centerpieces and place cards."

"I'm not so sure that's all you are. I remember your uncle was pretty nuts about making sure you knew how to take care of yourself. You're a better shot than me."

Queasiness lurched through her. "I'm not sure I want to talk about shooting right now." How many people had she hit? One? Two?

Lexie was watching her face, clearly trying to read her thoughts. "We all have sides of ourselves we keep locked away until they're needed."

"This guy…" Chloe stopped, considering how crazy she wanted to sound. "This man threw me through the air like a toy."

An angry flush crept over Lexie's cheeks. "Are you hurt?"

"Bruised."

"Did you lose consciousness?"

"Almost, but I don't think I have a concussion."

But what about her memory of Sam leaping on top of the gazebo? Sam running faster than her eye could follow? That flash of sharp, sharp teeth? Those had to be hallucinations. She was turning him, in her panicked imagination, into some sort of avenging beast. *That's it. I'm finally cracking up.*

Lexie reached across the table and felt Chloe's forehead. "I don't know, Chlo. You look pale as a mushroom. You feel a little feverish, too."

"I'm tougher than a bump on the head. I've been orphaned. I've been left at the altar. I've faced down Iris Fallon."

Lexie laughed at the last one. "Okay, Iris Fallon is proof positive you can take whatever life dishes out."

Chloe made an exasperated noise. "Until I met Sam Ralston. He's turned me into a basket case in a matter of days."

Lexie's mouth curled into a feline smirk. "He's got a little more oomph than you usually go for."

"Oomph?"

"You know. Swagger. Danger. Suits cut to hide the sidearms. It's an acquired taste, but you never go back."

That was what she was afraid of. "I always wanted a nice, quiet guy who liked antiquing and family picnics."

Lexie kept a neutral face. "Nice."

"I like nice."

"Nice is good. Nice is underrated."

"I think I want…" *I want my avenging beast.*

"Not nice?"

"A garnish. A bit of spice on the side." Chloe held up her thumb and forefinger, showing a sliver of air between. As she thought about Sam, the space widened. She wanted more than a little of whatever made him…him.

Lexie rolled her eyes. "Whoa, look at the wild child bursting out of her shell."

"Don't mock."

Her friend was suddenly serious. "I'm not mocking. I'm worried, Chloe. You had a close call. You got into something deeper than you were expecting. Remember I said I didn't trust your uncle's friends? Spice comes with a price."

Chloe shivered. Serious wasn't Lexie's style. Normally she would have carried on, making one off-color pun after the next. *What's going on? I don't know how much more*

I can take. "If it hadn't been for Sam, I would have been chopped to steak tartare. He's saved my skin more than once."

"We need to talk, Chlo. These guys aren't as squeaky clean as you seem to think."

A flush of anger heated Chloe's skin. She could feel Sam's strong arms picking her up, the shield of his body between her and danger. She wanted to defend his honor. She owed him that much loyalty.

Lexie must have seen it on her face. "Don't get mad at me. I'm trying to help you."

She was too tired to fight down her emotions. "Like I said, Sam saved me. I don't want to hear anything against him."

"You're defending him?"

"He defended me."

"You're the one who always wants information. Maybe now is the time to listen."

Chloe looked up, meeting Lexie's adamant gaze. She wanted to face whatever her friend had to say now, but she shied away. Too much had happened; her courage had been used up last night.

Lexie leaned close, putting her lips close to Chloe's ear. "How much do you know about Faran and his friends?"

"Only that they've been great. Mostly." Chloe suddenly wasn't sure what to say. "It's complicated."

Lexie put her finger to her lips. "Can we talk privately here?"

They leaned across the glass-topped table so they could speak softly.

"What's so hush-hush?" Chloe asked. Lexie hadn't wanted to talk on the phone, and now she was acting like Oakwood was littered with listening devices. Well, given the Gravesend Security connection, maybe it was.

Lexie bit her lower lip. "How much time do you have right now? For any of what I have to say to make sense, I have to go back to when Faran and I met. There's a lot to explain. *They're not people.*"

As if on cue, Faran walked in the room, his head bent as he finished texting on his phone. When he stopped and looked up, he froze, phone halfway to his pocket.

Chloe swore under her breath at the horrified look on her friend's face.

And Faran had seen Lexie. No, *seen* was the wrong word. From the bald pain that flickered across his face, it was more as if his soul smashed against the windshield of her sudden frosty reserve. The moment lasted long enough for Chloe to squirm. She'd warned him his ex-girlfriend would be in town, but he hadn't expected her here.

"Lexie." He drew himself up, chin lifting, his aspect suddenly one of studied calm. For all his laid-back manner, he showed iron control.

"You," Lexie said softly, but that one quiet word held a universe of anger. "What are you doing near my friend?"

"My job. I'm in security, remember? One of the good guys?"

"I hardly think that's possible."

"Lexie!" Chloe exclaimed.

They both glared at her, expressions nearly identical.

Her friend's stare was the more ferocious of the two. "Stay out of this, Chlo. What's between him and me, that's our business."

"Don't get involved," Faran said at almost the same moment. "It's old history. It doesn't need to be dragged up and turned over like old compost."

Chloe heard Lexie's indrawn breath. "Nice, Kenyon," she snarled. "Nice to know what we had rates the same as coffee grounds and kitchen scraps."

His eyes went an icy blue. "You broke it off."

"You lied."

Faran's eyes narrowed. "You pushed. I told you there were some questions I couldn't answer. I had no choice."

Her friend looked away. "Forget it. If you can't see the flaws in that picture, nothing I can say will make a difference."

Silence ached through the room. Chloe made a T gesture with her hands. "Time-out. I'm a wedding planner, not a couples therapist."

"And from what you said on the phone, you have a huge wedding to plan." Lexie stood, smoothing her skirt. "I'll get out of your hair."

Faran followed her every gesture, pain etched into his face, then looked away. Lexie paused, studying his profile, her mouth drawn into a tight line.

Chloe wished she could fix whatever was wrong, but didn't have a clue. "Lexie…"

"We'll talk later, Chloe," her friend said briskly. "Let's set something up at the hotel. I'm all yours for as long as I'm in town."

With that, she walked out. Faran seemed stranded in the middle of the floor, not sure what to do with himself.

"I'm sorry," Chloe said gently. "I had no idea it was that bad."

"No, I'm sorry. You didn't need to see that. I'm going to go for a walk." His voice was oddly throaty. "I think I need to eat something, and then I'll be all right."

"Blood sugar?" she asked.

Faran smiled wanly. "Kind of like that."

"Then take care of yourself."

"Yeah. Whatever."

His hands were clenched as he stalked from the room, shoulders hunched. Chloe watched him go, wondering what in blazes had happened between the handsome young man and her best friend. She realized she was sweating, her stomach in a tight, hard knot.

They're not people.

What the blazes did that mean?

Chloe opened her laptop and waited as the screen sprang to life. She was back in Jack's office. Outside, the light was fading.

For the past few hours, she'd been too upset to deal with Sam, Faran, Lexie or any of the rest of that part of her life. Instead, she'd spent the afternoon making wedding arrangements. As always, work helped calm her.

Her staff had been doing the legwork to fulfill Iris Fallon's every desire, but Chloe still had to make decisions. Phone calls to and from her suppliers kept her focused and busy, but now most businesses were closing down for the day.

Finally, her mind was free to roam back to the question of Sam Ralston. *Who is he, really?* And why did Lexie think he wasn't "people"? Did it have to do with the whole international Men-in-Black thing?

She clicked on a search engine and sat frowning for a moment. *What am I thinking? Do I have the right to check him out like this?*

Just because Lexie had warned her to stay away? Just because he'd done his best to keep her ignorant of everything he was doing? Just because he'd admitted he was an agent of some kind? *Um, yeah.* Just because she understood there were things about his work she couldn't know, that didn't make her any less curious about who he was as a man.

She was willing to believe that Sam thought he was doing the right thing. She did not believe she knew a quarter of what she ought to know about him.

She typed his name into the search engine. A bazillion hits came up and most looked relatively useless. A smattering of them, however, seemed to relate to a news story. She selected the first of those. She immediately saw a black-and-white portrait of a pretty blonde twentysomething wearing a fascinator. The caption below the picture identified the woman as Lady Beatrice Concarra. She stared at the picture for a moment, feeling an irrational jealousy. What did Lady Beatrice have to do with Sam? Then she read on.

Assassination Attempt at Emerald Sea

Lady Beatrice Concarra, eldest daughter of the famed shipping magnate, Arnaud, Duke of Nulanne, was fatally shot at 1:15 a.m. on Tuesday. The incident occurred at Emerald Sea, a dance club located in the Marcari capital. Lady Beatrice had arrived at the club around midnight as part of Princess Amelie's retinue.

Palace security has not yet released the name of the attacker. The gunman fired directly onto the dance floor, striking Lady Beatrice in the heart. Sam Ralston, security chief for the palace, claims the attack was an assassination attempt on the princess. Security at the dance club was reportedly breached, although no one in authority would give specifics. According to Ralston, "There are hostile elements we have been watching for several weeks now. The tragedy is that Lady Beatrice suffered as an innocent bystander." The palace would not comment on whether those "hostile elements" are Vidonese nationals.

However, unnamed sources claim the ancient feud between Marcari and Vidon is heating up again in reaction to the proposed marriage between Princess Amelie and the Vidonese crown prince, Kyle. Sepa-

ratists on both sides protest the prospect of unifica-
tion of the two kingdoms.

The article went on and Chloe read the rest with a growing sense of shock. Sam Ralston was security chief for
Princess Amelie of Marcari? *Seriously? He's part of the
palace staff?*

That explained so much. Guarding royalty? The responsibility was staggering. No wonder he took the whole bodyguard thing to the max. A lapse could be fatal. Look what
happened to poor Lady Beatrice.

When he'd said being a bodyguard could go wrong, this
must have been what he meant.

And this surely had some bearing on what had happened
to Jack. Would his security work have included working
for the Marcari government? Then of course security agencies would know about him because he was in the business of keeping crowned heads alive. And the wedding
dress? A connection to the princess went a little way to
explaining why he had it. *Why didn't you tell me any of
this, Uncle Jack?*

She clicked on a few more links, but they all seemed to
be about the same shooting. Otherwise, Sam Ralston kept
a very low profile. Or, *her* Sam Ralston did. There was also
a Sam Ralston, car dealer in Utah; a physics professor in
Toronto; and, a twelve-year-old playing the drums on You-
Tube. But now Chloe's curiosity was going at full steam.

Never mind snooping on the internet for information
made her feel like a love-struck teenager searching to find
photos of her latest crush.

She tried *"Samuel Ralston"* and got the less-than-helpful
hits again. Then *Samuel, Ralston* without the quotes. That
resulted in a bazillion hits to the power of ten. Chloe just
about closed the laptop and walked away, except she spotted

a row of thumbnail images partway down the screen—all pictures of various Samuels. She clicked the command to show her only images. The screen filled with tiny squares.

And there he was, in an old tintype photograph. A shock of recognition made her breath hitch as she sat up straighter, angling the laptop screen for a better view.

Same eyes, same chin, same delectable mouth. He was wearing a Union officer's uniform and that frozen expression people got from holding still for the old, slow cameras, but it was definitely Sam. Chloe zoomed in on the image until it started to blur. It had to be him. Even his long, dark eyelashes were the same.

She sucked in a breath, snapping herself out of the realm of impossibility. No, it was his ancestor, surely, but the family resemblance was marked. She clicked the link and it took her to a page hosted by a Pennsylvanian historical society. Ralston Samuel Hill had been a lieutenant colonel in the Civil War. Son of a career politician, graduated from West Point, married to Amy Weston, father of two sons and one daughter. Presumed killed in action, 1862.

They look so much the same. But that was silly. If he'd lived, he'd be how old? Over 180, anyway. Chloe stood up, pacing around the room to burn off a sudden burst of nervous energy.

Sure, the names and features were similar, but there was a good explanation. Sam must be a descendant of one of the children. That was all. And it was easily proved.

Chloe sat down again and logged into a genealogy database she sometimes used when a couple wanted a family tree in their wedding album. She looked up Ralston Hill there, but the only new information she could find was that his widow had remarried and the children had taken her new husband's name. There was no easy link between Sam's historical double and his present-day self.

The only useful thing she'd found out was that he'd been there when tragedy struck Lady Beatrice, a young girl who'd gone out to dance away the Mediterranean night.

That death was the only key she had to Sam's history. Otherwise, the internet had little to say on the present-day Sam. When a guy showed up only when someone died or was in danger of dying, she had to wonder just how much more she wanted to know.

But I think I'm falling in love with him.

Chapter 22

Sam stormed back into the house two hours later. Chloe wasn't absolutely sure he hadn't left sometime in the middle of the night. Wherever he'd been, it hadn't made him happy.

Long ago, her mother had advised Chloe, in a rare mother–daughter conversation, never to confront her man when he first got home from the office. He should have a drink and a relaxing moment alone with the newspaper before being presented with domestic problems.

As old-fashioned as it sounded—and a bit odd coming from a woman who had been about as domestic as a bobcat—it wasn't bad advice under certain circumstances. Chloe waited an entire hour before tracking Sam to his lair, Scotch on the rocks in hand. Her quarry was in the games room, chalking a pool cue with the air of Vlad the Impaler sizing up his next victim.

"Home from the office, dear?" she said sweetly, handing him the Scotch. She tried not to think about what Sam's workday might have entailed.

He put down the chalk and cue, an unsettled expression on his face, and took the drink. "Thank you."

"Bad day?" Chloe started a circuit of the pool table, giving him distance.

He didn't answer.

"You questioned that man, Pietro, after I left last night, didn't you?"

He didn't answer. It felt like a wall had sprung up, dividing the room between them.

"I know you probably took an oath of secrecy or something to do with your job. I get that now. And if you can't tell me what the creep said now, just say that someday you will tell me, so that I'll understand why my uncle died."

"Chloe—"

"Don't *Chloe* me." Her tone was sharper than she intended, and she took a deep breath to soften her words. "That man tried to kill me."

He watched her walk around the table for a beat, tracking her movement with his eyes. Chloe felt the wall between them pushing outward now, crowding her away.

He looked both sad and wary. "I know he did."

"Did he tell you anything useful?"

A dark expression crossed Sam's face. "No. So don't push. This time, it's not worth the effort."

She watched him take a sip of the drink, then set it down neatly on a side table. "That's it?"

The corners of his mouth twitched down. "I spent today tracking down where the Knights were staying. We tried before, but this time I finally found them. They were in a campground trailer park some distance away. They left around three this morning. They're in the wind. We have men trying to locate them again."

Chloe's breath caught. He was giving her real information. He was letting her in as far as he could. That was all she could ask. She took a step closer to him, wanting the discomfort between them gone.

Something slid behind Sam's careful expression. It looked to her like hurt and confusion. "Winspear's gone, too. No one knows where he is. I don't trust very many people right now."

She was going to take his hurt away if she could. If she could get close enough. "I just want to know one other thing. What's going to stop the thieves from coming back here?"

"The dress and the jewels go back to where they belong. If they're not here, there is no motivation for anyone to bother Oakwood."

"And when is someone coming to get the dress?"

"I'll take care of it." His eyes were hard and flat as iron. "I don't trust anyone else. That doesn't seem to work out for me."

She knew he wasn't referring to her; he probably meant Winspear. But his words still bothered her. "You can't judge everyone by what's happening here."

He braced his hands on the pool table, glaring at the green surface. "It's not the first time I've trusted when I shouldn't."

"Is that what happened with Lady Beatrice? You trusted people to help out with security and they failed?"

He looked up sharply. "I don't talk about that."

Chloe folded her arms against the sharpness of his gaze. "I'm sorry."

"Where did you hear about that?"

"The internet. It said the boy in the club wasn't the only one you caught. In the end three conspirators were charged and convicted. They found the bodies of the assassins torn to pieces in their cells. All but the boy who fired the gun." Her voice shook as she said it. The description of the scene was nauseating.

The tension in the room spiked. "Leave it alone."

"What happened?" Chloe replied, her fingers trailing along the polished edge of the pool table as she circled it slowly, working toward him. The hard, glossy wood felt a bit like the conversation—there was substance there, but it was slippery and hard to grasp.

"Leave it alone."

She stopped, close enough that they could reach out and touch. Proximity acted like magic. The wall between them crumbled. She couldn't explain how she felt it, but she did. They'd somehow reached an unspoken agreement. He would tell her what he could. She could ask for more, but agreed to accept it when he had to remain silent.

Sam gave a heavy sigh. He picked up the drink and took another swallow. "Lady Beatrice made the princess laugh. I think she was the only real friend Amelie had. I was supposed to keep both of them safe. I brought in others to help. Lady Beatrice died because I trusted them." He stopped abruptly, seeming to stop himself before he said more. "I don't like to talk about it."

"I'm asking because I want to know you. I'm not finding that an easy task."

"Yes, I know." The words were soft. "And you can't seem to get it through your head that I'm bad for you. If you have a type, I'm probably not it."

"French fries are bad for me, but I eat them anyway."

"Chloe." Her name was a growl.

Her whole being grinned, though she struggled to keep it off her face. "Now you sound like my dad."

This time he came toward her, moving in slow, prowling steps. Chloe watched him, not quite sure if she was excited or apprehensive. Either way, a fizz of anticipation settled in her stomach.

When Sam finally stopped he was so close that his pant legs brushed her knees. He leaned forward, putting one hand on either side of her, gripping the table. Chloe let her eyes drift closed so that she looked up at him from under her lashes.

"You're playing with fire," he said. "When it comes to you, I can't hold back."

The low tones of his voice resonated in her belly. She closed her eyes altogether for a moment, breathing him in. He smelled like whiskey and cool dusk in the lush green grass. He'd spent time outdoors that day.

"I know you're not going to stay," she said, words snagging in her throat. "You belong beside your princess. You have obligations."

"It would be worse for you if I did stay."

"You don't have a high opinion of yourself."

"I know what I'm talking about."

Chloe opened her eyes then. She stared right into his. She'd always known they were gray, but now she could see the individual streaks of dark and silver. A shiver ran up her backbone, something in her primitive brain sensing a danger her rational mind couldn't quite place. At the same time, desire for him ran hot in her blood. Whatever happened tomorrow, she wanted him tonight.

Fire and ice swirled inside her belly, goading her to lure him in. "So are you bad for me all the time, or just sometimes?"

"I'm bad for you right now." Sam took one hand from the chair and stroked her cheek. "Because I'm going to take what I want. I can't resist you."

"It's about time."

Sam didn't move at once, but let his fingers trail down the line of her jaw to the sensitive spot just below her ear. A trail of electricity followed his touch, leaving a tingling path. Chloe arched her neck against his cool fingers, wanting to feel more.

The next moment, his lips began the same journey, weaving tiny, quick kisses in a chain along her flesh. Chloe's breath hung suspended as he moved, unwilling to disturb the spell. Every press of his mouth sent a charge along her nerves, igniting sensations through her whole body. As he finished, the last kiss lingered, his lips soft and almost cool over the pulse in her throat. Shivering, she finally gulped in air, almost tasting the attraction between them.

Her hand cupped the back of his head, pulling him down so her mouth could find his. Thick and hot, her pulse felt slow, almost drugged. As she finally tasted him, a sweet ache infused her entire body. *And yet all he did was kiss me.*

Either Sam Ralston was a new gold standard of lover, or she'd been alone far, far too long. Only one way to be sure.

Chloe summoned her sweetest smile. "Are you going to aim for the eight ball, or do we get to find a bedroom first?"

His gaze raked over her as if weighing the inconvenience of relocation. It looked like sex on the pool table was winning the argument until finally something filtered through the lustful haze. "Bed."

Monosyllables would do. She gave his chest a shove so she could straighten up. He caught her around the waist, as if mere inches of airspace was a very bad thing. His thick sweater rubbed softly against her bare arms. She cuddled close, letting his arm wrap around her possessively. "My bedroom is closest."

"Go."

Holding hands, they stole up the stairs. Chloe dared not look at Sam, afraid she'd start to giggle. This was too much like a flashback to her school days, when she'd unsuccessfully tried to sneak boys up to her room under Uncle Jack's nose.

"Are you sure no one saw us?" she asked once Sam closed the door behind them.

"Yes."

"Not even your wolf?"

Sam's expression was a curious mix of horror and embarrassment.

"Forget about him." Sam slid onto the comforter next to her, pressing his mouth to hers, drinking in her mirth. Chloe melted into him, working her hands under the hem of that soft sweater, feeling the hard muscle underneath. She raked her fingernails lightly over his skin, earning a murmur of pleasure as she kissed him back.

His hands stole up her rib cage, lingering over every inch until he finally cupped her breasts. His thumbs brushed her aching nipples, making her arch against him, seeking more pressure to satisfy the pain. He pulled her onto his lap and she felt the hard evidence of his own ache. She reached down, but he brushed her hand away.

"Not yet. There's no need to rush."

She was about to rap out a snappy rejoinder, but he'd found the buttons down the front of her dress, and his mouth was on her breast. Chloe's head fell back as she gave herself over to the delicious feel of his tongue exploring the lace cups of her bra. The brush of his hair against her sensitized skin brought gooseflesh down her arms. As he closed on her nipple, her thoughts turned to the snowy blankness of a TV that has dropped its signal.

Somewhere in the following minutes, she lost her clothes. At the same time, she worked on Sam's, determined to find the beast within. She'd seen his chest before, but the sight bore repeating. He must have done some serious weight lifting, because muscles like that didn't happen by themselves.

She finally got the right angle to pull down his zipper. Sam rose from the bed, sliding off his jeans. He wasn't wearing anything underneath. Chloe wasn't sure where to look first. In the soft glow of the bedside lamp, he seemed made of marble, pale and sculpted, the shadows blurring the hard angles of his muscular flesh. As for the individual details—well, maybe there was some truth to the whole monster thing. As he fished in his wallet for a condom, Chloe sank back into the pillows, feeling like Christmas had come early.

The next moment, Sam was beside her. He held a lock of her hair between his fingers, teasing her skin with the ends. He brushed it over the curve of her breast, seeming fascinated by the roundness of it. Chloe ran her hand down his chest, pausing to circle his nipple in a mirror image of his movements.

"You are so beautiful." He let her hair fall free, pulling her close. At the same time, his fingers found the soft core of her, slipping inside to stroke the most sensitive places. Chloe writhed against him, wanting more, aching for completion. He brought her close but pulled away just shy of the brink. She wriggled closer, demanding, plunging against him.

The third time, Chloe ran a hand up the length of his shaft, and his attention shifted like the gears of a well-tuned race car. He trapped her in the cage of his limbs and entered her in one long, hard stroke.

Chloe cried out at the sensation. He was large enough that it was almost uncomfortable. He pulled out, and pushed in again, drawing another gasp. She shuddered, close to her peak but hanging on, taking him in and making it last as long as she could.

He seemed to read her thoughts, making the next stroke so long and delicious that she detonated. He had done too good a job preparing her, and she crumbled beneath his assault. She was his.

Falling to pieces was just the beginning, for she was adrift in a euphoria that seemed to spin endlessly. Chloe could feel Sam inside her, feel him working and pushing, possessing her as she had never been before. Like a territory to be conquered, no part of her went untouched, no inch untasted.

As he drove her again to climax, her muscles seemed to move entirely to his will, her body nothing but an instrument of desire. His own movements were growing faster, more ragged. She grabbed his shoulders, pushing to meet him, her skin a slick of sweat.

With a ragged cry, Sam gave a final thrust, spending himself inside her as she fell under another wave of mindless pleasure.

But not so mindless that she missed the fangs sinking into her throat.

Chapter 23

Chloe awakened with a start, her whole body gathering itself to spring free of the sheets. Her mind came online a beat later, befuddled by the adrenaline surging through her system. She rolled onto her side, groping for the edge of the big bed and tangling herself in the blankets.

"Hush!" A hand touched her bare shoulder.

Chloe froze, staring into the dim atmosphere of the bedroom. Enough sun leaked around the curtain to show it was morning, but not enough to make the room light. *Naked. Bed.* Her thoughts scampered like panicked mice. *Sam.* Memory returned with all the subtlety of a sledgehammer.

She flipped over, staring into the steel-gray eyes of the man beside her. "You bit me!"

It was out before she could stop herself. Fear skittered over her skin, and she stayed perfectly still for a long moment, barely daring to breathe.

Finally, he gave a slight shrug.

Chloe pushed the hair out of her eyes. "That's just rude."

"I didn't leave a mark."

Chloe's hand went instinctively to her throat. She was sure he'd drawn blood, but there was no soreness, no heat of a fresh bruise. *Impossible.*

"Not even a hickey," he said calmly.

"What did you do?"

He arched a brow. "Sorry, I thought you were enjoying it."

She had. Oh, yes. Chloe's insides turned to syrup at the suggestion. She felt the echoes of her last climax, shadows that could surge back to full force at any moment. Even the memory of his tongue and teeth was enough to send her over if she let herself revel in it.

A sigh escaped her before she could stifle it. His eyebrow quirked.

Not fair. Fear started to morph into irritation. *You just don't bite someone without their say-so!*

She tried to rise to her knees and keep the sheet drawn up around her at the same time. Unfortunately, that pulled the covers off Sam. There was suddenly more of Sam visible than she was prepared to deal with right then.

She twitched the coverlet over him, feeling a flush creep up her skin. "That was something else."

"You say that like it was a bad thing."

"It wasn't completely bad." She tried to keep a straight face. He was teasing her, the slant of his gaze a little bit mischievous, a little bit guilty. This was a different, playful side of him, and she wasn't sure she was ready for it. "But you…" She trailed off helplessly.

"You've got a good imagination."

"No. Forget the whole denial dance. That wasn't a daydream. You had fangs. It wasn't the first time I saw them."

The teasing started to look ragged around the edges. "What are you saying?"

He's strong. Fast.

"I don't know." *Hates the sun. Looks exactly like a picture that's a century and a half old.*

Oh, no way.

She put a hand on his chest. There was no heartbeat under the cool skin. "Are you dead?"

Annoyance twisted his features. "Excuse me? Did I seem dead last night?"

She'd spent too much time with Uncle Jack's mouldy manuscripts and plastic fangs to avoid the obvious conclusion. "You're a vampire!"

He sat up so quickly she had no time to scoot back. They were nearly nose to nose. Chloe felt her remaining blood drain from her face.

"Do I look like a vampire?" he demanded.

She studied him. She had no clue what to say. "You've got the broody looks down."

He collapsed back onto the pillows, covering his face with his hands. Chloe was glad for the moment of privacy, and hopped out of bed to grab her bathrobe. She wrapped the thick terry folds around her, hands shaking so hard she could barely knot the belt. Panic sang through her bones, locking muscles. Her jaw ached with it.

Vampire? Was she nuts? There were no such things as vampires. Not literally, anyway.

But, come on. She knew what she saw. She'd felt his teeth. Sure, the sex was good and all that, but did it cause hallucinations? Sex didn't make her see fireworks or flowers opening in slow motion and it sure as Vlad didn't make her see vampires.

She marched to the foot of the bed and gave him a furious glare. She felt oddly detached, as if she were floating above her own body.

"Don't you guys warn your lovers?" she snapped. "That's like the ultimate STD."

Sam emitted an exasperated groan, somehow still managing to look masterful while wearing nothing but bedclothes. "I thought I'd hypnotized you. You're not supposed to remember that part."

Chloe huffed. "Well, that's nice, isn't it? Snack and go."

"It was for your own good. I'm just not…the mind control talents are not my strength."

"Mind control?" she repeated in freezing tones. "What are you? Straight out of a B movie?"

He scowled back. "You're taking this rather calmly. Most people get hysterical."

"Most people?" His words riled her temper another notch. "Think about my last week, Ralston. My uncle was murdered. I inherited a wedding dress covered in stolen diamonds. Everyone who owns it winds up dead. I was attacked in my bed. Bad guys. Wolves. A wedding in three days. I don't mean to bruise your ego, but one night of hot sex with the living dead isn't as much of a shocker as you might think."

And then she burst into tears. Chloe jammed her fingers into the thick tangle of her hair, horrified by the hot ache in her eyes and the wetness trickling down her cheeks. She couldn't say another word. All the fear and anger since Jack's death jammed in her throat, choking off any explanations. All she could do was cry.

She heard the rustle of sheets, and then Sam was in front of her. Tenderly, he wrapped her in his thick, muscular arms and tucked her head under his chin. She fit there perfectly, her body cradled against the strong curve of his chest. Rhythmically, he rubbed her back, almost as if she were a colicky baby.

"Hush, sweet one." He kissed the top of her head, then tipped her head up to put gentle kisses on her eyelids. "Hush."

His touch was hypnotic, soothing the shivers from her limbs. No words, no excuses, no telling her how to think or feel—he simply held her. It was exactly the right thing. As his lips touched the spot just under her ear, she gasped, every cell in her body suddenly yearning for him. He slipped the robe from her shoulders, sliding his hands down the line of her back.

Chloe arched into him feeling his body wake, long and thick, against her. *He's a vampire!* But in the next moment, all she could remember was that he was Sam.

"I'm sorry, Chloe. I didn't mean for that side of me to come out. The more I want somebody, the harder it is to control. And I want you far too much."

She made a yearning noise deep in her throat. He grew harder, and his hands slid down to cup her backside. Chloe forgot everything but the taste of his mouth. "I need to know you."

"Now you do," he murmured. "You know everything."

Whether she fell back onto the bed or he pushed her was hard to say. He was on top of her, beside her, and then she was on top of him, taking possession of Sam.

His stomach tensed as she tasted him, letting her tongue linger in a slow circuit of his tip. Now he was the one making the throaty noise.

Yes, she was getting to know him. Getting to know exactly what he liked. She closed her lips over him, sucking and teasing him with her teeth.

"Chloe!" he protested through gritted teeth.

She bit down carefully, figuring turnabout was fair play. The salty taste of him grew stronger, the muscles in his thighs hard under her hands.

He shuddered, obviously at the edge of his control. Peeking up through her lashes, she could see his face. And there they were, the tips of sharp, white fangs just visible through his parted lips. Pleasure made them come out.

Fear and excitement knotted inside her. She released

him, dragging herself forward in one long, continuous movement, using as much of her skin as possible against the sensitive, engorged member.

Sam grabbed her, rolling her under him in a swift, predatory pounce. He was breathing hard, his nose buried against her neck. "You smell of fear and desire."

Chloe was beyond words. Instead, she arched her hips against him. And then he was inside her once more, stretching her, filling her, driving her to insanity. She felt the rhythm of her body milking him hungrily, responding with intensity she hadn't thought possible.

She could feel his teeth against her again, but this time he didn't drive them home. "Do it," she whispered.

"Too soon."

His words were nonsense to her. "Do it. Do it, please."

And he did. It wasn't painful, but an explosion inside her that seemed to come from deep in her belly, a sun of pleasure going supernova. Chloe cried out, tears of release trickling down her face.

"You're mine, Chloe." He stopped her cries with his mouth, and then thrust one last time, reaching his own climax. "All of you. Everything."

They lay boneless, exhausted. Chloe rolled into his arms, burying her face in his shoulder. "So. Vampires, huh?"

Her mind roamed to her uncle and his collection. The fact that he had it, that he'd shown it to her, was no coincidence. Just like the target practice, he'd been preparing her for something.

She sat up suddenly. "Uncle Jack was like you!" That explained so much—his strange hours, the secrets, the mysteries and the tasteless collection of rubber bats. "He never said anything."

Sam sighed, pulling her back down beside him. "We're not supposed to exist."

Her head spun. An insane desire to giggle rattled through her. She swallowed back the nervous laughter. "Are there many of you?"

"Maybe a thousand in the whole world."

Chloe sniffed, the storm of her emotions finally abating. A thousand. That was barely any, compared to billions of humans. "Don't you make more of your kind?"

"Not often. It's not as easy as it sounds, and not very smart if you're trying to stay invisible."

"How did you get to be Princess Amelie's bodyguard?"

Sam slipped his arm under her, curling her even closer. "Do you remember I told you about the two kings, and how they went to war when their brother brought the gems back from the Crusades?"

"Yes."

"The eldest brother, Vidon, loved his army and soldiers and dreamed of great conquests. Marcari, the younger, followed the path of alchemy and spells. Each secretly recruited magical beings—vampires, werewolves and demons. When they went to war, they used their magical creatures in the fight."

This sounds like a fairy tale. Yet Chloe paid attention. Fairy tales, it seemed, could come true.

"Many—human or not—were destroyed in the war. Staggered by guilt and remorse, Vidon blamed the supernatural creatures on both sides for the scale of the massacre. He demanded an oath from the Knights of Vidon, making them swear vengeance on nonhumans for all the generations of his royal house."

"That's where the Knights come in."

Sam nodded. She felt the motion of his chin rather than saw it. "Marcari offered the magical creatures protection instead, blaming himself and his all-too-human greed for his part in the war. Aching to atone, he swore to keep such madness from the earth forevermore. Recognizing his sense of honor, the vampires who survived the war banded together and pledged allegiance to Marcari."

"And you're still the princess's bodyguard."

"Not exactly *still*," Sam said with a smile in his voice. "The crusades were definitely before my time. I was born in 1830."

She pondered that. "How come you're tall?"

"Pardon?"

"I thought people were short in the old days." Perhaps it was an odd thing to ask, but she needed something to make sense. A hard fact she could hang on to.

He was silent for a long moment. "Size and strength are some of the gifts that come with the change."

"Oh."

His arms tightened around her. "Other things change, too. We're not men anymore. We're beasts."

Beasts? She pulled back just far enough that she could look into his face. His eyes had gone dark, the gray lost to the blackness of his pupils. Some of it had to be the dim light of the bedroom, but some of it was his obvious interest.

"Exactly what do you mean?" she breathed.

"For one thing, we don't choose our women lightly. Bedmates, yes, but not anyone we'd spend the night with. When we choose, we choose forever."

"You slept with me."

"Yes. And not lightly."

A shiver ran through her at the sound of his voice, half rasp, half growl. It was as if he'd let his human mask fall away, not needing it one second more. It left her with a cocktail of dread and thrilled anticipation.

You're saying I'm more than a one-nighter. That was supposed to be a good thing, but it made her break into a light sweat. *What does* forever *mean to a vampire?*

"And what do you do with your chosen women?" The words shook, her tone a little too high.

He gazed down at her, his eyes both hungry and tender. "Everything we can."

Instinctively, she reached up, caressing his cheek. He grasped her wrist gently, pressing a kiss to her palm. The gesture reminded her of the night he'd stopped her attacker and the first time he'd kissed her fingers. That was Sam, too. Courtly. A beast. Both, and more than both. He had claimed her. Somehow she'd claimed him, too.

He still had her hand, but now it was folded in his, pressed to his chest. His skin was cool, but not cold. Not at all unpleasant.

"What about this bite, then? Does it have any aftereffects?"

"No. Not unless I feed off you regularly."

"So you didn't hurt me."

"I'd never hurt you. I'm here to protect you."

She heard the fierce note in his words, the time-honored declaration of the male selecting his mate. He hadn't done anything—bite aside—she hadn't invited, but there was something savage a millimeter under the surface. *The men who shot Lady Beatrice were torn to pieces in their cells.* Was their killer the same man who held her now?

"What if you did feed off me a lot?" She had to know.

"There can be a psychic bond between a vampire and its human, um, friend."

Does the, um, friend happen to be named Renfield? She'd read plenty of vampire books that involved human servants and mind control.

"No, it's not like that," he said.

"You read my mind?" she asked sharply.

"No, but you had the question written all over your

face." One corner of his mouth turned up. "I'm not like that, Chloe."

But the hunger was in every line of his body. Not blood hunger, or at least not entirely that. Chloe could see so much more in the set of his head and shoulders as he leaned toward her, the tension around his eyes. It didn't take a lot of imagination to fill in the details. He wanted her in ways without number—the touch and warmth of a woman, the answering voice when he called out in the dark. He'd been alone a long time, and for some reason he'd placed that loneliness at her feet. He'd picked her to banish it.

But what would have happened if she hadn't remembered the bite? How long would he have let her go on thinking he was an ordinary man? Would he have walked away, taking his loneliness with him? His very nature was something he could not share. This was the secret behind everything about Sam Ralston. And yet, she had found him out.

She sat up, putting distance between them. "And if I say I can't handle this, what then?"

By now he understood her fears. *What you don't know could kill you. In this case, vampires.*

"When a human finds out what we are, erasing those memories is standard protocol," he said softly. "Standing orders. It's considered easier in the long run."

His expression said it wasn't going to be easier for him.

"You wouldn't," she breathed.

"I don't want to."

That wasn't the same thing as a *no*. Then she remembered he'd already tried. A cold, sick feeling surged through her. She slipped out of the bed and found her robe where Sam had let it fall to the floor.

She stared at him where he lay, dark hair and dark eyes stark against the white sheets. She knotted her robe shut with quick, sharp movements.

Guilt pinched the lines of his face. It wasn't hard to read.

"You're going to do it, aren't you? You're going to try again to wipe my mind."

"You're resistant. An expert would have to do the job." His voice held a world of unhappiness. He didn't want to face this any more than she did. But she knew enough about Sam to know he didn't flinch from duty.

"But you'll follow orders. Or try to. You—or your super-secret spy network—think you can make choices for me." Chloe drew herself up, gathering the shreds of her dignity. "Get out of my bedroom."

Chapter 24

Sam had to get out of this dilemma. He was supposed to be a straight arrow. Somehow, he'd wound up in knots.

It was hours later. Chloe stood across the room from Sam. Jack's study was quiet, the rain turning the day to a false twilight. For once she'd been the one to find him there, rather than vice versa. He'd been lingering amongst the old books and paintings, hoping she'd come. He'd made himself swear to leave her alone, but if they met by accident?

Be honest. He was stalking her like a lion in the long grass. He knew where the gazelle would wander. *She's mine.*

But that was the fastest way to get her forcibly brainwashed or killed. Humans who knew too much were considered enemies of the Company.

She was dressed now, her hair rolled up in that neat, elegant twist she had been wearing the day the wedding dress had come out of Jack's safe. The memory of it wrenched him. They'd come full circle, from shared mystery to mutual discovery to passion to…whatever this standoff was.

When we choose, we choose forever. He meant it. It had been dangerous to say it, but every word was true, regardless of the Company's rules.

"We have to find a compromise." Her voice cracked, all the vibrancy sucked out of it. "There is no way on earth I'm letting some stranger mess with my brain."

Sam kept his face a neutral mask. When it came to erasing memories, "let" wasn't usually a consideration, but he wasn't going to point that out. He remembered the feel of her in his arms, and his groin began to ache. She was his. The instinct to keep and claim warred with logic. Above all else, he had to keep her safe. "The Company isn't easy to fool."

"Who or what is the Company?"

"The group of us who serve the King of Marcari."

"Your boss." Red was creeping up her cheeks, her eyes turning from a soft summer-blue to a frozen winter sky. "Your friends. That fairy tale story about the king and his loyal vampires. They're the Company, aren't they?"

"Yes."

"This is madness." She paced to the window and back, her face pale as paper.

Sam's face was numb, grief and guilt crushing whatever spark kept him walking the earth. *You'd think a hundred-and-fifty-year-old could keep his fangs zipped up.*

But he owed her truth. She had railed against those who sought to protect her by keeping silent. He wasn't going to make that mistake. "The Company's reach goes further than you know. If they find there has been a security breach, they'll come after you. It doesn't matter where you are."

That caught her up short. "What?"

"You heard me." He said it gently. "They'll want to take your memories or your life."

Her eyes went round. "Kill me for just knowing you exist?"

"Yes."

She spread her hands into the air, a gesture of resignation. "Tell them to take a number. There are *already* people trying to kill me! And tell me this—How am I supposed to watch my back if I don't know about the Knights and the vampires and whoever else is out to get me? You're setting me up to die!"

"No!" Sam reached for her, but she shrank back. He dropped his arm to his side, his cold, still heart breaking in his chest.

Her mouth tightened, her eyes growing too bright in the half light of the room. The Company would kill him, too, for permitting the breach to occur. The rules about mating with human women were clear. But Sam didn't mention that. It was almost irrelevant. He wasn't sure he was going to exist if the memories of their union were erased from her lovely eyes.

Self-loathing scorched him. He had betrayed her the moment they kissed. He hadn't been able to control his yearning for her. He still couldn't. His body burned to feel her against him. From her scent, he knew she felt the same fire.

His world pivoted on its axis, changing utterly. Duty was everything, but his first obligation was to this woman who had held him in her slim, soft arms.

Words scraped through his aching throat. "I said I wouldn't let you come to harm. I mean it."

"How can I believe that?" Her eyes were bright with unshed tears. "You're asking an awful lot of trust for someone who's lied to me since the instant we met."

For a moment, Sam could find nothing to say. For the first time in his long existence, he was floundering. If he was going to solve this, he was going to have to break from everything he knew.

He grabbed her arms, pressing her back against the wall, capturing her body with his. He felt her breath on his face, the softness of her breasts against his chest. It was an act of pure possession. "Is this a lie?"

He crushed his mouth with hers, plundering the warmth of her with his lips and tongue. He left kisses along the corners of her mouth, her eyelids, the delicate line of her jaw. She tasted sweet, but there was also a trace of salt on her skin. She had been crying.

He broke away. No one made his woman cry. "I will protect you. I swear it. I am War. I am the strongest."

She studied him, her gaze flicking back and forth over his features. Her lips trembled for a moment. "How can you fight the whole Company by yourself?"

"I refuse to let you suffer for just knowing me."

"I'll suffer if you're hurt. Did you think of that?"

It was an effort to hide the stab of grief her words delivered. No one else worried if War was hurt. And yet standard orders said to wipe away her feelings like fog obscuring the clear window of duty. How could anyone ask that of him?

He set his hands on her shoulders, his touch as gentle as he knew how to make it. "My beautiful Chloe." *Forget obedience.* "I will take the two kingdoms apart stone by stone before I will allow anyone to touch you."

"I don't think that's a solution."

"Then what do you propose we do?"

Her jaw clenched, as if she were the one who was going to do the biting. "We don't do anything. We don't say anything. I have a wedding to put on here. I have to sell this house. You have to take the dress back to Marcari. We say goodbye. No one needs to know."

Sam narrowed his eyes. This plan required patience. Not his favorite thing. "You can keep me, the Company, everything a secret?"

"Of course I can." She swallowed hard. "I have to. Otherwise we'll have to find another end to this situation where

I don't end up a victim, and you don't have to fight the entire world." Her eyes pleaded with him, willing him to accept her plan.

This means I will disobey orders. He was the straight arrow, never deviating from his path. But breaking the rules made perfect sense. It would save them both—if she could keep his secret.

He growled a conditional acquiescence. "We walk away, then what?"

She hung her head, all the strength seeming to seep from her frame. "Are the rules going to change?"

"No." The word stuck in his throat.

She lifted her eyes to his, pain and anger mixed in her face. "Then nothing."

Nothing. If he loved her, if he wanted to be sure she was safe, he had to keep his distance. Never call her. Never touch her soft, warm body again. Never taste her again. *Unthinkable!*

He took her mouth again like a drowning man seeking a last gasp of air. He knew she was right. Carter was already suspicious that there was something between them. Until he had a better plan, silence was the safest course. But still…

"Forgetting isn't the worst thing that could happen," he said hoarsely. "Remembering will be a thousand times worse."

Her brows pulled together. "What's the alternative?"

He had no answer. No other plan. At least, not yet. He wanted to rage, beat something. Put his fist through a wall. Roar. "I will solve this."

"How?" She gave him a look that skewered him where he stood. It held despair, sadness, every raw and bloody feeling that was tearing him apart, too.

"I don't know yet, but I will take care of it. Trust me."

"I trust you to be wise and careful." Her eyes were gentle as she pulled his hands from her shoulders, kissed him chastely on the cheek and walked out.

Sam's first instinct was to haul her back, force her against the wall and mark her as his own all over again. She *had* to be his.

Except that way was disaster. That impulse to possess, to dominate was what got him in this mess in the first place. He was too much the vampire. Now she was at risk.

He watched her slim form walking away. *Wise and careful.* Careful wasn't his prime skill set. Battle was more his style. But for her, he could be anything.

Then, across the widening distance between them, he heard a sharp intake of breath. Chloe had been unspeakably brave, but she hadn't managed to stifle her tears.

No one cried for him. No one until now. *Nine hells.*

War had never shied away from battle. This was no exception. He *would* find a way to win.

Chloe drove to the Eldon Hotel, the SIG Sauer on the passenger seat. If she'd been pulled over it would have been a huge problem, but not as big a problem as angry vampires. Everything was relative.

She wondered if the rain-darkened sky meant all the undead could come out and play in broad daylight. Sam seemed to be able to get around in the day, but clearly didn't enjoy it.

Sam. Her eyes prickled again. She'd cried and cried until there were no more tears, but the pain of that last conversation hadn't dimmed one bit. She knew what they had was incredible and wonderful and, in effect, she'd said goodbye. And, at the same time, begged that she'd be allowed to remember she'd done it. How messed up was that?

There was no way she could say this outcome was for the best. It was just that the alternatives were worse. Die.

Forget Sam. Or, be miserable but at least remember their brief time together. Door number three sucked the least.

Chloe blinked tear-filled eyes and turned into the Eldon's parking lot. Rain left the hotel grounds looking dark and drab. She wondered what Hope's Reach looked like on a day like this. The memory of her lunch there with Sam sent a fresh wave of pain through her stomach.

There was too much she didn't know about the vampire world. Why did they mix with humans at all? Just for food? Or was there something else they gained from the contact? How big an impact did their kind have on the mortal realm? Chloe burned to know. Yet, if they had their way, she wouldn't have the time to ask questions before her memories were ripped out. *Over my dead body.*

Well, apparently that was an option.

When Lexie opened the door to her suite, she looked Chloe up and down with mounting dismay. "What happened to you?"

"It's raining out." Chloe stepped inside the living room of the suite. Done in pinks and greens, it looked like every other hotel anyplace, anywhere.

"I'm not talking about the weather. You look like you've just watched Bambi's mother die."

Chloe grabbed Lexie in a hug. "I just broke up."

"With Sam?"

Chloe staggered back, fighting off a fresh wave of tears. "He's a vampire."

Lexie looked sad and a little angry. "Like I said, they're not people."

"I had no idea what that meant."

"And how would you? We never had a real chance to talk. Is Sam aware that you know?"

She nodded. "How much do you know?"

Lexie sucked in a ragged breath. "Faran. Why we split up. Faran is a werewolf."

"Fido!"

Her friend gave her a puzzled look.

"That's what Sam called his wolf."

"Fido? Seriously?"

"That was Faran!" Chloe flopped onto one end of the overstuffed couch. "He turns into a wolf. How the blazes does that even work?"

Lexie put a hand to her forehead as if staving off a headache. "It's hereditary. The whole biting-contagion thing is a myth."

"Are you sure?"

"Yes. Faran has a lot of flaws, but he wouldn't outright lie about something like that." Lexie's face was serious. "You're in a lot of trouble, Chlo. You know about the whole memory-wipe thing?"

"Yeah. How come your memories were never erased?"

"No one knows I found out."

"Doesn't Faran?"

"We agreed to pretend it didn't happen. He was okay with that. He was never a rules kind of guy. We met at this resort in Cannes. I was photographing a swimwear collection and he was hanging around in the Casinos. I didn't find out till much later that he was working undercover. I thought he was just a rather nice part of the scenery."

Chloe gave her a long look, thinking how different Sam was from his friend, and yet they had ended up in the same predicament.

Faran, who was a werewolf. *I petted him!* And she'd sprayed him with Aunt Mavis's hair products. *Good grief.* "Faran trusts you not to spill his secrets."

"About that, yes." Her voice was thickly buttered with

irony. "We had other problems. I couldn't deal with the wolf."

They were both quiet for a time. The rain beat against the window of the hotel room. Chloe's whole body ached with tension. She was incredibly grateful to be able to talk to Lexie, but then they'd always kept each other's confidences. They were closer than sisters, and Chloe had never needed her friend more than now.

She finally broke the silence. "Sam and I have decided to pretend I don't know. That nothing important ever passed between us."

"Do you believe he'll stick to that?"

"That wasn't his first thought. He was more concerned about the power of the Company. He could change his mind or, worse, try and take on the whole world for my sake."

Lexie was curled up on the other end of the sofa, her long legs tucked under her. "I don't think it's as simple as whether he trusts you, or whether he thinks of the Company's power first. The fact that he even questions his duty shows how much he cares for you."

"Was Faran the same way?"

Lexie shook her head. "He's aware we've chosen a dangerous path, but Faran is a lone wolf. He obeys orders because he chooses to for the time being. Vampires are different. With them, it's all about hierarchy and obedience. If Sam picks a fight with the Company, it won't end well no matter who wins."

Chloe buried her face in her hands. "I can't believe this. What a nightmare. And yet I don't want to forget."

"The whole supernatural thing is pretty amazing stuff." Lexie gave a lopsided smile. "I don't, either."

"It's not that. It's Sam. I don't want to forget *him*."

"Also amazing stuff?"

"Very." Chloe felt a tremor pass through her. It was

more than memory, or just the replaying of sensation. It was her body's knowledge of Sam, bone-deep and howling with loss.

Lexie waved a hand in the air. "Then run for it. Don't wait."

"Before this wedding? I'll ruin my career, my business, everything I've worked for."

"So choose what's more important."

Chloe gave her a furious look. "This is ridiculous! Why am I in this position? Why should I have to choose?"

"Has Sam said anything to his friends?"

"I don't think so. Not yet."

"Good." Lexie drummed her fingers on the arm of the couch. "Watch out for that doctor, Mark Winspear. He has expert brainwashing skills. Apparently not all vampires can do it well. In that little pack of theirs, Winspear's the eraser. Once he played a trick on Faran, completely removing his memory of eating dinner so that he prepared and ate the complete meal over again three times. I wish I'd seen that."

Chloe huddled deeper into the cushions, anxiety pulling at her. The vampires had it all organized. There were chosen personnel who specialized in tearing apart human memory. *Sam wasn't exaggerating. They're serious about keeping their secrets.* "Winspear is on the outs with them. He's missing and Sam thinks he's working for their enemies."

Lexie raised an eyebrow. "Good to know."

"What does the Company think I'm going to do, anyway? Alert the media? They'd think I was crazy."

Lexie pushed back her long red hair. "The nonhumans have survived by being careful. If enough people spoke up, eventually the media would have to pay attention."

Chloe buried her face in her hands. "I hate this. I can't

just walk out of my life. I've worked too hard to let everything go."

Her friend's face puckered with worry. "It's your brain. What do we have besides our memories? It's kind of who we are."

"What if I just went home? Finished the wedding and left? Do you think Sam would stick to the plan?"

"You know him better than I do."

Chloe swore under her breath. She couldn't keep herself from remembering his first response had been to try to wipe her memories. How could she trust him? "This is insane."

"That's why I ended it with Faran. I couldn't live with all the cloak-and-dagger and, well, furriness."

"Sam knows tampering with my memory is the last thing I want." Yet the worm of doubt wouldn't quite lie still.

"Then give him a chance to be on the side of the angels. If he agreed to pretend nothing happened, he might just be honorable enough to do that."

Chloe nodded, her throat too tight to let her speak. She knew Sam wanted to find a better solution to their problems, but she couldn't imagine what that would be. In some ways, it would be a blessing if *he* forgot she existed.

"If you want to hedge your bets, leave before he expects you to. They can't erase your memories if you're not there. If you go just before the wedding wraps up, right in the middle of all the goodbye confusion, you can simply vanish. Lay low somewhere for a while. Give the bloodsuckers a chance to start worrying about other problems. Once the dust has settled, you can slip back home and carry on like nothing happened. If he's the right guy, no one will be the wiser and the Company will never darken your door again."

Is he the right guy? Of course he was. If he wasn't, would she be so desperate to remember him?

"I know, we'll go together," Lexie said. "I'll make sure you get away from the wedding. Plus, I have friends everywhere. We can be on the road forever without using a credit card or registering in a hotel. We'll be ghosts in the wind."

It was a terrible idea for a million reasons, but it was still better than having her brains vacuumed. Plus, it would still allow for her to keep her obligation to Elaine and Leo. "You make running away sound like a big adventure."

"Isn't it?" Lexie said with relish, leaning forward to poke Chloe's arm. "We've got to show the boys in black that we've got ideas of our own."

This was Lexie all over. Bolting was her number one way of dealing with difficult situations. There was a reason she was a globe-trotter, working freelance and living out of a suitcase.

Chloe drew her knees up to her chin. She hated the plan for the same reason that it was necessary: it took her away from Sam. They'd agreed to be apart, but these were concrete steps for putting miles between them. Her insides felt cold and heavy, as if someone had turned them to lead.

She sucked in a breath and her chest hurt with the effort. "Will you take a picture of Sam and me together at the wedding, just in case? If they do catch up with me and take my memories, I'll have something to show we were together."

"You want to remember him that much?"

Chloe rested her forehead on her knees, hiding her misery. "Whatever else he is, Sam is the once-in-a-lifetime guy."

Chapter 25

The rehearsal dinner was over, and all Chloe could think about was the fact that thirty-six hours from that moment, the wedding would be over.

Iris Fallon had been enchanted with the plans for the hors d'oeuvres. She had been okay with the dais and pavilions putting holes in Jack's garden lawn. She had been critical of everything else. Chloe had been at some pains to explain why poising a concert harp on the diving board of the swimming pool, while it would project the sound just dandy for the reception, would be objectionable to the harpist.

Some people are the clichés. Chloe closed her bedroom door behind her, kicked off her shoes and gathered up her supplies for a long bath. Unlike her old bedroom, this one didn't have an ensuite. She padded down the hall barefoot, reliving memories of Faran sliding across the floor in wolf form, of Sam coming to her rescue, gun drawn. That night seemed a thousand years ago.

Vampires. Werewolves. Okay, that's freaky. But I don't really care as much about that as I do the fact they have stupid rules keeping us apart. She'd finalized her plans with Lexie to leave during the wedding. If all went according to plan, she'd soon be far away from Sam, her memory intact and her heart in tiny pieces.

She shouldered through the bathroom door. It had a claw-foot tub deep enough to float in. A soak, a sleep and then she'd hit the ground running before the crack of dawn. Jack's mansion was stuffed with guests, staff and contractors. Even the palfrey was in the barn, having his hooves painted gold.

Chloe was stupefied with exhaustion. All she wanted was some quiet time. She wanted to sleep for a thousand years, without dreaming of Sam. She pushed the stopper into the drain of the tub and turned on the water, making sure it was good and hot.

She slipped off her clothes, donning her terry towel robe while she waited for the tub to fill, then lit a candle that sat on the counter. When she turned off the overhead light, the flame shimmered against the tiles and bounced off the mirror.

"Chloe," said the deep voice behind her.

She started. Big hands clamped her shoulders, holding her before she could wheel around to face the intruder.

"It's just me," said Sam.

"How did you get in here?" she demanded.

"I'm very good at sneaking around."

"It's a small room. I should have seen the door open!"

"I wanted to surprise you." He kissed the back of her neck. "No one knows I'm here."

Chloe hugged the robe around her, feeling more like she was wearing nothing at all. "Are you sure?"

His mouth was busy on her shoulder, tasting every inch of skin. "I'm not ready to let you go. I don't think I'll ever be ready." He turned her around. She could see his eyes now, black in the dim light. They held a world of promises.

His mouth crushed hers. It wasn't a kind or gentle kiss,

but devouring. Reflexively, Chloe's hands flew up to fend him off, but she only managed to press her palms against his chest. That gesture turned to a caress as he held her, pulling her so close against his body that only her toes touched the floor.

There was no room for talk in whatever Sam Ralston had planned. He parted her robe with one flick of his hand. A voice in the back of her mind protested. She had told him to leave her bed, and that applied to more than just that bed on that night. It had cost her all her courage to tell him they had to part. Now she would have to go through the agony of goodbye all over again.

Unfortunately, the small voice was drowned in the rush of her desire. Her body knew Sam, knew what he could do. Future pain didn't matter to her flesh, only the promise of pleasure.

She was already slick between her thighs. All it took was the sight of him, that musky scent of his, and she was ready. With a mind of their own, her fingers were unbuttoning his shirt. The touch of her skin against his, so slight, was enough to send shivers down her arms.

He nuzzled her neck, and she all but cried out in need, her nipples aching to be touched. He bent, his mouth closing around her breast. The warm, wet sensation mixed in her head with the rushing taps. She was drowning in the sensation of him, of the dark, warm room, of the wetness inside and outside of her body.

As he sucked, the sweet tension low in her belly was sharpening to hunger. She pressed against him, her body begging for more. He moved from one breast to the other, making his possession complete.

His shirt slithered to the floor. Chloe dragged her nails lightly down his back, feeling the curve of hard flesh, the sleek angle of his ribs. Sam truly was built like a god of battle, his chest deep, shoulders thick, his waist trim and ridged with muscle. She used her own tongue on his flat, dark nipples, flicking them to life.

Sam lost the rest of his clothes. When he sprang free from his pants, he was thoroughly armed for battle. A pleasant, tingling weakness passed through her, the breath of ecstasy to come. Sam turned off the taps of the tub. The sudden silence was broken only by the gentle lapping of the water and Chloe's own breathing. Sam climbed into the bath.

"Get in," he ordered, his voice a growl of desire.

She did. The tub was huge, deep enough that the water provided some buoyancy. Sam caught her around the waist, positioning her so that her back was to his chest. The hot water stroked her breasts, adding more fingers to the teasing sensations invading every nerve. She felt slightly weightless, tingling from heat and heightened sensitivity.

Sam angled her just so and entered her from behind. The size of him brought a sound of surprise from her throat. His hands closed over her breasts as he thrust, the lapping water echoing his motion. Chloe came on the third stroke.

Sam felt the pulses of her climax pulling at him, but he willed himself to resist his own climax. He pushed forward, bracing himself now on the edge of the tub, thrusting at a new angle, touching her inside and out in ever-changing ways. He could feel the tension building in her again, bringing her to the crest once more.

Was he being unfair, rekindling the fire they'd agreed to bank for the sake of safety? Perhaps. But he would not walk away from her. He had too much to lose. He had waited through lifetimes to find a woman like Chloe. Every instinct he had demanded that she stay glued to his side. *She's mine.*

Dimly, like a will-o'-the-wisp of reason in the wilderness of his pleasure, Sam knew he was lost. When vampires made up their minds about a mate, they claimed that person with every fiber of their souls. This had never happened to him before. In fact it rarely happened to anyone, but when it did, vampires were little better than wild beasts until their women accepted them.

I'm in trouble. He no longer belonged to himself. If Chloe was his, he belonged to her in an equally absolute equation. The Company's rules were no more than cobwebs to be brushed aside. Easier said than done, but there was no place in his brain for that now.

He thrust, and she dissolved around him, warm, sweet slickness milking him hard. Sam's fangs were out, the hunger for her blood—hers and hers alone—a painful cramping in every cell. As her mate, he was addicted to her.

His mouth found the softness of her neck and bit. Salty blood welled from the bite, filling his mouth with life. Chloe moaned, melting around him yet again. His saliva held the key to her pleasure, venom filled with erotic stimulants that also completely healed and hid the wound from his teeth. In hours, not even a discoloration would remain.

The pleasure cut both ways, giving to him as well as her. Sam felt aching, tightening and then an explosion that seemed to last an eternity of infinite, brilliant bliss. It tore him apart, killing him even as he was made new. He came long and hard, with everything he had.

He had never experienced orgasm close to this before. *Chloe!*

He rolled back to slouch against the tub, pulling her with him. He was sated, the raging need inside him fading down to a few glowing coals. Her blood churned inside, branding him with the very code that made her. That thought stiffened him enough that she moaned. He had to be careful.

She was only human. The vampire male was next to insatiable. His lust could hurt her.

Chloe lay quiet against him, lost in an exhausted haze between consciousness and sleep. Her breath fanned across his chest, teasing his nipples until the skin around them prickled with gooseflesh. The water was cooling now, the air of the bathroom seeming to grow colder with every drip of the tap.

Sleep. He was nowhere near the mind sage Winspear was, but he could guide her the rest of the way into slumber. *Sleep, Chloe.*

Her limbs grew heavier where she lay. He shifted, grabbing a towel to blot the water from her face. She was so beautiful, it made his chest ache. He pressed the towel gently to her cheeks and forehead, squeezing the water from her hair gone dark with its soaking.

When he had gazed his fill, Sam lifted her from the water, setting her gently on the thick white bathroom carpet. He dried the rest of her, and wrapped her in the robe he had dropped to the floor. Without bothering to do more than tie a towel around his hips, he carried Chloe to her bed and tucked her in it before she could catch a chill.

It was midnight. The witching hour.

Sam stood beside her bed, knowing what it was to be thoroughly bewitched. He had gone to Chloe planning to reassure her, to tell her somehow they'd stay together, even if that meant disappearing to places not even the Company could follow. War was still the best.

They'd never got to the talking part.

Surely she'd understood what he'd meant.

Chapter 26

Sam returned to the bathroom to dress. In the process, he found his phone and dialed a number. He started picking up wet towels while the cell rang, putting the bathroom back in some sort of order.

"Carter," came the gruff voice of his maker.

"It's Sam."

"When can I get the dress?"

The memory of Pietro's cracking neck bones came flooding back. *Why do you, the director of the Company, want to take it back on your own, with no escort?* That made no sense.

Sam had every intention of taking the dress back himself. If Carter was on the level, he would be annoyed but content as long as the dress made it home safely. If he wasn't—well, Sam didn't much care if he was angry, then. They'd be locked in a battle to the death.

The fact that he could even think that about the man he honored as a second father said too much about Sam's suspicions.

"I need to talk to you about something."

"You know I'm always here for you, boy." Carter's voice took on a homey singsong. A simple man with simple loyalties, it seemed to say.

"Had you ever met Pietro before?"

"No, of course not." His voice said clearly this wasn't the conversation he wanted to have.

Sam hung up the last towel. "He seemed to know you. He kept calling you boss. He didn't know Winspear's name."

"Like I said, Winspear must be using an alias. Winspear *is* an alias. You know as well as I do he's a Johnny-come-lately to the Company."

"Then how would the Knights know his information was of any value? You would think a strange vampire appearing at their doorstep would be staked. He must have credentials of some kind."

Carter was silent for a moment. "Winspear played a game darker than any of us really know. He was a trained assassin from the time of the Borgias. I'm sure he has credibility with all kinds of lowlife."

"True."

"Of course it's true."

"Unfortunate that Pietro died before we got more answers." Sam pushed a window open to let out the steam from the bath. The air smelled like Chloe's perfume.

"Don't criticize, boy. We were never going to get anything of value there."

How do you know? You broke his neck the moment he accused you of being a liar. Sam's gut knotted to a hard lump. "I worry Winspear is going to return here. He knows the layout. The staff trust him."

"You're worried about the girl."

"Chloe? Yes. She doesn't deserve any of this."

"She's a human and irrelevant. Vampires who moon after mortal women lose themselves."

"What does that mean?"

"They mate them. They feed so often they turn the

women." Carter's voice was thick with disgust. "Female vampires. No better than succubi."

But that woman and her mate are together forever. His heart lifted.

But Carter wasn't done. "And the men are useless afterward. Their loyalties are always with their women first. What good is that to the Company? They should owe their loyalty to me first and always."

Sam froze, really listening to what Carter was saying. Carter had made the rules about fraternizing with humans. The real reason he didn't like his warriors finding mates is because it eclipsed his authority. It was a question of power. *You keep us alone because you want to keep us obedient.*

Anger burned through Sam, his muscles tightening to the point of pain. Why hadn't he seen this before? Mind you, the only other time it had come up, Sam had barely become a vampire.

There had been his wife, Amy. He'd loved her fiercely, and still did. She'd been a woman of her time, gently raised and groomed to be a pillar of polite society. She'd had him wrapped around her delicate white fingers from the time he was in long pants.

After he'd been turned, he'd tried to go home, to find his wife in the country retreat up north where she'd taken the children. It hadn't worked. At the time, the thrill of having his new powers was impossible to conceal. After Carter had worked his dark magic, Sam had not only the semblance of life, but the strength of a Titan. He'd reveled in it. He hadn't tried to hide it.

His reunion with Amy had been the disaster of a single night. By dawn, she'd fled with the children, terrified that her husband had been possessed by devils. In some measure, she'd been right.

Carter intervened, blurring Amy's memories. She'd

spent the next year in a nurse's care. Grief, they'd called it. She'd only imagined that he'd come home because she wanted it so badly.

It had been then that Carter had given him the script. War wasn't made for love. Amy's mental breakdown was Sam's doing. And his children? Sam had watched them grow and have children of their own, but he hadn't dared come near them. What evil might he have sown in their lives? He had no choice but loneliness. He would destroy every human he loved.

Carter had known what damage a newly turned fledgling could do. He'd helped Sam convince himself of his own beastliness.

For centuries, Sam had felt a grief so deep it had no words.

"About the dress," Carter was saying.

Sam snapped back to the present, his gut a knot of hot, hard fury. "I can't get it right now. The place is crawling with humans. There is a wedding here in the morning. It will be much quieter after tomorrow."

Carter was silent for a moment. "We'll be in touch."

The line went dead, the silence filling Sam with disquiet. Personal issues aside, there were too many things that didn't add up. For one thing, if his maker had the authority of the King of Marcari behind him, why didn't he simply come forward openly? And where did Winspear fit into this? Were they working together?

He is my maker. He gave me life. He made me War.

The loyalties of so many years didn't die easily. His chest felt heavy, as if his heart had suddenly turned to a lump of iron.

Sam slipped back into Chloe's bedroom. She was curled on her side like a kitten, her knees drawn up into a ball. *We could be together forever.*

Carter forbade it.

Unless I break every rule in the book. Unless I find a way to be with her. Unless he turned his back on the Company. He would always honor the Throne, he had always been Marcari's ultimate champion, but how could he follow a maker who condemned him to darkness?

Maybe it was time War chose his own battles. It meant breaking every other bond he had, but what would he not give for a chance at real happiness?

She's mine. Did he seriously think he could give Chloe up? *Not bloody likely.* Straight arrows could have different targets, ones of their own devising.

Sam turned that idea over the way one might a candy melting on the tongue. Slowly, leisurely, tasting the pungent sweetness of disobedience.

He slid under the covers, curling around her, and held her as she slept.

Chloe woke alone. If her memories were befuddled for the first sixty seconds, her body was quick to remind her exactly what she'd been doing and how many times. For a moment, her breath left her, staggered by the memory. She fell back on the pillows, luxuriating in the sensations replaying themselves through her every cell.

The wedding!

She sat up so fast her head swam. Chloe stumbled to her dresser, groping for her phone. She hadn't set the alarm and panic was starting to ramp up inside her. What time was it? She had a wedding to put on.

At the same time, Sam's words replayed in her head. *I'm not ready to let you go. I don't think I'll ever be ready.*

Okay, so that was pretty straightforward, but what did it mean in practical terms? The mind-blowing sex was lovely, but when her life and her brain were at stake, she needed specifics. She had to talk to him.

She finally found her phone and thumbed it to life. Seven o'clock. She'd meant to get up at four. *Geez!* Chloe ran for her closet.

When she reached the teeming kitchens, Faran was already there. He'd been better than his word, not just helping with the menu but helping to cook it, too. His whites were splashed with food and he was piping something into tart shells at lightning speed. "These are savories," he said with a grin. "My own recipe. The venison is locally sourced. I, uh, hunted it myself."

Racks of finished tarts were set out to cool. They looked and smelled delicious, the crusts exactly the right shade of golden-brown. Chloe gave him her best smile, refusing to grapple with the image of Fido versus Bambi. *I hope there aren't any dog hairs in it.* "They smell fabulous," she said.

"Thanks." With only a cloth to protect his fingers, he pulled an enormous pan of the tarts out of the oven, releasing a mouthwatering cloud of warm spices. "I'll serve these with a piquant currant coulis."

"Sounds perfect." She had to shout over the clamor of pots and urgent voices bouncing off miles of stainless steel. It was at least a thousand degrees in there.

"The cake arrived," he put in. "It's in the walk-in for now."

"Did you look at it?"

"It's a bit purple, but it's a bit late to do anything about it."

Chloe took a look inside the fridge. *Okay.* The cake was huge, and when assembled would create a castle a good five feet tall. Chloe had asked for something in a mauve, but Faran was right. The baker had got into the spirit of the moment. The cake was a psychedelic purple, the surrounding hill a lime-green. The dragon clinging to the main tower was every bit as tall as the castle itself. When the dry ice was activated, curls of smoke would drift from the creature's nostrils. It was playful, colorful and full of personality. Elaine was going to love it.

Faran pushed through the crowd and stood beside her, wiping his hands on his apron. "When do you need to serve this?"

"It has to be on display by three o'clock. That's when the reception starts."

"All you can do now is embrace it's quirky spirit." He was staring at the cake, doing his best to keep a straight face.

"Mrs. Fallon is going to freak."

"Well, she likes unicorns. Unicorns *might* live in a bright purple castle."

Chloe kissed his cheek. "I've got it covered. I found dozens of tiny medieval toys. Knights. Unicorns. Fair ladies. The display is going to be a fabulous tableau."

Faran gave her a high five.

Outside, the sky was hazy with cloud, but it looked like the kind that would burn off after a few hours. Her staff was putting up the ribbons and bunting, decorating the chairs where the ceremony would be held, and setting up sound equipment under one of the pavilions. The champagne fountain was going to be a popular spot, so Chloe ordered another few cases be brought up just in case. Then she stopped to change the location where the string quartet was supposed to go. At the last minute, Iris Fallon had fired the harpist, since she wouldn't play suspended over the pool in a mermaid costume or wearing angel wings. The string players had thankfully been left unmolested in their tuxedos.

Chloe stopped in the barn to check on the faux unicorn. The horse, despite the shiny gold hooves, looked reasonably content. All in all, things were going fairly well.

By the time the ballroom, large dining room and the retiring rooms for the wedding party were perfect, the clock had jumped forward to noon. Guests were arriving in droves. Chloe felt like a mechanical car racing around a track, moving faster with every lap.

The wedding party was arriving. *Oh, crumb.* That meant Mrs. Fallon was on-site.

Chloe got the bride and her maids into their dressing room, ducked Iris and scurried off to make sure the group of madrigal singers knew where they were supposed to go.

One group of security had set up by the twin oak trees at the gate of the drive. They were stopping every car that came in, checking identification against the guest list. It was more stringent scrutiny than any other wedding Chloe had managed, but with the diamonds, the cream of the business and social worlds, and stray maniacs on the loose, it seemed prudent. Thankfully, the visitors were accepting it with good grace.

As she passed the gate, Sam caught her arm. He was wearing his industrial-strength sunglasses, and she realized they no longer bothered her. Now she understood exactly why he wore them. According to everything in Uncle Jack's vampire memorabilia, the undead were nocturnal creatures.

"How are you doing?" he asked, his voice like a caress.

"Good." Chloe leaned in to his touch. She wanted to talk about last night, but now wasn't the moment to discuss it. Until the ceremony had started, she would barely have time to think, let alone wrap her head around something as important as their future. "The guests are coming thick and fast. How's the security? Do we have enough bodies?"

Sam nodded, slipping back into guard mode. "I've called

Gravesend to send out a few dozen more. I think we have enough on-site, but I'd rather overdo it. After all, Oakwood has two hundred acres to keep track of. As it is we can't cover the whole perimeter. I'd rather set up patrols just in case."

Whatever Sam thought was a good idea was fine with her. "Perfect. Thanks. I'll find you later." She kissed him lightly and hurried off, leaving him alone in the shadow of the shattered oak tree where Jack had died.

She checked her phone again. Half an hour until the ceremony started. Everything was in place. Now she just had to cross her fingers and hope. She started back for the house, taking the shortcut between the overflow garage and the building where maintenance had its workshop.

A man was leaning against the side of the garage, smoking a cigar. She didn't recognize him, but given the crowd that wasn't a surprise. She nodded and smiled. He smiled back and stepped into her path.

"Hello, my girl," he said in a gruff voice. The man had a mane of gray-streaked hair and sunglasses much like Sam's. "Are you Chloe, Jack's niece?"

She stopped, wanting to get past him so she could begin herding the bridal party into place. Something always went wrong at the very last moment. But she fell back on good manners. "Yes, sir, I'm Chloe Anderson."

He rolled his cigar between thumb and forefinger. "My name is Aldous Carter. I was a friend to your uncle as I am to young Sam."

Chloe tensed. Anyone who described Sam as young either didn't know him very well, or was himself one of the undead. "I'm pleased to meet you."

"I'm sure you are." He took a puff on the cigar, the pungent scent of it tickling Chloe's nose. "Jack left you something I want. Sam seems reluctant to get it for me."

Chloe's alarm bells went off. It was too far to run back to the gate, especially in the shoes she was wearing, and the space between the two buildings was hidden from view. Anyone making a circuit of the grounds was sure to walk past without noticing.

Chloe decided to brazen it out. "I'm sure I don't know what you mean. I am organizing this wedding, Mr. Carter. I need to get back to the house. The ceremony is going to start shortly."

She started forward, prepared to shoulder her way past, but he raised his arm, planting his hand against the side of the workshop. Chloe stopped, her way effectively barred.

"I don't think so." Carter smiled. "You're my bargaining chip. Sam won't listen to me, but he wants you badly. If he's as far gone as I think, a fortune in diamonds is nothing compared to a chance to get between your legs again."

Chloe gasped, not at the vulgarity of what he said, but at the feel of cold iron against the back of her dress.

"Oh, yes," said Carter. "I brought some friends with me. I think you already met the late Pietro. Let me introduce you to his brothers."

"You were working with him?" she gasped. They'd all thought Mark Winspear was the traitor, but they'd been wrong.

He leaned forward, his face an inch from hers. "Still pleased to make my acquaintance, little girl?"

The words, and the way he said them, resonated through her. This was the man she'd shot in the foot the night she'd followed Sam into the garden! Chloe's throat closed with terror.

Chapter 27

Where am I?

Chloe gasped as the hood was pulled from her head. The air was stale, but far better than the sour-smelling cloth that had been jammed against her face. Her momentary relief was almost instantly replaced by fresh apprehension. Wherever they were, it was dark and damp and all too dungeonlike for comfort.

Anger choked her before she could frame any questions. Anger, laced with panic. Chloe struggled against the zip tie Pietro's brothers had used to bind her hands. They'd mercifully left her feet unbound, but she wasn't running anywhere. They'd shoved her into a chair, and Carter was looming over her, a flunky to either side. She was a bird surrounded by hungry cats.

"Now down to business," he said.

Her mind groped for what business that might be. She'd been standing by the garage, and then she was here, in this tiny dark room. She didn't remember anything in between. Zero. Nada. They'd taken her to their lair, and she had no idea where that was.

Disorientation swam through her. "Did you mess with my mind?"

He gave a sardonic smile. "I thought you might prefer hypnosis to being knocked over the head. It worked just as well on the security Sam had posted on the north gate. Good men. No match for me."

Chloe wasn't prepared to accept any of this. "There had to be hundreds of people at Oakwood. You can't just kidnap a person from the middle of a crowd! Somebody would have noticed."

He tsk-tsked. "People see what they want to see. Typically, they ignore anything that will cause inconvenience. Don't think the cavalry is going to come charging in to save you."

"Sam will."

"Will he?" Carter snorted. "True enough—I can smell Sam's presence on you. You've been his dinner before this."

"So?"

Carter's eyes widened, and she realized she'd made a mistake. She should have been doubtful or horrified, not accepting. She wasn't supposed to know what Sam was.

"Interesting." The tone of his voice made the flunkies stir. They'd been so quiet she'd almost forgotten them. "Sam, Sam. The boy never listens."

"What do you care?" She was growing colder, but she couldn't tell if it was the room or just the frozen depths of her fear. Her lips felt numb, too clumsy to work properly.

He fell back a step, face clenched in a look of pure frustration. "You should ask rather why *you* should care. As long as I direct his actions, the world is safe from him. You are safe."

"Who are you?" she asked, fighting to keep a quaver from her voice.

He ripped off the sunglasses, revealing furious, ice-blue eyes. "I *made* him. I found him all but dead, a great soldier shackled by the obligations of his species. He put everything between his potential and the great things he could achieve. A woman. His mewling brats. The poxy rabble he called his men. In the end, those obligations dragged him into the mud, his guts on the ground. I freed him of that. I made him War."

He grabbed a fistful of her hair, dragging her head back so that she was forced to look up at him. Chloe cried out, pain and fright struggling for supremacy.

"He's mine. He belongs to me. I hold his leash."

That made her blink. "His leash?"

"Vampires aren't house pets, my dear. They are machines of destruction, dedicated to the great work of the Company. But without a dominant influence, they are simply monsters. I do what I can to teach my boys the face of their evil, but learning can be slow. I never thought Sam would go back for seconds. Not after the first time."

"The first time?"

"His wife went mad." Carter released her, stomping in an agitated circle.

Chloe's head snapped forward, her scalp throbbing where he'd grabbed her hair. *His wife went mad.* She remembered. Amy, the wife of Ralston Samuel Hill. Sam's wife. *What happened to the poor woman?* "She eventually remarried."

"I took her memories."

Chloe shuddered, her own mind reeling. A wad of panic was trying to work its way up from her stomach. Already, her heart was starting to pound too fast.

Carter was pacing, his flunkies watching him. One had an automatic rifle cradled in his arms. Suddenly Carter wheeled, glaring at her. "You don't understand. What makes us powerful makes us beasts. It is the influence of demons. Only evil can come of this infection. Our souls are long destroyed."

"But Sam is a good man!"

"None of us is good." His face was a horrible mask of agony, as if he saw something that cracked his reason into splinters. "When the bloodlust was on me, I slaughtered my own wife and brats."

Chloe cringed, as much from the pain and rage in his voice as from what he said. She heard Pietro's brothers shift uneasily.

Carter leaned down, bringing his face far too close to hers. "I can't let Sam slide down that unholy path. I must bring him to heel. And you, you are too much temptation. He forgets his duty to me."

She could do nothing but stare back into his glassy eyes. She wasn't even sure he was seeing her, but might have been gazing on some spectacle from the sewers of his own brain.

The flunky with the gun pushed forward, breaking his trance. "Then take your revenge on him, or on her, I don't care. But do it later. Right now, we have a small opportunity to retrieve the diamonds."

Carter didn't take his eyes from her, but his expression focused to something more sane. "Where is the dress?"

Forcing herself to take a deep breath, she tried to still the tiny earthquakes of fear shaking her insides to pieces. "I'm not going to tell you. Once you have the dress, I'm as good as dead."

She watched him digest this. As long as she kept this maniac talking, that gave Sam more time to find her. He would find her. That's what Sam did.

But she miscalculated. He was done with conversation.

Carter's blow knocked her sprawling from the chair. One of the flunkies had to jump aside to avoid her body as it hit the floor.

* * *

Sam looked at his watch.

The natives were getting restless. He could hear their muttering all the way down at the gate. According to Chloe's timetable, the ceremony was about to start. All the guests seem to have arrived, because no cars had come by for a good quarter hour.

He looked up at the shattered tree, wondering what Jack would have thought of turning his place over for a wedding like this. He probably would have liked it. Jack had always been up for a party.

Sam, however, was not enjoying himself. He was worried about Chloe. She'd greeted him warmly enough just now, but the look in her eyes spoke of unfinished business, of serious conversations yet to be had. Maybe she still thought he was going to erase her mind and abandon her, no matter what he had told her with his body.

Sam heaved an inward sigh. Women were so bad at interpreting wordless devotion. With them it was always talk, talk, talk. In his youth, they had begged for letters and poems. Sam had received a good education, but no schoolmaster had prepared him for writing love poetry. By the nine hells, he was thankful modern women were over that fashion.

He turned to the security guard standing a dozen feet away. "I'm going up to the house."

"See if they can send down some sandwiches and water," the guard suggested. "This is going to be a long day."

Sam agreed and started up the road. He entered the house as soon as he could to get out of the penetrating sun. Most of the crowd had shifted to the lawn where the ceremony was to take place, but Iris Fallon was still at the house, storming from room to room. She wore a peach chiffon pantsuit that billowed as she moved. It made him think of old paintings of the Furies, drapery aflutter as they chased their victims down and ripped off their heads.

Iris slid to a halt in front of Sam, her heels scraping on Jack's hardwood floor. "Where is that chit of a planner? Where is she?"

Chit? "I don't know, ma'am," Sam replied, centuries of good manners forcing him to be polite. "I last saw Chloe about an hour ago." *Call her a chit again and I'll forget that I was raised to be a gentleman.*

"I need her here now!" she seethed. "I've had the security men look everywhere for her. This is insupportable. I'm paying her to be on the spot!"

"I'll find her," Sam said soothingly. He was looking for Chloe anyway.

"And bring that unicorn from the stables."

Sam didn't reply to that one. Despite his calm tone, doubt nagged at him. He knew how important this event was to Chloe. If she wasn't here, where was she?

Taking a guess, Sam headed for the kitchen. Kenyon was there, filling trays with tiny bites of this and that. "Have you seen Chloe?"

The werewolf looked up. He was dusty with flour but looked completely happy. "She was here a while ago." He glanced at the clock on the wall. "She should be with the wedding party."

Sam felt his doubts grow sharp claws. "She's not there. It sounds like they've looked everywhere."

A strained look came over Kenyon's face.

"What?"

"Chloe's under a lot of pressure, what with the thieves and the wedding and…whatever."

Sam grabbed the front of the werewolf's whites. "What are you saying?"

Kenyon's eyes held pools of sadness. "I'm sorry, I've been where you are."

"What are you talking about?" Sam forced himself to let go of his friend.

"I just can't help remembering what happened when Lexie and I got close."

"What do you mean?"

He almost saw Kenyon clam up, as if a steel wall had slammed across his face.

"What do you mean?" Sam growled.

"Well," he said carefully. "When things didn't work out, Lexie took off. Dropped off the face of the earth for months and months. You know those two women are like sisters, right?"

Sam just stood there, feeling whatever semblance of life he had draining away.

Kenyon looked around the room as if checking for eavesdroppers, and then leaned close. "Is there any chance that Lexie might have talked Chloe into running away?"

Chapter 28

Pain shot through Chloe's shoulder as she landed, followed moments later by a burning in her jaw. Tears leaked from her eyes as she clutched the floor, afraid to get up in case he knocked her down again.

Her mind was a turmoil of fear, but anger had taken control. They could take her life, but she could cling to her will—at least for a little bit longer. Yes, everyone broke eventually, but Jack Anderson's niece was going to make them work for it.

Rough hands heaved her up and dropped her back into the chair. It was one of Pietro's brothers. "Where is it?" the man asked in heavily accented English.

Chloe tried to open her mouth, but her jaw hurt too much. She started to cry from pain and exhaustion. Mortified, she pressed her bound hands to her face.

"This is useless," Carter grumbled.

The other Knight spoke up. "Can't you pull it out of her mind?"

"I can erase something. Finding a fact is different."

"Is it impossible?"

"It takes time. Once something passes from short- to long-term memory, it becomes hard to find."

The one with the gun broke in. "Don't worry about being neat. Do it, then kill her."

"No!" Chloe managed to get the word out. *The least you can do is let me die with my mind in one piece!*

Someone pounded on the door. The men fell silent.

"It's security! Anyone in there? We're looking for Chloe Anderson."

Chloe took a breath to cry out. The next instant, one of the Knights clamped a hand over her mouth. He bent, putting his mouth to her ear. "Wrong move."

The security guard turned the door handle and rattled it, but it was locked.

"You got a key?" someone asked.

"Not to this room," another voice answered.

The pressure of the Knight's hand pained Chloe's bruised jaw. She whimpered, tears leaking from the corners of her eyes. With a shiver, she felt the cold iron of a gun under her right ear. The others stood silent, barely breathing, until she heard the footsteps of the security guards move away.

The Knight with the gun growled. "Try and call out again and you can watch your brains redecorate the wall."

She squeezed her eyes shut, giving herself the blessed relief of not seeing those three horrible faces. She was on the edge of throwing up. But a thought niggled—security men had been just outside that door. Where was she?

With her eyes closed, she could hear how badly her breathing rasped with tension. For a moment that filled her world, but another sound began to press in on her. Voices. Many, many voices.

Chloe opened her eyes and studied the wall in front of her with renewed interest. It was old, unfinished concrete, but there was shelving along one side. She let distant memory fill in the rest of the scene. Once, that shelving had been full of wine crates. *We're beneath Oakwood!*

That meant the voices she heard were upstairs, probably in one of the reception rooms. Now things were beginning to make sense. There was an underground utility passage from the basement to the workshop where they had grabbed her—it would have been easy to bring her here unseen.

Relief, almost a fierce joy, revived her dwindling will.

She worked her jaw to see if it would move. It was still horribly stiff, aching worse than any root canal she could remember.

The man with the gun dug the barrel into her skull. "Where is the dress?"

"It's in the study," she mumbled.

Carter's head snapped in her direction. "The study?"

"In a safe. Behind the painting of a soldier."

There was indeed a hidden compartment in the study. The dress, however, was in the safe in Jack's bedroom. But she was in the business of buying time, not providing accuracy.

"What's the combination?" Carter demanded.

"It's written down. I don't remember." *Where is Sam?* It was past time he put his superhero tights on and showed up.

"I can get anything open," said the smaller Knight. "The problem is getting through the house unseen."

Carter looked thoughtful. "This is a big wedding. There are so many strangers and workmen in the house, no one will notice a few more. Not even men carrying tools."

The men looked at each other. The Knight with the gun spoke. "One cracksman, two lookouts minimum in a busy location. Someone has to watch the prisoner. We're a man short."

She watched Carter's face and could see him make the

decision. "You'll have to make do with one lookout. Tie her to the chair and go. If she's wasting our time, I'll shoot her."

Sam was stunned. Would Chloe leave?

He stormed out of the kitchen, ignoring the sunlight that slammed against his skin like the blast from an oven. Iris Fallon swooped down on him.

"Mr. Ralston, where is Chloe?"

He stopped short, struggling to put his fangs away. The woman was in his way. He barely stopped himself from sweeping her aside. "I don't know."

"Well, who is going to fix this?"

"Fix what?

"The madrigal singers are wearing green. I distinctly said the color theme of the wedding was mauve and gold."

He felt his instinctive manners unraveling at a dangerous rate. "Are they any good?"

"Of course they are. I chose them."

He clenched his jaw a long moment before he spoke. "Then no doubt people are listening too hard to notice the outfits."

She inhaled in short, jerky gasps. Sam could tell she was about to start crying, or perhaps shrieking with rage. In time-honored male fashion, he looked around for another woman to handle it.

Elaine was standing in the hall, touchingly beautiful in her wedding gown. She looked lost. "Chloe was supposed to tell me when to start the procession. They've seated Grandma, Leo's there at the altar, but—" She waved her hands helplessly.

Sam swallowed. He knew the look. He'd seen it on soldiers who needed a leader. They knew what to do, but they needed somebody to point them at the target. "Now. Do it now. You're the bride. Everyone will follow your lead."

"But I can't get on that horse without help! Not in this skirt."

Sam thought of Chloe, and how badly she'd wanted this wedding to work. Fixing this was the least he could do.

"Come with me," he said to Elaine, giving her his arm.

They walked onto the lawn. Elaine's father was holding the head of the white horse. The stuffed unicorn horn Mrs. Fallon had demanded was thankfully absent. Against all odds, good taste had prevailed.

"Hang on," Sam said to the bride, and lifted her onto the saddle.

Elaine settled easily, obviously comfortable with horses, and lowered her veil. "Thank you, Mr. Ralston."

Iris appeared at Sam's elbow and handed up the bouquet. She stared at her daughter a long time, her expression growing soft.

"You're beautiful," she said. "Never forget that."

"Thanks, Mom," Elaine said in a quavering voice, and her father led her away. The horse began the long procession that would lead it to the aisle. The whole path was strewn with flowers, the way marked by tall, ribboned poles crowned with tumbling sprays of roses.

Iris stood for a moment, her lower lip trembling. Then she swallowed. "That cake is purple. And it has toys on it."

"Forget the cake," Sam said. "You're going to miss the wedding. Go watch your beautiful daughter get married."

Iris gave him a long look. "You're right."

And she went to watch the ceremony she had so meticulously planned.

A few minutes later, the wedding was under way. Now that it was in motion, the event would unfold as it should. Chloe had organized everything down to the last ice cube.

Sam slipped from the back of the crowd, ready to resume

his search of the grounds. He caught the flash of a camera. Lexie Haven was darting around the sidelines, catching the candid moments between the bride and groom. If she had planned to leave with Chloe, it hadn't happened yet.

Then Chloe is still here! Sam quickened his pace, moving toward the house. The Fallon woman said security had looked "everywhere." Jack's security guards were human, though. They weren't him.

Sam stopped cold. There was a man standing in the shadow of the porch. *Winspear.*

The doctor beckoned.

Suspicion, anger and worry collided. Sam stormed toward him with the brute fury of an avalanche. He hadn't seen him since the night of the firefight at the gazebo. The night Winspear had snatched the fake wedding dress.

He grabbed Plague by the front of his shirt and slammed him against the side of the porch. "What in the nine hells are you up to?"

The doctor looked tired, his already pale face bone-white with strain. "Hello to you, too, Sam."

"You've gone over to their side. Why?"

"Have I?"

"You shot at us. You shot at Chloe!"

"And the little minx shot back and actually hit me. Believe me, if I wanted you dead, you'd be pushing up daisies. For centuries I earned my livelihood taking out oafs like you."

There was every chance that someone could pass by and see their argument, but there was no one around right then. That was good enough for Sam. He closed one hand around Winspear's windpipe, lifting him enough that his feet dangled free.

Sam realized the low, vibrating growl was coming from

him. Fury swirled in his gut. Chloe was in danger, and so much of it seemed woven around the doctor's betrayal.

Within seconds, Plague began to struggle, a strangled noise rattling from his throat. Suffocation wouldn't kill him, but a crushed windpipe would be painful. Severing his spine would finish the job.

"Wait!" he managed to croak.

Sam released him, but just enough so that he could speak. With a violent push, Winspear broke the hold the rest of the way.

"Listen to me, Ralston. Two Knights are ransacking Jack's study. They're looking for the diamonds. I caught a glimpse of Carter, too. He's the leak. He's betrayed us to the Knights."

Sam had suspected it, but Winspear's words still fell like a blow. "So have you."

"No. I've been working both sides to find out who the informant is. That's why I was at the gazebo. When the grapevine hummed with word that you were going to hand off the dress, I had to know who showed up. I also wanted to make sure the diamonds were safe."

Irritation flashed through Sam. "The dress was a decoy. I'm not that stupid."

"I couldn't take that chance. You've always followed orders to the letter."

"It seems we're getting bad orders these days."

"I'm sorry. I know Carter was your maker. I couldn't take the chance that you'd side with him if I decided to take him down. You're loyal, Sam."

Sam's brain was righting itself, feeling as bruised and sore as someone who'd fallen down a long flight of stairs. Winspear had been undercover. It made sense. It was also a huge relief. Something unknotted in his heart, and he stepped back, giving the doctor room.

"I'm loyal to the Horsemen."

"Good." A smile flickered over Winspear's face, and was gone.

Sam gripped his friend's arm, an apology without words. "Carter knows our names, how we work, everything. If he tells the Knights of Vidon…"

Winspear nodded slowly. "Our vulnerabilities will be exposed. He wants to take the diamonds and run. If he slips through our fingers today, we may never catch him."

Sam spoke the words that had been pounding through him like a pulse. "Chloe's missing."

Winspear's face grew paler still. "They think she's the key to the dress. We have to find Carter *now*."

Chapter 29

Carter prowled the room. Chloe followed the restless movements, her stomach squeezing a little tighter every time he changed direction. It was as if he were winding himself up, the spring of his nerves—and hers—cranking tighter with every circuit.

Carter was her only guard. Before they'd left for the study, the two Pietros had lashed her feet together and bound her to the chair with thick nylon rope. Then they'd cut the zip tie binding her hands and then secured her hands behind her with her own silk scarf. Someone had forgotten to bring extra zips. It didn't matter. They knew their business; there was no way she was loosening the knots.

Carter went back and forth. He looked as if he was as tense as she was. Unless he snapped out of it, all those demons he ranted about might come out and play.

Chloe took a shaking breath. "Mr. Carter?"

His head snapped around in a disturbingly snakelike motion.

"Why are you working with those men? Pietro's brothers?"

He was silent long enough that she thought he wouldn't answer, but then he spoke in a quiet voice. "I have worked for the Company for centuries, but nothing changes. I would say that whatever experiment Marcari has run has been allowed to go on long enough."

"I don't understand."

"Vampires, even with the most rigorous discipline, cannot be wholly tamed. They've been allowed to exist long enough. My intention is that the Knights of Vidon prevail."

Chloe didn't pretend to understand, but she grasped enough to almost feel pity. Carter had murdered his family, and his sense of guilt had eventually driven him crazy. Somewhere in the kaleidoscope of that madness, he'd decided controlling other vampires with an iron fist was no longer enough. Only the ultimate act of control—killing them—was going to satisfy his self-loathing. It would mean destroying himself, but not until he'd done as much damage to the Company as he could.

But she still had one question. "What do you want with Princess Amelie's wedding dress?"

The overhead light cast harsh shadows over the rough-hewn lines of his face. "To level the playing field. Marcari has monsters. Vidon has few resources to match that. The diamonds will go a long way to buying humankind a fighting chance."

As he spoke, he'd moved closer and closer until she could feel the brush of his clothes against her. By the look in Carter's eyes, his demons were feeling frisky. Involuntarily, she jerked, scooting the chair an inch to the right.

He didn't seem to notice, but just stared down at her like a bird sizing up a worm.

I have to keep him talking. "Then where did my uncle fit in?"

He scowled, distracted.

Good.

"Jack? He suspected what I was doing, so I stopped him before he could interfere."

Her brain stopped for a moment, frozen by sheer fury. Then heat began creeping up her body, like a flame of rage rushing up from her belly. "You killed him!"

She flung herself against her bonds.

"No." Carter's look was almost a sneer. "But I caused it to be done."

Her chest shredded inside. The pain and loss felt like pieces of her soul falling away, leaving only an ache in their place. "I hate you." Her voice was dull, the words spoken without much emotion at all. She hurt beyond ranting.

Carter's eyebrows lifted slightly. "It's an understandable reaction. Nevertheless it had to be done."

"I loved him. He looked after me." All of a sudden her anger began to rush back. Her throat began to close, choked by a need to scream and cry. Maybe tear Carter's head off his shoulders.

"When faced with true darkness, love doesn't matter."

Chloe looked into his face, studying it hard. There wasn't any remorse. *He's crazy. Absolutely mad.*

A cold, clinical need to survive took over. Rage wouldn't help her. Her wits might. "What about Jessica Lark?"

Carter shrugged. "I don't know who killed her. I don't know why. She didn't have the diamonds when she died. Lark didn't matter anymore."

"Did you know Uncle Jack had them?"

"Not until you pulled them out of his safe, little girl. That was one deadly inheritance."

"How did you know out about the safe?"

"We had a man on the inside."

The one Sam had found dead in the car. *So many dead.* Chloe swallowed down fresh horror. Details were falling into place, but there was no time now to think about what they meant. Not unless she wanted to join the body count.

Carter reached out to touch her, maybe put a hand on her shoulder. Chloe jerked again, the chair skidding farther to the right. Carter stepped forward, reaching, and she tried to repeat the motion. Instead, the chair overbalanced, tipping her over backward.

Chloe yelped, trying to tuck and roll. Bound as she was, she was helpless as a doll. The impact drove the slats of the chair into her back. Pain fountained through her hands as they were crushed between the chair and the floor.

Nausea swam through her, not helped by the fact she was nearly upside down, her head toward the wall and the empty shelving partially obscuring her view. They'd tied her feet together, but hadn't bound them to the chair legs. They dangled awkwardly, her right foot minus its shoe.

Carter loomed over her, hands on his hips, but she couldn't see anything above his collar. "I think we've talked enough, little Chloe." His hands moved to linger over the weapons strapped to his sides.

Sam, now would be a good time to rescue me.

A twitch of Carter's fingers sent adrenaline rushing through her. Her feet kicked up, knocking the long wooden shelves from their brackets. Chloe angled the move forward, so the clattering boards flew at Carter. He jumped back to avoid them. A few of the brackets unhooked from the strapping, falling to the floor with a ring of metal. One skidded under Carter's heel, sending him tumbling to the ground.

The move also rolled the chair. The knots in the fat nylon rope slipped enough to let her wriggle upward, working the loops of rope over the top of the chair. She tucked her legs up, catching her heels on the seat of the chair and pushed.

The chair scraped along the floor, and then she was free of it. The entire maneuver took no more than seconds.

She managed to push herself to her feet. Her ankles were lashed too tightly together to do more than wobble. Bracing herself against the wall was the best she could do.

Carter was already standing, watching her with grim amusement. Letting the mouse run a bit before he batted it with his paw. *Fine. Let him.*

"Hope can be such a sad emotion in the end," Carter said, reaching her in two strides.

He grabbed her throat and began squeezing. He could have shot her, but something in his face said hands-on murder would be so much more satisfying. He would drag it out by inches.

Chloe felt her pulse pounding, echoing through her skull. Breath wouldn't come. She writhed, feeling the delicate architecture of her throat begin to crush. She made a gagging, gurgling noise she'd never heard any creature make before.

He was just too strong to fight back.

I'm going to die.

They caught two Knights of Vidon in Jack's study, sizing up the safe. Moments later, Sam and Winspear were dragging the two down the service stairway.

"Where's Carter?" Sam tightened his grip on the captive man's arm to a crushing pressure. "Where is Chloe Anderson?"

The question reverberated in the empty stairwell. Sam was aware of the distant murmur of voices, the smell of cooking, the pale beige paint of the walls. Most of all, he was conscious of the bruising flesh beneath his fingers. Soon, it would be breaking bone.

He had to find Chloe.

The man let out a ragged groan. Winspear's Knight

winced, his eyes flying wide at the sound. "Stop it! You already killed one brother!"

Sam saw his opportunity. "Who?"

"Pietro!"

"I didn't kill him. Carter snapped his neck to keep him from talking."

"Impossible!"

Sam met the man's gaze. He had limited sympathy for slayers, but Carter had murdered their brother when he was helpless and then lied about it. That offended his sense of honor. "Believe what you like, but I'm telling you the truth."

The Knight doing the talking didn't say another word, but grew deathly pale.

Sam knew he had him. "I'll let this brother live if you answer my question."

One word escaped the bloodless lips. "Basement."

Sam released his grip, feeling his prisoner sag in relief. "Let's go."

Once they were down the stairs, it took little encouragement to extract which room Chloe and Carter were in.

"How about we use their heads for battering rams?" Sam growled when confronted with the storeroom's locked door.

"Too mushy." Winspear banged it open with one well-planted kick.

Sam tossed the Knights through the door. They flailed nicely until the floor stopped them. Mark drew his weapon, training it on the men. Sam pushed past them, a half dozen strides taking him into the cellar. As he moved, he swept the area with the nose of his gun. There were shelves and metal brackets strewn across the floor.

Sam turned just in time to see Chloe dangling from Carter's hand. She crumpled to the floor when Sam's maker released her throat.

He froze, not wanting to comprehend what he was seeing. *Chloe!* Memories, feelings, hopes smashed together, leaving him blind and deaf for a split second. Everything he cared about was plummeting into the abyss, about to shatter beyond repair.

She wasn't dead—yet—but she was badly hurt, breath rasping through her horribly bruised throat. And, with Carter armed and only inches away, she was still in terrible danger. Sam ached to run to her, but first he had to destroy the threat.

His fangs came out. *"You hurt my woman."*

"You're mine," Carter said. "My tool. My War."

"Never again." Sam's voice came out in a rasp.

"Your duty is to me."

Words. Words didn't have a place in Sam's head right then. Rage reared up inside him like a dragon unfurling huge, black wings.

Carter didn't seem to understand that he was about to perish. "You know I'm right. You're the straight arrow."

"You betrayed us to the Knights. That makes you the target."

Sam moved in a blur, closing the distance between them and smashing his fist into Carter's face. He didn't hold back. In one wrench, he tore his maker's shoulder holster apart, flinging his weapons across the room. The move had been easy because Carter had not expected it. The older vampire blocked the next blow, showing his teeth in a savage hiss. The fight was on.

It had to end quickly. Chloe was hurt. Drawing his gun, Sam aimed for the head, but Carter kicked it from his hand in a move even Sam's vampire sight didn't catch. A roundhouse kick followed, forcing Sam to fall back. Behind him, Mark was yelling something. Sam could feel the tide of the fight struggling to turn against him.

No. He dove forward, ducking under Carter's guard to

grapple him. For a moment it was a battle of raw power, strength against brutal strength. Sam had the physical advantage, but Carter had fought him time and again on the training field. There were few moves he didn't know.

Except Carter didn't practice with a werewolf. Sam twisted, thinking to fling the other man down. It was the same move he had used on Kenyon the last time he'd run the testing field.

But Chloe sat up. Sam's heart leaped with relief.

It was the distraction Carter needed. He slammed Sam to the ground instead. Sam's teeth rattled with the force of the blow. Carter's eyes were wild as he tried to pin him, but Sam rolled, breaking Carter's grip. Cold metal pressed into his hip. He groped, hoping for a blade.

It was a metal bracket, the type that held up cheap shelving. Sam barely registered the fact before he plunged it into Carter's throat. Blood spurted, showering Sam, the floor, the walls and ceiling.

A wound to the throat wasn't enough to kill a vampire, but it would slow him down. Or so he thought. Carter pounced. This time Sam grabbed him, wrestling his maker to the floor like he had the wolf. This time, there was no mistake.

He wrenched the bracket from Carter's throat, and then plunged it into the vampire's heart. Rage began to separate into distinct thoughts and images. The wreck of Jack's car. Carter's lies that night at the Salmon Tail. Chloe crumpled on the floor.

Mark kicked Sam the gun he had dropped. He picked it up. "No one hurts my friends." Sam aimed the piece. "And no one hurts the woman I love."

Carter's head exploded. The blast rang through the tiny room like a grenade. Sam rose and looked down at his handiwork. Not even an undead was coming back from that.

Instantly, he went to Chloe, who was staring at him with wide, amazed eyes. She had pulled herself to a sitting position, propped against the wall. She held herself stiffly, taking quick, shallow breaths. She was obviously in pain. He fell to his knees beside her. "You need a doctor. Winspear!"

"Holding bad guys prisoner over here. If you want to cover them, I'd be delighted to help."

Sam wanted to go and needed to stay. He wrenched apart the silk scarf binding her wrists. Chloe clutched his sleeve, her grip weak as a baby's. He covered her chilled hand with his own, feeling the ache in her swollen, red fingers like it was his own.

"Just hold me," she whispered. "That's all I need."

"I'm filthy."

"I don't care." She leaned into him, and he gathered her in his arms and held her as she wept out the aftermath of fear and pain. "You came when I needed you."

"Always." He pressed his lips to her hair and clung to the light that had finally broken the chains of his lonely darkness.

Chapter 30

This is Gossip Quest TV News Magazine, *bringing you the latest update on the surprise event of the season. Kidnapping! Stolen diamonds! Who knew that a wedding could be the scene of so much derring-do? A week has passed, and we still have so few facts. Will we ever find out what was really behind the supersecret showdown in the basement of Oakwood Manor? Every branch of law enforcement this news reporter contacted refused comment.*

What we do know is that this event has made the front page of bridal magazines everywhere. As drama unfolded below ground, an utterly fabulous event was happening in Oakwood's gardens. News cameras could not help capturing the decorations, the food and that fabulous cake! According to those in the know, society weddings haven't seen such fresh and natural elegance in decades. You can bet that Chloe's Occasions, the wedding design firm responsible for the spectacular nuptial event, is now on every bride-to-be's speed dial....

Chloe clicked off the TV, silencing the hyperventilating news anchor. A brief, rueful chuckle escaped her. Ironically, after planning the so-called event of the season, she had missed most of the actual wedding.

After a stay in the hospital—the injuries to her neck and throat had given the doctors pause—she was finally setting her old bedroom to rights, removing the last traces of the night she was attacked. The housekeeper had replaced the mattress and bed linens, and sunlight poured through the curtains, turning everything bright and cheerful. It looked as though nothing had happened.

Except that it had, and things kept happening. This afternoon, she had received a request from Mark Winspear to meet her in Jack's study.

Is this the moment when Mark erases everything about the Company and its personnel from my mind? Or just parts of it? Who decides what I get to keep?

Her stomach clenched with anger. It was unfair. For a moment she envied Lexie, but there was no way she could point to her friend as an example of a human woman who could keep a secret. That would get Lexie and Faran in trouble, too.

Nevertheless, she would somehow prevail. If she'd found a compromise between Iris and Elaine, she could negotiate a compromise with the Company. They owed her that much after their director had kidnapped and nearly strangled her.

Slowly, painfully, Chloe pulled on a light linen jacket that hid the multicolored bruises on her arms. Some of her fingers were taped, the joints sprained and a few small bones fractured when she'd fallen on her bound hands. Her neck was badly bruised, too, but a soft scarf hid the worst. She had no intention of looking like a victim.

Just before she left her bedroom, she slid a small digital recorder into the pocket of her jacket. If Mark Winspear did tamper with her memory, she meant to have some clue to follow so that she could reconstruct these past few weeks.

She walked into Jack's study as firmly as her aching body would allow. A glance around told her that Mark was alone, sitting at the desk with his dark head bent over a sheaf of papers. He rose when she entered the room. To her surprise, she saw the wedding dress draped over one of the overstuffed chairs, diamonds shimmering in the dim light.

"What are you doing with that?" she asked tightly. "Why isn't it in the safe?"

"I thought you might want to say farewell," Mark replied. "Half a dozen of the most trusted palace guards will be here tonight. With your permission, Faran and I will return with them as escorts for the dress."

"Not Sam?"

Mark was silent. She crossed the room to where the dress lay, touching the soft layers of silk and lace. It was good to think she'd fulfilled her uncle's request to see the gown returned to the princess, but watching it go would be like saying goodbye to Jack all over again.

"I thought we should talk," he added. "I'm leaving tonight, and there are things you and I have to settle."

He walked around the desk to face her. She reached into her pocket and switched on the recorder.

"It seems strange talking to you," she said quietly. "I thought you were the evil genius behind everything."

He gave a bark of laughter, turning his face away to hide who knew what emotion. He wasn't an easy man to read, but the moment gave Chloe a chance to study his body language. He was more slightly built than Sam, but no less deadly. A rapier instead of a broadsword. And every line in his body said he was more than a little uncomfortable.

Finally, he shrugged. "I don't blame you for being suspicious."

He reached over, plucked the recorder out of her pocket and switched it off.

"I was working both sides of the game," he said. "And by the way, Vampires can hear these things working. I wouldn't try that again if I were you."

Chloe colored and took the recorder as he handed it back to her. "You were a double agent?"

"More or less. Your uncle and I knew something was wrong. I was the logical choice to go undercover."

In the past few days, Sam had told her about Jack's role with the Horsemen. It had made her proud and sad. She wished she could talk to her uncle about what he'd done and seen. "Not Sam?"

"No one would believe Sam as a turncoat."

Which implied they would believe it of Mark. She couldn't quite tell what he thought about that.

She waited a beat, wanting to get on to the subjects that interested her most, like whether he was going to scrub her brain. He didn't say anything but seemed to be waiting for her to speak.

Finally, she asked a question just to break the silence. "Did you know it was Carter from the start?"

"Not at first. We knew there was a leak at Company headquarters. We began to suspect half the scandals around the prince's love affairs were untrue, created to damage his reputation and his relationship with Princess Amelie. Then there was an attempt on the princess right after the wedding was called off. It served its purpose to finish destabilizing the truce between Marcari and Vidon."

Despite herself, despite the reason she was there, that piqued her curiosity. "When Lady Beatrice was shot?"

Mark gave her an appraising look. "Yes."

"I read about it." She shifted painfully from one foot to the other. She was still in too much discomfort to stand for long.

He caught the gesture and motioned to the couch. "Please, sit. I am forgetting all my courtesy."

They both sat, each in one corner, with a neutral distance between them. Mark still looked uneasy but carried on with his story. "The shooter was mesmerized by a powerful mind. There aren't many of us who can do such a seamless job. That's when I began to wonder about Carter. The fact that the shooter got by Sam's security net was suspicious in itself. He doesn't make that kind of mistake."

"Why didn't you warn Sam?"

"Warn him of what? I had no proof. Carter was our superior. I don't accuse anyone of treason without solid evidence. Accuracy is serious when the wrong word could cost a life. So I did what I could. I went to find answers."

Chloe heard the edge of steel in his words. "I see."

"Perhaps." He didn't sound convinced. "Perhaps your adventure in the cellars gives you a glimpse of what kind of danger we deal with."

"I don't kid myself that it was more than a glimpse."

"Good. If you'd answered any other way, I would have thought you a fool." He gave her a long, narrow look.

She didn't know Mark Winspear, but something told her he would be a bad enemy to have.

"Will putting an end to this affair help smooth things over between Marcari and Vidon?" she asked.

"The Knights will not tolerate a truce with Marcari, regardless of what treaties are signed. The King of Vidon plans to break publicly with the Knights once a purge of the palace guard is complete. I'm sure the treachery will be harder to stamp out for good, but at least it will not continue under the palace roof."

"Is there any chance the royal wedding might go ahead?"

Mark's dark face was thoughtful. "I don't know."

She nodded, looking down at her bandaged hands. "It

would be a shame for that dress to go to waste. A lot of people put themselves on the line to get it back to the princess. Who will take Carter's place?"

"I don't know," Mark replied. "There will be an inquest, but no one blames Sam for what he did. Once that is over, the King of Marcari will appoint someone new."

A silence fell between them.

"I want you to know something," Mark said quietly. "Vampires are not human. We do everything more intensely. When we make war, entire cities die. When we love, it's forever and with every cell of our beings."

The intensity of his words rattled her. "You sound like you know what you're talking about."

He pressed his lips together, giving a slow nod. "I see what's going on between you and Sam. I've lost one good friend this month, and I don't have many left."

Apprehension quivered in Chloe's chest. "I don't understand."

"You know it is my job to erase your memories of the Horsemen."

The words fell like a hammer blow, and she felt her insides coil tight. She should have listened to Lexie. She should have run before the wedding. She could have run after, but she had foolishly believed shedding her own blood to protect the dress would make the vampires spare her.

Chloe nodded, unable to speak. If she did, her pride would fail her. She would grovel.

"Carter made those rules." Mark said the name as if it tasted foul. "He believed vampires were intrinsically evil. Much of that fear came from his own early experience. He had been turned and abandoned by his maker. There was no one to help him make the transition, things went horribly wrong and that trauma festered over time. Yet there was a certain truth to his beliefs."

"How so?"

"A vampire in love is more than a little crazy. He will find it hard to put anything before his beloved. In effect, he would give up everything for her sake."

Chloe finally found her voice. "Humans aren't that different."

Mark raised an eyebrow. "Would you leave everything for a man you love?"

"Is that a trick question?"

"No tricks. I'm just curious."

"I believe in love that strong."

Something in his face grew harder. "Would you leave everything for Sam? If we asked, would you give up everything to be with him?"

The odd tone of his voice made her turn around, her injured neck protesting at the movement. Sam was standing in the doorway, his face carefully schooled, not a shred of emotion showing.

Anger sliced through her. "What does it matter what I am willing to give up if you're going to steal my memories?"

"It's the only thing that matters," Sam said, his rough voice giving away the pain his face was hiding.

Chloe weighed what she was going to say next. She was here to have her memory wiped. Until that was off the table, nothing else made sense. "I don't want to say goodbye to you, or Mark, or Faran. It's like an entire world has opened to me. I'm living and walking and talking with miracles."

"I've not been called that before." Sam gave a wry smile.

"You are miraculous. You've saved my life time and again. You kept Elaine's wedding from falling to pieces. You defend the people you love and protect things you care about. That's more than wonderful all on its own. So you're a creature of legend. That's gravy."

"I bet you've not been called 'gravy' before, either," Mark said dryly.

"I'm not going to talk about sacrifice." Chloe rose, circling the room to face both men. The movement put her next to the dress. She reached out and stroked the frothy skirt. "I know my job. I know what makes couples work. Every relationship is a compromise, but love doesn't count costs. If you feel that bad about what you're giving up, you'd better take a step back and ask yourself if you're really in love after all."

She turned to Sam and touched his face with her bruised, bandaged fingers. Everything she felt, every pain, every joy throbbed in her voice. "I don't think the real question is what I give up, but what I bring. What you bring. We're infinitely richer by being in love. We don't lose by being together."

Sam caught her hand so gently that she barely felt the pressure of his touch. And then he kissed it, pressing his lips to her damaged fingers with infinite care. "But you might lose. Carter was only one person. There is an entire army of Knights."

"I know," she replied softly. "But I will manage as long as you don't keep secrets from me. Don't shut me out."

Sam blinked. "I promise not to do that."

"Then believe in the joy we'll have, and we'll take the rest as it comes."

Sam's gray gaze caressed her. "Nine hells, I love you, Chloe Anderson."

Chloe turned to Mark. "Does this mean you're not messing with my head? I mean—"

The doctor held up a hand to stop her words. He looked as if he wished he could vanish under the couch. "Those were Carter's rules. I don't feel obligated to rescue Sam from your depraved clutches."

Chloe released the breath she'd been holding. With a low chuckle, Sam pulled her to the safe space within the circle of his arms.

Mark shook his head. "I think he likes those clutches just the way they are."

Chapter 31

Later, Chloe and Sam went for a walk in the moonlit garden.

She was as irritated as a woman madly in love could get. "Mark had no intention of wiping my memories. Why on earth didn't you just say so?"

Sam was quiet for a moment. "Lexie left Kenyon. It was entirely possible you'd want to back out of any association with the Company. There would have been more to consider then."

"I hadn't thought of that." She was suddenly sorry for Lexie. What had gone on that the two of them couldn't work it out?

"I'm glad you didn't walk away."

"Just glad?"

He turned to look down at her. "Ecstatic."

"Well, you said you'd find a way for us to be together. You did it. You solved the case, and more."

Nothing more needed to be said. They walked a little farther, moving slowly to compensate for Chloe's bruises. The night was silent but for their footsteps on the gravel path, the odd sound of something small rustling through the grass. She had a thick shawl pulled over her shoulders.

Even though it was summer, this close to the ocean the night breeze was cool. Above, the sky was strewn with stars, a half moon pinned in the velvet dark.

"I'm going to be sorry to leave this place," she murmured. "Uncle Jack loved this garden."

"He did." Sam was silent for a few steps. "He was a good friend."

"How long did you know him?"

"Since the Great War."

She tried to imagine Sam and Jack, flying biplanes or airships or strolling beneath the crystal chandeliers of the great luxury steamers like the *Titanic*. "You shared a lot of history."

"Yes."

"And with Carter, too."

"Yes."

The set of his mouth told her there was loss and pain he didn't want to talk about. It wasn't that he was keeping secrets; part of him was still Ralston Samuel Hill, born in a time when men didn't share their feelings the same way they did now. She'd work on that, right along with training him to give answers of more than one word.

"Chloe," Sam said. "About your parents. I asked some questions. Did you know what they were working on when they died?"

"All I know was that they were biochemists with a drug company. They died in a home invasion."

"But you've always believed they were killed because of their work."

"Yes. The house was torn to pieces, but as far as I could tell, nothing was taken. Mom's jewelry was still there. No one had touched Dad's wallet. Most of the damage was in the home office. The killers were looking for something, and judging from the mess they didn't find it. I have no idea what they wanted. My parents never discussed their work with me."

"They couldn't. They were protecting you. They worked for the Company."

She stopped. "What?"

Sam put an arm around her shoulders. Someday, he vowed, he would find out who took Chloe's family from her. He would see justice done. "Jack knew how talented they were. He convinced our research and development department to take them on, even though they were human."

"What were they working on? What was so important that they were killed for it?" Chloe suddenly realized that Sam probably couldn't tell her, either. "Generally speaking, of course."

He gave her a wry smile. They started to walk again, drawing near the gazebo. "Mark could give you a more informed answer. I'm not the science guy. As I understand it, they were trying to figure out, biologically, what makes a vampire a vampire."

"Dreamy eyes and a rockin' cape?"

Sam winced. "They were separating myth from fact. We're fast healing, not technically dead even though we are often at death's door when we're turned. Although it's rare, vampires can produce children."

Chloe's step hitched, realizing that they'd used a condom only the first time they'd been together. After that, she'd assumed it wasn't an issue. *Sam's babies?* Her whole body flushed with the idea.

"Your parents believed we're actually a separate species, genetically altered through union with a symbiotic microorganism."

Chloe caught her breath, fascinated. "Were they right?"

"As far as anyone can tell me, they barely scratched the

surface of the question. There is as big a mystical component as a scientific one."

She shivered, and Sam pulled her closer. "But why kill them for researching that?"

"Sometimes people fear information as much as they desire it. People like the Knights. They would love to know what makes us tick so that they could kill us more efficiently. Or maybe they want to know how to make themselves just as fast and strong."

Chloe thought about her parents, and how she had sometimes resented their silence. "So it was volatile enough information that they couldn't risk telling a teenaged girl."

"No. And Jack couldn't tell you about it, either. He broke all kinds of rules just showing you his collection of vampire knickknacks."

"I'm glad he did. I think my head would have exploded in these last few weeks if he hadn't prepared me to consider the existence of vampires."

He bent down and kissed the top of her head. "Just so you know, not all the Company are vampires. There are a handful of werewolves like Kenyon and one or two humans like your parents."

Chloe thought about that. "Was Jessica Lark one of you?"

"She worked for the Company on special assignment. That's really all I know. We may never find out exactly why she died, or…" He trailed off, eyebrows drawing together.

"Or?"

"I saw a picture of her with somebody I know. I'm just wondering if there was more to it than I assumed."

"Are you worried?"

He shook his head, his face clearing. "No, it's someone I trust."

They'd reached the gazebo, which hadn't been Chloe's

favorite spot since the night they'd captured Pietro. She tried to look at it now with fresh eyes, willing the bad associations away. Sam mounted the steps, holding Chloe's hand. It was warmer there, the rock face behind it blocking some of the wind.

"A private spot," Sam said approvingly.

"There are still security guards roaming the grounds."

"But not here."

He guided her to one of the wooden benches with the ornate, wrought iron frames. Chloe sat, glad of the opportunity to rest. She kept forgetting how much her encounter with Carter had taken out of her.

Sam sat beside her, cuddling her close. "I, um, suggested to the guards that they leave the patrol of this area up to me tonight."

"Are we patrolling?"

"I'm your personal guard. Forever."

She poked his side playfully. "Be careful what you wish for. That means a steady stream of wedding clients to deal with."

He smiled, but it was quickly replaced by his serious face. "When we bond, it's as much biochemical as emotional. The two get mixed together. We're as good as addicted. I'm going to need you always."

She felt the weight of his solemn mood. "I'm mortal. I won't last."

Sam took a deep breath. "I love you, Chloe. More than anything. But you should know that if you stay with me, you will become like me."

She wasn't even sure of everything that becoming a vampire would mean, but she knew she wanted Sam. She could handle the rest. She'd proven she could survive when the going got tough. And being with Sam? That was the opposite of tough.

She leaned close to whisper in his ear, not because it was a secret, but the words were meant only for him. "I promise to love you and be with you always."

Sam held her close, burying his face in her hair. She recalled Carter's words: *When faced with true darkness, love doesn't matter.* It deserved a rebuttal.

"When there is love, there is no such thing as true darkness," she said. "When there is love, darkness doesn't matter."

They made love in the grass, Chloe's shawl spread out beneath them. Sam moved tenderly, taking care not to touch the bruised places on her skin. As he peeled back the fabric of her blouse, her skin pebbled where his breath fanned across it. Her nipples rose hard beneath the silk of her camisole. With so many bumps and bruises, she hadn't been wearing a bra.

He cupped her face in his, tasting first one lip, then the other, leaving kisses at the corners of her mouth where her dimples lay sleeping. And then he plundered her, bold as any pirate, stealing the secrets of her kiss. She moaned beneath him, tasting him, capturing his tongue with hers.

Sam's hands were busy with other buttons and zippers, so he pulled down the tiny strap of the camisole with his teeth. Chloe's shoulder was lovely, a perfect feminine roundness, neither too plump nor too slender. He wished he could draw just so that he could capture that graceful curve.

He captured it with his lips instead, proving he was an artist in another medium. The smell of her skin made him slightly dizzy, as if every synapse in his brain were firing at once. "Chloe," he said to the butter-soft skin of her shoulder.

"Hmm?" she replied, fumbling with the belt and button of his trousers. The roughness of her bandages making an interesting friction in male places. It was a phenomenon worth experimenting with in future.

"Chloe," he repeated, following the scalloped neck of the camisole to that heavenly hollow between her breasts.

His fangs were down, and he let them scrape along the curve of her breasts, not so hard as to injure, but enough to make her squirm with the sensation. The squirming did little for his self-control. The ache in his groin was enough to stop his breath.

Chloe pulled down the zipper of his pants. It gave some relief, but that only encouraged his lower brain to hurry things along.

"I want you," she demanded.

In the moonlight, her skin looked pale as milk, almost luminous. The patch of lawn they had claimed was surrounded by roses, their scent lingering like the memory of sun in the air. He plucked one, a full-blown white bloom tipped with a pink core.

He straddled her, knees on either side of her slim waist, and touched the petals to her skin. She shivered enticingly, her hands on his as he trailed the flower over the curve of her belly to the slick folds below. Her hips arched beneath the silken touch, aroused and sensitive. She was ready, wet, inviting.

Pulling her legs around his waist, he found the core of her with his tip. She took him greedily. The hot slickness of her engulfed him, and he pushed more and more. Each thrust earned him a little moan. Those sounds were almost more than superhuman strength could bear.

He stopped thrusting. Her eyes opened, wide and unfocused, searching his face. With the rose, he stroked her cheek, trailing the petals across her lips. Then he bent to taste her mouth. There was nothing innocent left in their kiss. They ate at each other hungrily, all but heedless of his sharp teeth.

His hands found her breasts, kneading them, suckling the nipples. Chloe's back arched to meet him, the movement nearly shattering his control. His hips moved in response, triggering the pulsing of her first climax. Sam's breath was ragged, his thoughts shredded to nothing but skin and sweat and desire. He thrust again, fighting the impulse to finish, wanting to draw it out, but needing, wanting, aching to make her his.

Chloe cried out beneath him, and he could hold on no more. His body shuddered with the need to move, the urge to feel her flesh tight around him. He pushed, and pushed again, falling into a rhythm as ancient as birth and death. *Chloe. Chloe. Chloe. Chloe.*

He roared as his own release came, taking her with him. Her body pulled at him, milked him, sucked him under a mindless wave of possession and surrender. Sam let himself drift on the feeling, aware of the stars above, the grass beneath them.

"You're mine," he said again, speaking the words before the witness of heaven and earth. He sucked in a great breath of air, feeling the power of his claim.

When they had finished, he curled around her, wrapping the shawl over her to keep her from the cold. This time, after tasting her blood, he pierced his own wrist, offering it to her.

"It will heal you," he said, stroking her hair.

There was a moment when he was not sure if she would turn away, revolted, or trust him enough to take it. Then she wrapped her hands around his wrist and bent to the wound, lapping at what he offered.

The sensation of it made him hard again, but he waited patiently, drinking in the scent of the rose they had crushed beneath their weight.

Chapter 32

They woke the next morning in Chloe's bed. The first thing she felt was Sam's arm curled over her hip. The second was an absence of pain.

Slowly, carefully, she stretched each limb. She didn't hurt anywhere. Whatever magic was in Sam's blood had cured her wounds. In fact, she felt wonderful.

Oddly excited, she rolled over, curling against the hard slab of his chest. The scent of him made things clench low in her belly.

"Hello," he growled in her ear.

"Hello." She gave him a kiss. "I had an idea."

"I have a lot of ideas." He rolled her onto her back, following so that he landed on top, braced on his elbows.

It didn't take an anatomist to guess what his ideas involved. He pressed against her with distracting emphasis.

Chloe cleared her throat. "I could help you."

"Indeed you could," he purred with a smile.

"With your spy stuff."

The smile deepened a touch. "Planning all our weddings? You'd better bring unbreakable dishes for the werewolves."

She narrowed her eyes. "I'm serious. Think about how

many people go to weddings, anniversaries, whatever. What better cover to get into places? To get into homes where you'd never otherwise secure an invitation?"

Sam's eyebrows drew together. "We don't need invitations to cross a threshold. That's myth."

"You know what I mean! You could show up and do your spying while you were mixing drinks. Bartenders hear everything. Or mix in the crowd serving appetizers. It's a no-brainer."

"It's not a bad idea. In my youth, the best spies were the servants. They had an excuse to go anywhere, overhear any conversation. They were invisible."

"Then you'll think about it?"

"It could be a useful tool." One corner of his mouth curled up. "It would give us plenty of opportunities to work together."

"Exactly."

They had just finished a thorough kiss when Chloe's phone went off with the ringtone that said there was an emergency at the office. Sam swore as she rolled over to grab her cell from the bedside table.

"Hello?"

"Check your email," said her assistant's voice. She sounded stressed. "This is one I can't handle."

"Why not?"

"It's from the Crown Prince of Vidon. I didn't think I should open it myself."

Chloe hung up and switched on her laptop. The message was actually a video clip. She set the laptop on the bed so Sam could watch, too.

The clip started with a sweeping view of the Mediterranean. White beaches. White buildings framed by palms. Blue sky. Blue water. She could just make out the top of a railing made of swirls of black iron.

"That's from the balcony of the palace in Marcari," Sam said. "What's he doing there?"

The camera pulled back to show a young couple sitting at a table for two. She recognized them at once. Kyle Alphonse Adraio, Crown Prince of Vidon, looked more like a striker for one of the Italian football teams than he did royalty. He was dressed nicely, but his clothes were casual. His brown hair curled past his collar, and his mobile mouth looked ready to laugh. She could see why he had a reputation as a charmer.

Beside him sat a slim, dark-haired woman Chloe recognized as Princess Amelie. The most striking feature of the princess was her large, thick-lashed violet eyes, which made her look meltingly vulnerable. The two were laughing and lifting flutes of champagne toward the camera.

She caught her breath. "They're together."

Sam rolled onto his elbow to get a better look. "She looks happy. That's good."

Prince Kyle smiled broadly at the camera. "Greetings, Ms. Anderson. And to Sam Ralston. My informants tell me where I find one of you, I shall find the other."

"Salut!" the Princess chimed in, clinking her glass against Kyle's.

Amelie spoke in a charming, soft accent. "First of all, thank you so much for your part in seeing the dress home safely. It arrived this morning, along with Plague and Famine. And you deserve to know a piece of the puzzle we discovered here in Marcari. The idea to put the diamonds on the dress came from my grandmother."

"By all nine hells." Sam made a noise of both amusement and exasperation. "That's the dowager for you."

Amelie went on. "She envisioned her granddaughter sparkling on worldwide television as she walked down the aisle of the cathedral. Spectacle. Theater. A billion cameras snapping. My grandmother was ever the genius when it came to the showmanship of state."

Chloe was still a beat behind. "The dowager queen removed the crown jewels without telling the rest of the royal family?"

Amelie answered as if she heard the question. "It was the dowager's taste for a surprise that started this whole affair. She knew the king, my father, would never risk the gems by removing them from the treasury, so she convinced Jack Anderson to spirit them out of the castle and take them to Jessica Lark. He was just enough of a rogue to agree. So you see, this is how my wedding dress came to be in the eye of this storm."

She gave Kyle a significant look, and the camera shifted slightly toward him.

"I have two points of business," he said. "First, I have made an offer on Oakwood Manor. I have every reason to believe it shall be accepted by your solicitor, the esteemed Mr. Littleton. He shall make the title deed out to you, my dear Chloe. Please accept it in thanks for your generous, brave spirit and the courage you showed protecting my Amelie's treasure. I have a feeling, with your business going so well, you will need a place befitting your future station in life."

"I can't accept that!" Chloe gasped.

"Of course you can," Sam said calmly. "You don't say no to a prince."

"Second," Kyle went on blithely, with what seemed a cheerful certainty that no one could deny him, "our wedding shall be on Valentine's Day."

He stopped to kiss Amelie. They were a beautiful couple, the Mediterranean wind twining their dark locks together. It would be nice to get a wedding shot of them, just like that.

Sam's hand closed over Chloe's thigh. If he kept that

up, whatever Kyle had to say next would rapidly diminish in importance.

Kyle resumed in the nick of time. "We heard what an incredible job you did on the Venuto-Fallon wedding, and what professionalism you showed in extremely trying circumstances. So highly have your praises been sung, we want you to plan our wedding."

Chloe's heart stopped in her chest. "Huh?"

"You can do it," Sam said, patting her leg.

Amelie leaned into the frame. "We hope you will bring that rogue Samuel Ralston with you. Perhaps you would consent to be our guests for your own Mediterranean wedding?"

Chloe's jaw dropped. "Do they have spies or something?"

"Yes." Sam's hand traveled up her thigh.

"Remember," said Kyle. "Valentine's Day. Send your reply as soon as you get this."

The clip ended as they both lifted their glasses in a toast. Sam closed the laptop and set it on the nightstand before the last word was done. "He can wait."

Chloe slid into Sam's embrace. "A royal wedding. What do you think?

Sam gave her a devouring look that promised her reply to Kyle would be very, very late. "I think Marcari is the perfect place for a honeymoon."

Afterword

For a number of years, I played with several Celtic and early music ensembles that performed at weddings—occasions big and small, formal and costumed, in fancy hotels and backyards. It was great fun, even though I always tear up during the vows, whether or not I know the couple—go figure—and that is definitely not a helpful habit when trying to read music.

Each wedding was unique, but there were some especially memorable moments, like the time a bagpipe-playing uncle insisted on a duet. Yes, those pipes are excruciatingly loud up close.

Through it all, I came to completely respect the heroic individuals who organized those wonderful celebrations, whether they were professional planners or dedicated family and friends. Let it be said that the stories of the Four Horsemen of the Apocalypse are fantasies. Even with all her contacts, Chloe Anderson puts on a huge wedding in a sliver of the time that it would normally take. All I can say is: you go, girl. Why should vampires get all the superpowers?

And while we're asking questions, how did Mark Winspear know Jessica Lark? What did the Knights of Vidon plan on doing with the money from the stolen diamonds? Princess Amelie has her dress back, but what happened to the designs for the rest of the bridal trousseau? Although Sam and Chloe found each other, the story of Amelie and Kyle's star-crossed royal wedding has just begun. Be sure to look for *Possessed by an Immortal,* available next month.

Please visit me at www.SharonAshwood.com. I love to hear from readers!

* * * * *

A sneaky peek at next month...

NOCTURNE™

BEYOND DARKNESS...BEYOND DESIRE

My wish list for next month's titles...

In stores from 16th April 2014:

❏ Demon Wolf – Bonnie Vanak

❏ Possessed by an Immortal – Sharon Ashwood

In stores from 6th June 2014:

❏ Night of the Shifter – Caridad Piñeiro,
Megan Hart, Linda O. Johnston,
Doranna Durgin & Katie Reus

Available at WHSmith, Tesco, Asda, Eason, Amazon and Apple

Just can't wait?